GEPT

Listening Test

全民英檢初級
聽力測驗題庫解析

英檢出題方向來自日常生活
40個英檢最常見情境融入題型訓練

Step 1

● 看圖辨義

迅速瀏覽圖中所有元素，分析 什麼樣的元素可能會有什麼樣的 問法，在題目播出前不浪費任何 一分鐘。

Step 2

● 問答

迅速瀏覽每個選項的答案，由 選項可猜測待會問題的方向是什 麼。甚至可先以消去法把最不可 能的答案排除。

Step 3

● 簡短對話

用五大WH問句How? Who? What? Where? When? 的要領，仔細聆 聽一段英文對話，面對問題時不 會手忙腳亂。

Step 4

● 短文聽解

獨家搶先收錄99年最新題型『短 文聽解』，讓你比別人早一步進 入狀況！在你瀏覽插圖時，甚至 可預測出『下一題會怎麼問？』 ，盡速聽出關鍵字並完成作答。

Step 5

● 聽力
PASS！！

1000題「聽解能力」密集訓練

到底能幫我**增強**哪些**能力**呢？

▼ 速見P.8

自然反射訓練

每個主題情境都有3個經典問句與經典答句，每種問法一定都有固定的回答句型，可訓練你聽出句中的關鍵語，把回答變成一種自然而然的反射能力。課前先暖身一次，對稍後的聽力練習會有很大的幫助。

經典問句

問法① What is this?
問法② What are these?
問法③ What can people find in here?

經典答句

問法① This / It is a / an _____.
問法② These / They are _____.
問法③ People can find

▼ 速見P.50

快速上手句

每個主題情境最重要的必背語句。它提供了一般常用的慣用對話範本，讓你熟悉什麼樣的問法，一定會有固定的回答方式。句子簡短卻能貼切表現口語的習慣。不用再死背文法、句型，常常跟著唸，把回答變成自然脫口而出的能力。

Hint 快速上手句

A: How's it going? 近況如何？
B: Not bad. 不錯。

A: How are you doing these days? 最近過得怎麼樣？
B: Pretty good. 很不錯。

A: How's everything? 一切都好嗎？
B: Everything's OK. 都還不錯。

A: How's life? 生活過得怎麼樣？
B: Same old thing. 老樣子。

▼ 速見P.9

看圖預測關鍵字

看圖辨義以及短文聽解的題目不印在試卷上，你必須先瀏覽插圖再依CD播放的問題作答。訓練你找出圖中的關鍵元素，並依經典問句的固定問法，預測待會CD會怎麼問，在等待中不浪費一分一秒，瀏覽插圖時，即可完成猜題並搶先作答。

Q2 （請聆聽 CD所播放的題目）
CD 1-12

Q3 （請聆聽 CD所播放的題目）

▼ 速見P.51

答題時間提示

這可不是恐怖15秒！而是要讓你習慣考試節奏，平時練習時就必須意識到每題答題的時間。只要掌握等待播出題目前的猜題技巧，聽見播音前就可拿到60%的分數，再根據題意做出最適切的回答，要拿高分絕對不是問題。

請聆聽錄音機播出的英文句子，再從試題冊上在選項 A、B、C
選項中，選出一個與題意最相符的答案。
題只播一次，請仔細聽。）

答題時間 約 15 秒/題

low are you?
ine. And you?
's fine.

ow do you do it?
am doing well.

CD 1-12

CONTENTS

第三部分 簡短對話

第四部分 短文聽解

解答篇

全民英檢聽力測驗

第一部分　第二部分　第三部分　第四部分

看圖辨義

作答提示

▶試題上有數幅圖畫，每題請聆聽錄音機播出的題目和三個英文句子之後，在選項[A][B][C]中選出與所看到的圖畫最相符的答案。

（每題只播出一次，請仔細聽）

看圖辨義

| 主題 **1** | 物品・動物 Article ・ Animals |

課前暖身 以下是經典問句與經典答句，各有 3 句。請先瀏覽一次。對稍後的聽力訓練會有很大的幫助喔！

經典問句

問法 **1** What is this?

問法 **2** What are these?

問法 **3** What can people find in here?

經典答句

回答 **1** This / It is a / an ＿＿＿＿＿＿＿＿＿＿.

回答 **2** These / They are ＿＿＿＿＿＿＿＿＿＿.

回答 **3** People can find ＿＿＿＿＿＿＿＿＿＿.

聽力練習 試題上有數幅圖畫，每題請聆聽錄音機播出的題目和 3 個英語句子之後，在選項 A、B、C 中選出與所看到的圖畫最相符的答案。
☞（答案請見 **P.186**）

8

答題時間
約 **15** 秒/題

Q1

🎧 MP3 **1-1**

（每題只播一次，請仔細聽。）

B This is a sheet of paper.

Q2

🎧 MP3 **1-1**

（每題只播一次，請仔細聽。） B They're furniture.

Q3

🎧 MP3 **1-1**

（每題只播一次，請仔細聽。） B Sea animals.

一定要學會的生活場景必考題 **9**

經典問句

問法 ❶ What is she / he doing?

問法 ❷ What's happening here?

問法 ❸ What is she / he going to do?

 經典答句

回答 ❶ She / he is V-ing.

回答 ❷ People / They are V-ing.

回答 ❸ She / he is going to V.

課前暖身　以下是經典問句與經典答句，各有 3 句。請先瀏覽一次，對稍後的聽力訓練會有很大的幫助喔！

聽力練習　試題上有數幅圖畫，每題請聆聽錄音機播出的題目和三個英語句子之後，在選項 A、B、C 中選出與所看到的圖畫最相符的答案。
☛（答案請見 **P.187**）

答題時間 約 **15** 秒/題

主題
2
活動
Activities

Q1

MP3 **1-2**

（每題只播一次，請仔細聽。） B. He is taking a bath.

Q2

MP3 **1-2**

（每題只播一次，請仔細聽。） A. People are watching a game

Q3

MP3 **1-2**

（每題只播一次，請仔細聽。） B. She's going to go shopping.

課前暖身 以下是經典問句與經典答句，各有 3 句。請先瀏覽一次，對稍後的聽力訓練會有很大的幫助喔！

 經典問句

問法① What is this place?

問法② Where are these two girls?

問法③ Where are they probably going?

 經典答句

回答① This is a _____.

回答② They are in / at / on a _____.

回答③ They are probably going to the _____.

聽力練習 試題上有數幅圖畫，每題請聆聽錄音機播出的題目和三個英語句子之後，在選項 A、B、C 中選出與所看到的圖畫最相符的答案。
☞（答案請見 P.190）

答題時間
約 **15** 秒/題

Q1

（每題只播一次，請仔細聽。） B This is a library.

MP3 **1-3**

Q2

（每題只播一次，請仔細聽。） C They're in a stadiem.

MP3 **1-3**

Q3

（每題只播一次，請仔細聽。） B They're prebebly go ti a hospital.

MP3 **1-3**

一定要學會的生活場景必考題　13

時刻 Time

以下是經典問句與經典答句，各有 3 句。請先瀏覽一次，對稍後的聽力訓練會有很大的幫助喔！

 經典問句

問法 **1** What is the time?

問法 **2** What time is it?

問法 **3** When does the ＿＿＿ start?

 經典答句

回答 **1** It's ＿＿＿ o'clock.

回答 **2** It's ＿＿＿ to / past ＿＿＿.

回答 **3** It starts at ＿＿＿ a.m. / p.m..

試題上有數幅圖畫，每題請聆聽錄音機播出的題目和三個英語句子之後，在選項 A、B、C 中選出與所看到的圖畫最相符的答案。
☛（答案請見 **P.194**）

答題時間
約 **15** 秒/題

Q1

MP3 **1-4**

（每題只播一次，請仔細聽。）C It's five o six.

主題
4

時刻 Time

Q2

MP3 **1-4**

（每題只播一次，請仔細聽。）A It's a quarter to three.

Q3

MP3 **1-4**

（每題只播一次，請仔細聽。）C It's start at six pm.

以下是經典問句與經典答句，各有 3 句。請先瀏覽一次，對稍後的
聽力訓練會有很大的幫助喔！

課前暖身

經典問句

問法 **①** How is she / he feeling?（問心情）

問法 **②** How does she / he look?（問表情）

問法 **③** What does she / he look like?（問身材、外表）

經典答句

回答 **①** She / He is _____.

回答 **②** She / He looks _____.

回答 **③** She's / He's _____.

　　　　 She has / He has _____.

　　　　 She looks / He looks _____.

聽力練習

試題上有數幅圖畫，每題請聆聽錄音機播出的題目和三個英語句子
之後，在選項 A 、 B 、 C 中選出與所看到的圖畫最相符的答案。
☛（答案請見 P.196）

答題時間
約 **15** 秒/題

Q1

MP3 **1-5**

（每題只播一次，請仔細聽。） B She is worried.

Q2

MP3 **1-5**

（每題只播一次，請仔細聽。） B He looks excited.

Q3

MP3 **1-5**

（每題只播一次，請仔細聽。） B She has a thin face.

課前
暖身

以下是經典問句與經典答句，各有 3 句。請先瀏覽一次，對稍後的
聽力訓練會有很大的幫助喔！

 經典問句

(問法❶) What happened to him / her?

(問法❷) Why is she / he here?

(問法❸) What is wrong with him / her?

 經典答句

(回答❶) She / He hurt her / his _____.

(回答❷) She / He has got _____.

(回答❸) She / He has a _____.

聽力
練習

試題上有數幅圖畫，每題請聆聽錄音機播出的題目和三個英語句子
之後，在選項Ａ、Ｂ、Ｃ中選出與所看到的圖畫最相符的答案。
☛（答案請見 **P.199**）

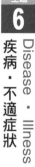

答題時間
約 **15** 秒/題

Q1

MP3 **1-6**

（每題只播一次，請仔細聽。） A He hurts his toos.

Q2

MP3 **1-6**

（每題只播一次，請仔細聽。） C He hurts his leg.

Kyle

Q3

MP3 **1-6**

（每題只播一次，請仔細聽。） C He has a caugh.

課前暖身 以下是經典問句與經典答句，各有 3 句。請先瀏覽一次，對稍後的聽力訓練會有很大的幫助喔！

經典問句

問法**①** What is she / he eating / drinking?

問法**②** What does she / he want?

問法**③** What would she / he like?

經典答句

回答**①** She / He is eating _____.

回答**②** She / He wants _____.

回答**③** She / He would like _____.

聽力練習 試題上有數幅圖畫，每題請聆聽錄音機播出的題目和三個英語句子之後，在選項 A、B、C 中選出與所看到的圖畫最相符的答案。
☞（答案請見 **P.201**）

答題時間
約 **15** 秒/題

Q1
MP3 **1-7**

（每題只播一次，請仔細聽。）C. She is eat fast food.

Q2
MP3 **1-7**

（每題只播一次，請仔細聽。）B She wants some bread.

father   daughter   mother

grandfather

Q3
MP3 **1-7**

（每題只播一次，請仔細聽。）He would like a black coffee

以下是經典問句與經典答句,各有 3 句。請先瀏覽一次,對稍後的
聽力訓練會有很大的幫助喔!

 經典問句

問法 **①** What is she / he wearing?

問法 **②** What is she / he carrying?

問法 **③** What is she / he going to buy?

 經典答句

回答 **①** She / He is wearing _____.

回答 **②** She / He is carrying _____.

回答 **③** She / He is going to buy _____.

試題上有數幅圖畫,每題請聆聽錄音機播出的題目和三個英語句子
之後,在選項 A、B、C 中選出與所看到的圖畫最相符的答案。
☛(答案請見 **P.204**)

答題時間
約 **15** 秒/題

Q1

MP3 **1-8**

（每題只播一次，請仔細聽。） A. He's wearing a shorts.

Q2

MP3 **1-8**

（每題只播一次，請仔細聽。） A. He's wearing a necktie.

Q3

MP3 **1-8**

（每題只播一次，請仔細聽。） B She's going to buy shoes.

個人資料 Personal Data

課前暖身

以下是經典問句與經典答句，各有 3 句。請先瀏覽一次，對稍後的聽力訓練會有很大的幫助喔！

 經典問句

問法 **1** How old is she / he?

問法 **2** How heavy is she / he?

問法 **3** How tall is she / he?

 經典答句

回答 **1** She / He is _____ year(s) old.

回答 **2** She / He is _____ kilogram.

回答 **3** She / He is _____ tall.

聽力練習

試題上有數幅圖畫，每題請聆聽錄音機播出的題目和三個英語句子之後，在選項 A、B、C 中選出與所看到的圖畫最相符的答案。
☛（答案請見 **P.206**）

答題時間
約 **15** 秒/題

主題
9
個人資料

Personal Data

Q1

MP3 1-9

（每題只播一次，請仔細聽。）

B. He's 7 years old.

Q2

MP3 1-9

（每題只播一次，請仔細聽。）

A. She's 56 kg.

56 kgs

Q3

MP3 1-9

（每題只播一次，請仔細聽。）

C He's 1.5 meters tall.

150cm

課前暖身 以下是經典問句與經典答句,各有 3 句。請先瀏覽一次,對稍後的聽力訓練會有很大的幫助喔!

 經典問句

問法 **1** What season is it?

問法 **2** What month is it?

問法 **3** What time of the year is it?

 經典答句

回答 **1** It's winter / spring / summer / fall.

回答 **2** It's January / February /....

回答 **3** It's New Year / Halloween / Christmas /....

聽力練習 試題上有數幅圖畫,每題請聆聽錄音機播出的題目和三個英語句子之後,在選項 A、B、C 中選出與所看到的圖畫最相符的答案。
☛（答案請見 **P.209**）

答題時間
約 **15** 秒/題

Q1

🎧 MP3 **1-10**

（每題只播一次，請仔細聽。）

B. It's winter.

（每題只播一次，請仔細聽。）

A. It's April.

Q2

🎧 MP3 **1-10**

April

（每題只播一次，請仔細聽。）C It's a new year.

Q3

🎧 MP3 **1-10**

主題 **11**	日期 Dates

課前暖身

以下是經典問句與經典答句，各有 3 句。請先瀏覽一次，對稍後的聽力訓練會有很大的幫助喔！

經典問句

問法① What day is today / it?

問法② What is the date today?

問法③ What date is _____?

經典答句

回答① Today / It is （Monday ～ Sunday）.

回答② Today / It is （Month ／ date）.

回答③ It is (on) （Month ／ date）.

聽力練習

試題上有數幅圖畫，每題請聆聽錄音機播出的題目和三個英語句子之後，在選項 A、B、C 中選出與所看到的圖畫最相符的答案。
☛（答案請見 **P.212**）

答題時間
約 **15** 秒/題

Q1

🎧 MP3 **1-11**

（每題只播一次，請仔細聽。）B. Today is Thursday

主題 **11** 日期 Dates

（每題只播一次，請仔細聽。）C. It's Fabrary second.

Q2

🎧 MP3 **1-11**

二月 **2** 星期五

（每題只播一次，請仔細聽。）B. On June eleventh

Q3

🎧 MP3 **1-11**

NOTE	
Jane's birthday	1979/10/15
Annie's birthday	1975/8/30
Terry's birthday	1976/6/11
Mary's birthday	1974/3/7

| 位置 Positions

以下是經典問句與經典答句，各有 3 句。請先瀏覽一次，對稍後的聽力訓練會有很大的幫助喔！

經典問句

問法 **1** Where is the _____?

問法 **2** Where does _____ live?

問法 **3** What is under / on /... the _____?

經典答句

回答 **1** It is _____ the _____.

回答 **2** A / The _____ is under / on... the _____.

回答 **3** She / He lives _____ the _____.

試題上有數幅圖畫，每題請聆聽錄音機播出的題目和三個英語句子之後，在選項 A、B、C 中選出與所看到的圖畫最相符的答案。
☞（答案請見 **P.213**）

答題時間
約 **15** 秒/題

Q1

🎧 MP3 **1-12**

（每題只播一次，請仔細聽。）

B. It's in front of a car.

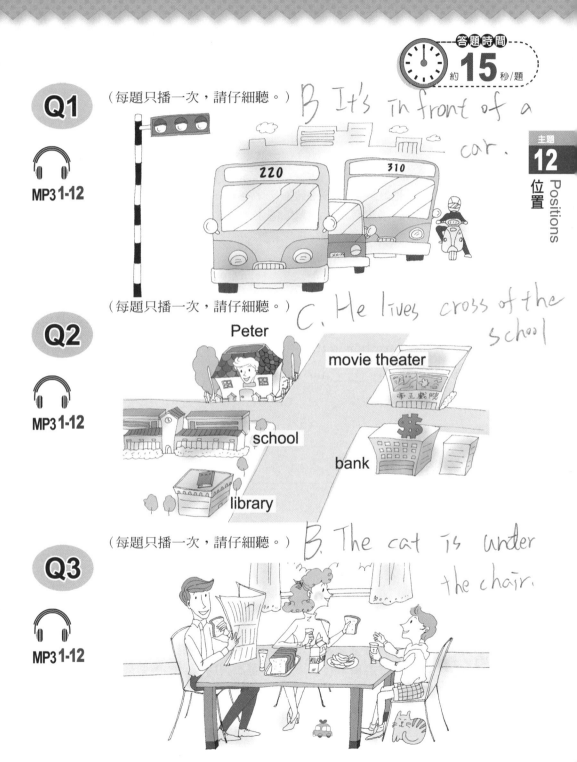

Q2

🎧 MP3 **1-12**

（每題只播一次，請仔細聽。）

C. He lives cross of the school

Peter

movie theater

school

bank

library

Q3

🎧 MP3 **1-12**

（每題只播一次，請仔細聽。）

B. The cat is under the chair.

數量 Quantity

以下是經典問句與經典答句，各有 3 句。請先瀏覽一次，對稍後的聽力訓練會有很大的幫助喔！

經典問句

問法❶ What number is it?

問法❷ How many _____ are there?

問法❸ Who is first?

經典答句

回答❶ It is number _____.

回答❷ There are _____.

回答❸ _____ is first.

聽力練習

試題上有數幅圖畫，每題請聆聽錄音機播出的題目和三個英語句子之後，在選項 A、 B、 C 中選出與所看到的圖畫最相符的答案。
☛（答案請見 **P.215**）

答題時間 約 **15** 秒/題

Q1

MP3 **1-13**

（每題只播一次，請仔細聽。）

B. Thirty-one

Lottery

Q2

MP3 **1-13**

（每題只播一次，請仔細聽。）

B. There are two children.

Q3

MP3 **1-13**

（每題只播一次，請仔細聽。）

C. Sally is first

Sally　　Helen　　Emily

價錢 Prices

以下是經典問句與經典答句，各有 3 句。請先瀏覽一次，對稍後的聽力訓練會有很大的幫助喔！

經典問句

問法 **1** How much is it?

問法 **2** How much does it cost?

問法 **3** How much did she / he spend?

經典答句

回答 **1** _____ dollars.

回答 **2** It costs _____ dollars.

回答 **3** She / He spent _____ dollars.

聽力練習 試題上有數幅圖畫，每題請聆聽錄音機播出的題目和三個英語句子之後，在選項 A、B、C 中選出與所看到的圖畫最相符的答案。
☛（答案請見 **P.217**）

Q1

MP3 **1-14**

（每題只播一次，請仔細聽。）

Ticket Fare

To Tainan................$ 856

To Taichung...........$ 412

To Keelung.............$ 165

Q2

MP3 **1-14**

（每題只播一次，請仔細聽。）

Q3

MP3 **1-14**

（每題只播一次，請仔細聽。）

課前暖身 以下是經典問句與經典答句，各有 3 句。請先瀏覽一次，對稍後的聽力訓練會有很大的幫助喔！

 經典問句

問法 **1** How's the weather?

問法 **2** What will the weather be like?

問法 **3** What's the temperature?

 經典答句

回答 **1** It's _____.

回答 **2** It will be _____.

回答 **3** The temperature is _____ degree.

聽力練習 試題上有數幅圖畫，每題請聆聽錄音機播出的題目和三個英語句子之後，在選項 A、B、C 中選出與所看到的圖畫最相符的答案。
☛（答案請見 **P.218**）

Q1

MP3 **1-15**

（每題只播一次，請仔細聽。）

Q2

MP3 **1-15**

（每題只播一次，請仔細聽。）

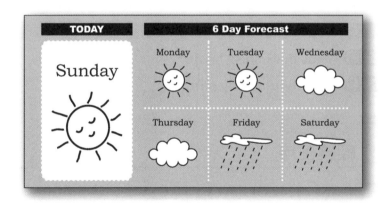

Q3

MP3 **1-15**

（每題只播一次，請仔細聽。）

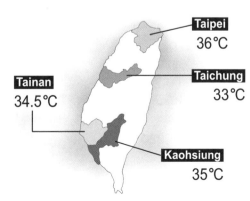

以下是經典問句與經典答句，各有 3 句。請先瀏覽一次，對稍後的聽力訓練會有很大的幫助喔！

 經典問句

問法 **1** What is she / he?

問法 **2** What does she / he do?

問法 **3** Who should they call?

 經典答句

回答 **1** She / He is a _____.

回答 **2** She / He works as a _____.

回答 **3** They should call _____.

聽力練習 試題上有數幅圖畫，每題請聆聽錄音機播出的題目和三個英語句子之後，在選項 A、B、C 中選出與所看到的圖畫最相符的答案。
☛（答案請見 **P.220**）

答題時間
約 **15** 秒/題

主題
16
職業 Occupations

Q1

MP3 **1-16**

（每題只播一次，請仔細聽。）

（每題只播一次，請仔細聽。）

Q2

MP3 **1-16**

（每題只播一次，請仔細聽。）

Q3

MP3 **1-16**

課前暖身

以下是經典問句與經典答句，各有 3 句。請先瀏覽一次，對稍後的聽力訓練會有很大的幫助喔！

 經典問句

問法 **①** What is more expensive?

問法 **②** What is the cheapest way to _____?

問法 **③** Who should pay the most?

 經典答句

回答 **①** _____ is more expensive.

回答 **②** By _____ / Take a / the_____.

回答 **③** The _____ should pay the most.

聽力練習

試題上有數幅圖畫，每題請聆聽錄音機播出的題目和三個英語句子之後，在選項 A、B、C 中選出與所看到的圖畫最相符的答案。
☞（答案請見 **P.222**）

答題時間 約 **15** 秒/題

Q1

MP3 **1-17**

（每題只播一次，請仔細聽。）

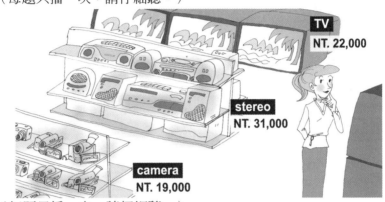

TV NT. 22,000

stereo NT. 31,000

camera NT. 19,000

（每題只播一次，請仔細聽。）

Q2

MP3 **1-17**

3 Ways to Kaohsiung

By Plane.................$ 2000
By Train.................$ 600
By Bus...................$ 550

（每題只播一次，請仔細聽。）

Q3

MP3 **1-17**

$80　$40　$50

課前暖身 以下是經典問句與經典答句,各有 3 句。請先瀏覽一次,對稍後的聽力訓練會有很大的幫助喔!

經典問句

問法**①** Who is the person ...?

問法**②** Who is the man / woman in _____ ?

問法**③** What is their relationship?

經典答句

回答**①** She / He is _____.

回答**②** She / He is his / her _____.

回答**③** They are _____ and _____.

聽力練習 試題上有數幅圖畫,每題請聆聽錄音機播出的題目和三個英語句子之後,在選項 A、B、C 中選出與所看到的圖畫最相符的答案。
☛（答案請見 **P.225**）

答題時間
約 **15** 秒/題

Q1

MP3 **1-18**

（每題只播一次，請仔細聽。）

Rosa

Philip

Maria

Mark

Lily

Q2

MP3 **1-18**

（每題只播一次，請仔細聽。）

Q3

MP3 **1-18**

（每題只播一次，請仔細聽。）

Excuse me...

一定要學會的生活場景必考題　**43**

課前
暖身

以下是經典問句與經典答句，各有 3 句。請先瀏覽一次，對稍後的
聽力訓練會有很大的幫助喔！

經典問句

問法❶ Where can people probably find this?

問法❷ Where should this / these things be put?

問法❸ What goes with this?

經典答句

回答❶ People can probably find this in _____.

回答❷ It / They should be put in _____.

回答❸ ____ goes with _____.

聽力
練習

試題上有數幅圖畫，每題請聆聽錄音機播出的題目和三個英語句子
之後，在選項Ａ、Ｂ、Ｃ中選出與所看到的圖畫最相符的答案。
☞（答案請見 **P.227**）

Q1

MP3 1-19

（每題只播一次，請仔細聽。）

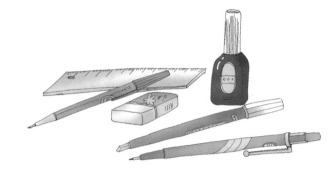

Q2

MP3 1-19

（每題只播一次，請仔細聽。）

Q3

MP3 1-19

（每題只播一次，請仔細聽。）

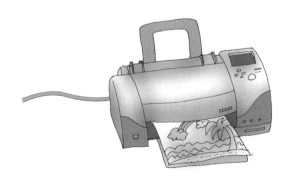

課前暖身 以下是經典問句與經典答句，各有 3 句。請先瀏覽一次，對稍後的聽力訓練會有很大的幫助喔！

 經典問句

問法**①** What does she / he need most?

問法**②** Who needs / uses this most?

問法**③** What's her / his trouble?

 經典答句

回答**①** She / He needs _____ most.

回答**②** A _____ needs / uses this most.

回答**③** She / He _____.

聽力練習 試題上有數幅圖畫，每題請聆聽錄音機播出的題目和三個英語句子之後，在選項 A、B、C 中選出與所看到的圖畫最相符的答案。
☞（答案請見 **P.228**）

Q1

MP3 1-20

（每題只播一次，請仔細聽。）

Q2

MP3 1-20

（每題只播一次，請仔細聽。）

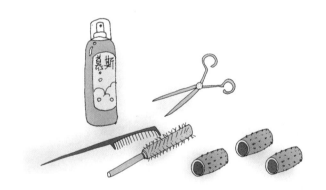

Q3

MP3 1-20

（每題只播一次，請仔細聽。）

全民英檢聽力測驗

第一部分　第二部分　第三部分　第四部分

問答

作答提示

▶每題請聆聽錄音機播出的
英文句子之後，再從試題冊
上的[A][B][C]選項中，選
出一個與題意最相符的答案。

（每題只播出一次，請仔細聽）

問答

第一類 招呼與問候

主題 1　見 面

Hint
快速上手句

important sentences

A: How's it going? 近況如何？
B: Not bad. 不錯。

A: How are you doing these days? 最近過得怎麼樣？
B: Pretty good. 很不錯。

A: How's everything? 一切都好嗎？
B: Everything's OK. 都還不錯。

A: How's life? 生活過得怎麼樣？
B: Same old thing. 老樣子。

A: How are you getting along? 近來如何？
B: Keeping busy. And you? 一直很忙，你呢？

A: Hey, What's up? 嘿，有啥新鮮事？
B: Nothing new. 一切如舊。

A: Hi, what's new (with you)? 有啥新鮮事？
B: Nothing much. 沒什麼。

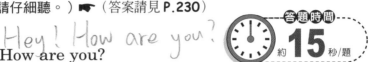

聽力練習 每題請聆聽錄音機播出的英文句子之後，再從試題冊上的選項 A、B、C 三個選項中，選出一個與題意最相符的答案。（每題只播一次，請仔細聽。）☞（答案請見 P.230）

答題時間 約 **15** 秒/題

MP3 **2-1**

主題 **1** 招呼與問候 v 見面

B **1** *Hey! How are you?*
A. How are you?
B. Fine. And you?
C. It's fine.

C **2** *How are you doing?*
A. How do you do it?
B. I am doing well.
C. I am doing my homework.

C **3** *Hi! Tom! A How have you been?*
A. Well, about the same.
B. They are the same.
C. I don't know what I'm doing.

B **4** *Hi! Good to see you again.*
A. Yeah, how have you been?
B. It's good to meet you.
C. I'm O.K.

C **5** *Hello! Sue!*
A. I'm Sue.
B. How do you do?
C. Hi, Jack. What a surprise.

B **6** *Mark, is that really you?*
A. It's yours.
B. Yes, Sam. It's me.
C. Yes, it's mine.

7 _Did you have a good holiday?_

A. It was wonderful.

B. Wish you a happy holiday.

C. No, it's good.

MP3 2-1

8 _Hi! I'm Johnson. Are you Maria?_

A. Maria is a good girl.

B. Hello, Maria. How do you do?

C. Yes, that's right. Hello Johnson.

9

A. How do you do, Ms. Davis?

B. Who is Betty Davis?

C. Do you know her?

10

A. Goodbye, Rose.

B. Hi, Rose. It's nice to meet you.

C. It's nice of you, Rose.

主題 2　道　別

Hint 快速上手句

important sentences

機場道別用語

1. It's very nice of you to come and see me off.
   您來給我送行，真是太客氣了。

2. I hope to see you again.
   希望能再見到您。

3. I'll be seeing you.
   再見。
   ※〔註〕是美國人喜歡使用的告別語。

4. Happy landing.
   祝您平安！
   ※〔註〕是送行者向上飛機的人說的告別語。

5. Bon voyage!
   祝您一路平安！
   ※〔註〕本句是法語。

（答案請見 P.232）

聽力
練習

每題請聆聽錄音機播出的英文句子之後，再從試題冊上的選項 A、B、C 三個選項中，選出一個與題意最相符的答案。（每題只播一次，請仔細聽。）☞

答題時間
約 **15** 秒/題

MP3 **2-2**

1
A. Bye. Take care.
B. What did you buy?
C. By train.

2
A. Go away.
B. I come here sometimes.
C. Thanks, I will.

3
A. Thank you.
B. We're going on a trip.
C. Yes, we had a nice trip.

4
A. Happy birthday.
B. Enjoy yourself.
C. Who is coming?

5
A. You, too.
B. It's a nice day, isn't it?
C. Hi, I'm back.

6
A. Yes. Bye.
B. Yes, you can see it too.
C. Oh, I see.

7
A. Sure thing.
B. Here you are.
C. I will get there by three.

 MP3 **2-2**

主題 **2** 招呼與問候 v 道別

 8
A. Same here.
B. I missed the bus.
C. Did I miss anything?

 9
A. Yes, it's a good knife.
B. Have a sweet dream.
C. Have some sweet.

 10
A. You go first.
B. Yes, I will go.
C. Yes. I'm sorry.

聽力練習

每題請聆聽錄音機播出的英文句子之後，再從試題冊上的選項 A、B、C 三個選項中，選出一個與題意最相符的答案。（每題只播一次，請仔細聽。） ☛（答案請見 **P.234**）

 答題時間 約 **15** 秒/題

 MP3 2-3

1

A. Sorry, I don't have time.
B. Of course I can count.
C. Yes, I am Ken.

2

A. I don't have enough time.
B. Thanks. I will.
C. We will make good use of our time.

3

A. Not this time.
B. I won't be late.
C. You first.

4

A. I'd love to.
B. I am with you.
C. We are together.

5

A. What for?
B. I'd love to come.
C. Thank you.

6
A. I'm having a good time.
B. I'm doing my homework.
C. I'm twenty years old.

MP3 2-3

 7
A. I like drinking tea.
B. No, thanks. I'm fine for now.
C. Be careful with what you eat.

 8
A. I can make it home.
B. Thanks, I will.
C. Nobody's home.

 9
A. Best wishes.
B. Thank you.
C. Because I have no money.

 10
A. Let me see you out.
B. Welcome. Please come in.
C. Thanks very much. It was a great party!

祝賀與道喜

每題請聆聽錄音機播出的英文句子之後，再從試題冊上的選項 A、B、C 三個選項中，選出一個與題意最相符的答案。（每題只播一次，請仔細聽。）☛（答案請見 **P.237**）

答題時間 約 **15** 秒/題

MP3 2-4

1
A. Mary and Chris are happy.
B. Merry Christmas to you, too.
C. Happy New Year!

2
A. Happy birthday!
B. How are you?
C. Oh! How nice.

3
A. Thank you, girl.
B. Wonderful! I'm graduated.
C. Great! I have a daughter!

4
A. You are? Congratulations!
B. You are married?
C. Molly is a good girl.

5
A. Have a nice trip.
B. Did you see that?
C. I see.

6
A. Good day.
B. Good luck.
C. I can't wait to play the TV game.

MP3 2-4

7
A. Why were you off for a week?
B. Have a nice trip.
C. That's too bad. I hope you get well soon.

8
A. That's very kind of you to say so.
B. Can I get past, please?
C. I'm afraid not.

9
A. What do you believe?
B. I hope we have the key to this lock.
C. Honey, I'm so happy for you.

10
A. Same to you.
B. I saw the news.
C. How are you?

聽力練習 每題請聆聽錄音機播出的英文句子之後,再從試題冊上的選項 A、B、C 三個選項中,選出一個與題意最相符的答案。(每題只播一次,請仔細聽。) ☛(答案請見 **P.239**)

答題時間 約 **15** 秒/題

MP3 2-5

1
A. It's nothing.
B. You look kind of pale.
C. I'm not feeling well.

2
A. It doesn't matter.
B. I'm in trouble.
C. I have a headache.

3
A. You have the wrong number.
B. It's not correct.
C. I broke my tooth.

4
A. It will take you three days.
B. Three times a day; after meal, please.
C. I have three meals a day.

5
A. We have to get to a hospital.
B. So that's what happened!
C. Well, I couldn't sleep well.

6
A. I have a cold.
B. What can go wrong?
C. You'd better see a doctor.

MP3 2-5

7
A. Ouch! It hurts.
B. Did you see a doctor?
C. What's your favorite subject?

8
A. Too bad.
B. You need to blow your nose.
C. You have bad teeth.

9
A. Oh, I'm getting better.
B. I've been feeling sick all week.
C. Yes, it's the cold.

10
A. My nose is running.
B. Not much.
C. Please call an ambulance.

電話用語

電話號碼唸法及技巧

★在電話號碼中 "0" 讀作字母 "O"，就像在單詞 "go" 中的母音發音。

★一個特定地區的電話，一般來說只有 7 位或 8 位數字。7 位的號碼，讀的時候前三位一組連在一起，後四位一組連在一起，中間有一個停頓，比如：625-4598 讀作："six-two-five ， four-five-nine-eight"；8 位的號碼，可以 4 個一組來讀。

★兩個相同數位或三個相同的數位可以用 "double" 或 "triple" 來代替，比如 224-6555 可以讀作："double-two-four ， six-triple-five"。

★若末尾出現 3 個零，可以用「千」來發音，如：979-6000 讀作："nine-seven-nine ， six-thousand"。

每題請聆聽錄音機播出的英文句子之後，再從試題冊上的選項 A 、
B 、 C 三個選項中，選出一個與題意最相符的答案。（每題只播一
次，請仔細聽。）☛（答案請見 P.242）

答題時間
約 **15** 秒/題

MP3 **2-6**

主題
6
招呼與問候 v 電話用語

1
A. I'm here.
B. This is Grace.
C. Hi, how are you?

2
A. Yes, it is. Who's this?
B. What's the price?
C. No, I'm Erin.

3
A. I'll get her. Hold on, please.
B. Sharon is talking.
C. Yes, you can talk.

4
A. Hello, May.
B. I'm pleased.
C. I'm sorry, but he is out.

5
A. I'll be right back.
B. Thank you. I'll call back later.
C. OK, tell me later.

6
A. This is her friend, Lily.
B. This is her.
C. I'll call you.

7

A. Yes, please.
B. Yes, take it.
C. No, you can't.

MP3 2-6

8

A. Hold on, I can't take it any more.
B. Hold on, let me get a pen and paper.
C. Hold it still, please.

9

A. Don't be afraid.
B. I'm terribly sorry.
C. You look terrible.

10

A. What do you call him?
B. I'm number 23.
C. Is this 2222-3333?

第二類 稱謂與關係

主題 7 名字、人名與職業

聽力練習 每題請聆聽錄音機播出的英文句子之後,再從試題冊上的選項 A、B、C 三個選項中,選出一個與題意最相符的答案。(每題只播一次,請仔細聽。)☛(答案請見 **P.244**)

答題時間 約 **15** 秒/題

MP3 **2-7**

1
A. He's a famous actor.
B. He's Gray Davis.
C. He's a super star.

2
A. Nice to meet you.
B. The Chen's.
C. Helen Chen, C-H-E-N, Chen.

3
A. I can't, either.
B. No, I don't.
C. So do I.

4
A. Mine, too.
B. I am, too.
C. Who's your teacher?

5
A. It's a lucky dog.
B. We call him "Lucky."
C. My father gave him a name.

MP3 2-7

6
A. It's name is "Micky."
B. It's a "mouse."
C. I don't like it.

7
A. I'm fine. Thank you.
B. How do you do?
C. I'm a computer engineer.

8
A. Neither, I'm a vet.
B. Either a doctor or a dentist.
C. Both of them.

9
A. I am a firefighter.
B. I want to be a teacher.
C. I want to grow up.

10
A. No, I don't want to be.
B. No, I won't be a doctor.
C. No, I want to be a reporter.

主題 8 所有格關係

聽力練習 每題請聆聽錄音機播出的英文句子之後,再從試題冊上的選項 A、B、C 三個選項中,選出一個與題意最相符的答案。(每題只播一次,請仔細聽。) (答案請見 P.246)

答題時間 約 **15** 秒/題

MP3 **2-8**

1
A. That's right.
B. That is a dog.
C. No, it's not yours.

2
A. Yes, it's new.
B. We have a few.
C. I think so.

3
A. Yes, this is Jim.
B. I don't know.
C. I didn't know it's James'.

4
A. The red one.
B. I want this one.
C. Watch.

5
A. Which one?
B. Never think about it.
C. It's no use.

6

A. This is mine; that is yours.
B. I don't know when.
C. Two for each.

MP3 2-8

7

A. Who?
B. Wait for my call.
C. Give me a call.

8

A. This is mine.
B. That's my sister.
C. She's not my sister.

9

A. Yes, very well.
B. No, he doesn't.
C. I know what you mean.

10

A. No. Wife.
B. It's him.
C. Not me.

主題 9 自 己

聽力練習　每題請聆聽錄音機播出的英文句子之後，再從試題冊上的選項 A、B、C 三個選項中，選出一個與題意最相符的答案。（每題只播一次，請仔細聽。）☛（答案請見 **P.248**）

答題時間 約 **15** 秒/題

MP3 **2-9**

1
A. It's mine.
B. It's me.
C. I am.

2
A. It's me.
B. This is mine.
C. Here I am.

3
A. I'm not.
B. This is Bryan calling.
C. It's me, Bryan.

4
A. Answer me, please.
B. I know Ann, sir.
C. I do.

5
A. Yes, I see.
B. Here I am.
C. I heard from Cathy yesterday.

6
A. Just call me Alex.
B. Stop calling me.
C. What a shame.

MP3 2-9

7
A. Hi, Jane. Yes, it's really me.
B. You're really a good friend.
C. It is really dark.

8
A. I will.
B. I did. Sorry.
C. I brought it.

9
A. Help yourself, please.
B. Yes, I did.
C. Didn't you?

10
A. What else?
B. No, I'm the only one.
C. Yes, I need glasses.

主題 **10** 個人資料

毎題請聆聽錄音機播出的英文句子之後，再從試題冊上的選項 A 、 B 、 C 三個選項中，選出一個與題意最相符的答案。（每題只播一次，請仔細聽。）☞（答案請見 P.250）

答題時間 約 **15** 秒/題

MP3 **2-10**

1
A. I'm from China.
B. Yes, I'm a Chinese.
C. Just a little.

2
A. No, I live alone in Taipei.
B. We live in Taipei.
C. Yes, I love my family.

3
A. Yes, I'm Charlie.
B. No, I'm not your son.
C. No, but I'm an only son.

4
A. Oh? How many people are there?
B. We are family.
C. Now you have a new family.

5
A. What grade are you in?
B. Really? An elephant school?
C. What time do you go to school?

6
A. No, my mother works.
B. Yes, she's a teacher.
C. No, she's a factory worker.

MP3 2-10

7
A. Yes, with two children.
B. Yes, I'm Marian.
C. No, I'm not single.

8
A. So it's near your house?
B. So you're going for a walk?
C. So you're off now?

9
A. I want to have a computer.
B. I love surfing the net.
C. I think it's wasting time.

10
A. Why not me?
B. Sure. I'm a good swimmer.
C. Yes, she's sweet.

第三類 情境

主題 11 　　　 餐 廳

Hint 快速上手句

important sentences

西餐常用字彙

牛排熟度	咖啡	可樂/披薩
rare 生的/一分熟	black 純/黑咖啡	small 小
medium rare 三分熟	with cream / milk 加奶精/加牛奶	regular 中
medium 五分熟	with sugar 加糖	large 大
medium well-done 七分熟	**牛排醬料**	
	black pepper 黑胡椒	
well-done 全熟	mushroom 蘑菇	
用餐地點	to go = take out　外帶 for here = eat in　內用	

聽力練習 每題請聆聽錄音機播出的英文句子之後，再從試題冊上的選項 A、B、C 三個選項中，選出一個與題意最相符的答案。（每題只播一次，請仔細聽。）☛（答案請見 **P.253**）

答題時間 約 **15** 秒/題

MP3 **2-11**

1
A. Three, please.
B. Yes, sir.
C. Are you sure?

2
A. I like May.
B. I'd like to see the menu, please.
C. Put these things in order, please.

3
A. Yes, I'll have a Sirloin steak.
B. No, you may not.
C. Here, take it.

4
A. Medium level.
B. In the medium.
C. Medium rare, please.

5
A. Well, I like black pepper.
B. I like sausages.
C. Yes, I sold it.

6
A. Never mind.
B. Nothing else.
C. I'll have coffee, please.

7

A. After the meal, please.
B. It's a letter.
C. Get me a ladder, please.

MP3 2-11

8

A. Who is it?
B. I'd like just one.
C. One cheeseburger, to go.

9

A. That's enough.
B. Nothing special.
C. What a thing it is!

10

A. What did you eat?
B. Certainly, what would you like?
C. What's your phone number?

每題請聆聽錄音機播出的英文句子之後，再從試題冊上的選項 A、B、C 三個選項中，選出一個與題意最相符的答案。（每題只播一次，請仔細聽。）☛（答案請見 **P.256**）

答題時間 約 **15** 秒/題

MP3 **2-12**

1
A. He's 23 years old.
B. He's very fat.
C. He's 172 cm.

2
A. What's your weight?
B. Who is heavier?
C. How do you like it?

3
A. My brother is taller than me.
B. He is as tall as me.
C. The tall one.

4
A. He likes sports.
B. He is a tall young man with long hair.
C. He is fine.

5
A. No, she's not beautiful.
B. No, she's not.
C. She did pretty well.

6
A. A purse.
B. A dress.
C. Luggage.

主題
12
情境
∨
外表打扮

7
A. You're gown up.
B. Go to get a belt.
C. You should wear a tie.

8
A. Put on a hat.
B. Get dressed.
C. Socks will keep them warm.

9
A. A little.
B. Yesterday.
C. Every day.

10
A. Do I?
B. Don't you?
C. Do you?

結　帳

important sentences

付款時的口語用法

1. We'll go Dutch. 各自付帳。

2. Let me take care of the check. 我來付。

3. This is on me. 算我的。

4. This is on the house. 本店請客。

5. The company will pay for it. 公司會付。

6. Bill, please. （我要）買單。

7. Where is the cashier? 在哪裡結帳？

8. Does this price include tax?
   這個價錢有含稅嗎？

9. Is it duty free? 這是免稅品嗎？

10. Can't you give me a discount?
    你可以給個折扣嗎？

聽力練習 每題請聆聽錄音機播出的英文句子之後，再從試題冊上的選項 A、B、C 三個選項中，選出一個與題意最相符的答案。（每題只播一次，請仔細聽。）☞（答案請見 P.258）

答題時間 約 **15** 秒/題

MP3 **2-13**

主題 **13** 情境 V 結帳

1
A. Oh, no. Let me get it.
B. Got it?
C. You'll pay for it.

2
A. Oh, thank you. I'll get the next one.
B. You can't cheat.
C. Oh, no. It's too bad.

3
A. One moment.
B. Is the money right?
C. I'll pay by check.

4
A. It's a credit card.
B. I'm in a rush.
C. Cash.

5
A. I want to pay with a credit card.
B. How much is it?
C. Money isn't everything.

6
A. How much do you charge?
B. What's wrong?
C. Oh, it's too expensive.

7
A. You're 3 years older than me.
B. I own it.
C. That'll be fifty-five dollars and twenty 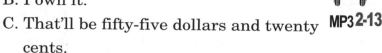 MP3 2-13
   cents.

8
A. It'll be $120.
B. It's $120 each.
C. We'll get 120 altogether.

9
A. I don't want to change it.
B. Oh, keep the change.
C. Catch the chance.

10
A. Yes, it is.
B. I got a flu.
C. We have good service.

主題 14　個人好惡

聽力練習　每題請聆聽錄音機播出的英文句子之後，再從試題冊上的選項 A、B、C 三個選項中，選出一個與題意最相符的答案。（每題只播一次，請仔細聽。）☞（答案請見 P.260）

答題時間 約 **15** 秒/題

MP3 **2-14**

1
　A. Yes, a movie.
　B. I like it.
　C. I like the movie theater.

2
　A. Yes, I like them.
　B. I have a camera.
　C. Very much.

3
　A. Yes, it's my favorite.
　B. Yes, I love doing sports.
　C. I like jogging, swimming and skating.

4
　A. What kind?
　B. What do you like?
　C. Are you interested in music?

5
　A. Not so good.
　B. Right on! I'm going to buy some new CDs.
　C. I can't sing.

6

A. I'd rather wear jeans than a dress.

B. Do we have a choice?

C. Be my guest.

MP3 2-14

7

A. I'm afraid she would.

B. She didn't tell me.

C. No, I don't think so.

8

A. I love it very much.

B. This university is famous.

C. You're unlike me.

9

A. Just a haircut.

B. Cut it short all over.

C. I'd like a shampoo.

10

A. Yes, I do. I'll go there one day.

B. I'll be there in a second.

C. I visited the city several times.

第四類 數字

主題 15 詢價

Hint 快速上手句

important sentences

討價還價的說法

1. Would you lower the price?
   你可以算便宜一點嗎?

2. Could you cut the price a little?
   你可以少算一點嗎?

3. Can you give me a discount?
   你可以給我一些折扣嗎?

4. Sorry, it's one price for all.
   對不起,這是不二價。

5. Our price are all fixed.
   我們的價格都是不二價的。

6. I'll buy it if it's under 50 dollars.
   如果這不到 50 元我就會買。

聽力
練習

每題請聆聽錄音機播出的英文句子之後，再從試題冊上的選項 A、B、C 三個選項中，選出一個與題意最相符的答案。（每題只播一次，請仔細聽。）☛（答案請見 P.262）

答題時間
約 **15** 秒/題

MP3 **2-15**

1
A. It's about $ 1,200 for one night.
B. We'll stay for 3 nights.
C. This is for rent.

2
A. It's $ 70.
B. It's $ 70 per hour.
C. It's fair.

3
A. Yes, they are.
B. You are free.
C. Yes, there are four.

4
A. Three meals a day.
B. $100 a meal.
C. No, they aren't.

5
A. US$ 10.00 a day.
B. US dollars.
C. Nothing.

6
A. Can I change to another room?
B. I have a 25-cent coin.
C. US$ 25.00 a week.

7
A. Oh, it's free.
B. Oh, you have to pay in cash.
C. Should I?

MP3 2-15

8
A. You're worth it.
B. I have a lot of it.
C. Yes, I bought you a coat.

9
A. I won't pay for it.
B. I pray before going to bed.
C. It's too much.

10
A. This is a country.
B. Please count it.
C. I'm sorry, but not.

聽力練習 每題請聆聽錄音機播出的英文句子之後，再從試題冊上的選項 A、B、C 三個選項中，選出一個與題意最相符的答案。（每題只播一次，請仔細聽。）☛（答案請見 **P.265**）

答題時間 約 **15** 秒/題

1

A. Why did you get up so early?
B. It's time to go to bed.
C. I usually get up at six thirty.

MP3 2-16

2

A. At the store.
B. At ten o'clock, sir.
C. The store is open.

3

A. It's time to start the class.
B. He's a big star.
C. It starts at three thirty in the afternoon.

4

A. Keep early hours.
B. It is 9:00 a.m. to 5:30 p.m.
C. I worked from 9:00 a.m. to 5:30 p.m. yesterday.

5

A. Sundown is about 8:30 here.
B. My son came at 8:30.

C. The sun goes down in the west.

6

A. 9:25 on Track 12.
B. It takes 9 hours by train.
C. We will leave Los Angeles by 9 o'clock.

MP3 **2-16**

7

A. We plan to leave at 11:45.
B. It should be close at 11:45.
C. It should be here at 11:45.

8

A. Check-in time is 11:00 a.m.
B. Please check out before 11:00 a.m.
C. We'll check the plane at 11:00 a.m.

9

A. The show is good.
B. She showed up on time.
C. I have no idea.

10

A. About ten minutes.
B. About ten meters.
C. About ten long ropes.

🎧 **聽力練習** 每題請聆聽錄音機播出的英文句子之後，再從試題冊上的選項 A、B、C 三個選項中，選出一個與題意最相符的答案。（每題只播一次，請仔細聽。）☞（答案請見 **P.267**）

答題時間 約 **15** 秒/題

MP3 **2-17**

1
A. Is it seven o'clock already?
B. It's seven o'clock.
C. I get up at seven o'clock.

2
A. At 9:00 last night.
B. Nothing is right.
C. I'm afraid not.

3
A. The house is made out of wood.
B. Just a second. I'll have to check.
C. O.K. I'll check the house.

4
A. What is the time?
B. I hope so.
C. Yes, you are here on time.

5
A. Okay, I will.
B. Will you come tonight?
C. Yes, I can hear.

6
A. At one o'clock in the afternoon.
B. Winnie's not leaving.
C. I don't know why.

MP3 2-17

主題
17

數字
v
時間約定

7
A. I think you'll make it.
B. When does the train leave?
C. Try to catch me.

8
A. Turn on the light.
B. It's getting late.
C. For how long?

9
A. Ok, bye.
B. I come home at 5:00 in the evening.
C. Did you see?

10
A. You name the time.
B. Ten times.
C. In old time.

詢問時間

聽力
練習

每題請聆聽錄音機播出的英文句子之後，再從試題冊上的選項 A、B、C 三個選項中，選出一個與題意最相符的答案。（每題只播一次，請仔細聽。）☛（答案請見 **P.269**）

答題時間 約 **15** 秒/題

MP3 **2-18**

1
A. It's the time.
B. See you next time.
C. It's half past eight.

2
A. It's one o'clock sharp.
B. Don't touch. It's sharp.
C. Don't ask.

3
A. Can't you?
B. Are you sure?
C. Sure. It's twenty to nine.

4
A. Yes, it's a quarter to seven.
B. Please be quite.
C. Show me.

5
A. I won't tell Tom.
B. It's not for Tom.
C. It's four o'clock.

6
A. It's two hundred and twenty.
B. It's two twenty.
C. Two times twenty is forty.

MP3 2-18

7
A. Time flies.
B. It's fifteen minutes fast.
C. It's fifteen minutes past seven.

8
A. I don't think it is five o'clock yet.
B. I don't think so.
C. No wonder.

9
A. My watch says two o'clock.
B. Watch what you say.
C. Watch out.

10
A. I'm sorry, I have no money.
B. I'm sorry, I have no watch.
C. I'm sorry, I have no change.

11
A. It has struck one.
B. It's a clock.
C. Good luck.

主題 19　詢問地點

聽力練習　每題請聆聽錄音機播出的英文句子之後，再從試題冊上的選項 A、B、C 三個選項中，選出一個與題意最相符的答案。（每題只播一次，請仔細聽。）☞（答案請見 P.272）

答題時間　約 **15** 秒/題

MP3 **2-19**

1
A. Yes, we're from Australia.
B. No, I'm from Canada.
C. No, I'm an American.

2
A. I'm in Hualian.
B. I live in Korea.
C. I live in school housing.

3
A. I'm fine.
B. I'm a housewife.
C. I'm at home.

4
A. We were not there.
B. We are lost.
C. You are losing it.

5
A. He's going to the library.
B. Yes, he's going to the library.
C. Yes, he's going.

MP3 2-19

主題 **19**

慣用句型 v 詢問地點

6
A. Not me.
B. Not yet.
C. I can't.

7
A. We're on the bus.
B. You're right.
C. We're right here.

8
A. Don't go.
B. It's in the airport.
C. The airport, please.

9
A. Do you like spaghetti?
B. I know that place.
C. How pretty!

10
A. People around the world know about it.
B. Canada has the most islands in the world.
C. Is it China?

聽力練習　每題請聆聽錄音機播出的英文句子之後，再從試題冊上的選項Ａ、Ｂ、Ｃ三個選項中，選出一個與題意最相符的答案。（每題只播一次，請仔細聽。） ☛（答案請見 **P.274**）

答題時間 約 **15** 秒/題

MP3 **2-20**

1
A. Just take a chance.
B. My father drives.
C. Take it easy.

2
A. Go ahead.
B. I'll take it.
C. Take bus 202.

3
A. By MRT.
B. It's by the zoo.
C. By heart.

4
A. Easy. Just call her.
B. Easy come; easy go.
C. On foot.

5
A. Here is $2,000 cash.
B. Here you come!
C. Here we are!

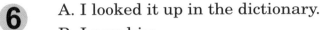

6
A. I looked it up in the dictionary.
B. I saw him.
C. I didn't talk to him.

MP3 **2-20**

7
A. Jason told me.
B. You're telling me.
C. Let me tell you why.

主題
20
慣用句型 v 詢問方法

8
A. Help me, please.
B. You can do the dishes.
C. Why didn't you help me?

9
A. You can leave now.
B. I'm doing housework.
C. I'd like to see the ties.

10
A. Just leave.
B. Just a minute.
C. I made a cake.

詢問原因

解釋語氣的開頭語

1. There's a (good) reason for this:...
   這是我做這件事的理由……。

2. Here's what happened:...
   讓我來告訴你發生了什麼事……。

3. Let me tell you why...
   讓我來告訴你為什麼……。

4. Let me explain...
   讓我來解釋……。

5. The reason is...
   理由是……。

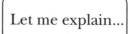

Let me explain...

聽力練習 每題請聆聽錄音機播出的英文句子之後，再從試題冊上的選項 A 、 B 、 C 三個選項中，選出一個與題意最相符的答案。（每題只播一次，請仔細聽。） ☞（答案請見 **P.276**）

答題時間 約 **15** 秒/題

MP3 **2-21**

1
A. What's the matter?
B. That's not good.
C. It's a good idea.

2
A. Excuse me.
B. You'll be sorry.
C. Did you catch a cold?

3
A. I can't open this box.
B. He's fine.
C. Watch your mouth.

4
A. I did it myself.
B. That sounds great.
C. Nothing.

5
A. Oh, are you? Why?
B. How can you say that?
C. Don't worry.

6
A. I was ... busy.
B. I came by a taxi.
C. Yeah, sure.

7
A. Why me again?
B. That's right.
C. Don't mention it.

MP3 **2-21**

8
A. You name it.
B. No, you don't understand.
C. Sure. What is it?

9
A. Yes, I'm.
B. What for?
C. Yes, I have.

10
A. It's cool!
B. Why not use a comb?
C. Why not?

主題 22	感官動詞

Hint

快速上手句

important sentences

感官動詞慣用句法

◆常見的感官動詞：
see / hear / smell / taste / watch / feel

❶ 感官動詞的用法：

1. 感官動詞 + 形容詞：
   I **feel** cold. 我覺得冷。

2. 感官動詞 + 名詞：
   I **heard** the thundering. 我聽到打雷聲。

3. 感官動詞 + 受詞 + 原形動詞 / 動詞 -ing：
   I **saw** the train come / coming into the station. 我看到火車進站。

❷ 特殊用法：

4. 感官動詞 + like + 名詞：……起來像～
   You **look like** a doctor. 你看起來像個醫生。
   She **felt like** a fool. 她覺得自己像個大笨蛋。

答題時間 約 **15** 秒/題

MP3 **2-22**

1
A. O.K. I'm here.
B. Yes, very well.
C. I'm pretty well, thank you.

2
A. It's filled of water.
B. He feels sick.
C. It feels nice and soft.

3
A. Yes, I like you.
B. Yes, it tastes good.
C. No, it's not like that.

4
A. Wow, beautiful lady.
B. Umm, it smells good.
C. I ate already.

5
A. Can't you see?
B. You're so nice.
C. Very handsome.

6
A. I can't hear it.
B. It smells good.
C. It smells like garbage.

7
A. Never. You just surprised me.
B. I'll never see you again.
C. I have a sore throat.

MP3 2-22

8
A. So are you joining us?
B. I was glad to talk with you.
C. You have a beautiful voice.

9
A. How does it feel?
B. Then why not stay longer?
C. How do you feel?

10
A. Yeah, I can't feel my feet anymore.
B. It's not good for you.
C. I'm not feeling well.

主題 23 驚訝與驚喜

Hint 快速上手句

important sentences

驚呼語氣

1. Hooray! = Yippee!
   萬歲！（歡呼聲）

2. Oops! = Oh, no!
   糟糕！

3. Ouch!
   唉唷！痛啊！

4. Yuck! = Gross!
   討厭！噁心！

5. Oh, my goodness!
   噢，天啊！

Oh, my goodness!

聽力練習

每題請聆聽錄音機播出的英文句子之後，再從試題冊上的選項 A、B、C 三個選項中，選出一個與題意最相符的答案。（每題只播一次，請仔細聽。）☛（答案請見 P.281）

答題時間 約 **15** 秒/題

MP3 **2-23**

主題 **23** 強調短句 v 驚訝與驚喜

1
A. Oh, no. Is it?
B. How many?
C. Do you have the time?

2
A. Already?
B. Here we are.
C. It' the wrong time.

3
A. What a surprise!
B. You can't do this.
C. It's mine.

4
A. What's the matter?
B. Do you believe it?
C. How can you do this?

5
A. That's surprising. He's never late.
B. Why were you late?
C. Give me one second.

6
A. I can't believe it.
B. You won't believe it.
C. Believe it or not.

7
A. Are you joking? She looks so young.
B. No kidding? She's your sister?
C. Wow. What a good kid!

MP3 2-23

8
A. Good guess.
B. They all laughed at him.
C. No kidding.

9
A. I'm afraid it is.
B. Yes, it's real.
C. For real this time?

10
A. Hi, long time no see.
B. It's not just you.
C. Yes, I'm really busy.

主題 24　命令與警告

聽力練習 每題請聆聽錄音機播出的英文句子之後,再從試題冊上的選項 A、B、C 三個選項中,選出一個與題意最相符的答案。(每題只播一次,請仔細聽。)☞(答案請見 **P.283**)

答題時間 約 **15** 秒/題

MP3 **2-24**

1　A. What are you talking about?
　　B. The teacher is speaking.
　　C. I'm sorry.

2　A. All right.
　　B. I'm all ears.
　　C. We're in a library.

3　A. You're too careful.
　　B. I do care.
　　C. Yes. What is it?

4　A. OK. OK.
　　B. Come on. Let's leave.
　　C. Go away.

5　A. Would you hand me that vase?
　　B. Hey, take it easy.

C. It's easy as pie.

6

A. Hey, I'm not stupid.

B. You will what?

C. I'll see you out.

7

A. I won't.

B. I'm sorry.

C. I forgot.

8

A. Are you O.K.?

B. I'm feeling better.

C. Thanks.

9

A. Oh, thank you.

B. Better safe than sorry!

C. How are you?

10

A. Please don't hurt me!

B. Don't worry. I will.

C. Ouch! It hurts.

主題 25 催促與延緩

聽力練習 每題請聆聽錄音機播出的英文句子之後，再從試題冊上的選項 A 、 B 、 C 三個選項中，選出一個與題意最相符的答案。（每題只播一次，請仔細聽。）☞（答案請見 **P.285**）

答題時間 約 **15** 秒/題

MP3 **2-25**

1
A. OK, coming.
B. Gook luck!
C. Take your time.

2
A. Just a minute.
B. Help yourself.
C. Oh, that's all right.

3
A. Sure. What is it?
B. Slow down.
C. Don't push me.

4
A. Time's up.
B. No problem. I'll wait.
C. Don't go away.

5
A. What do you plan to do?
B. Let's head out.
C. O.K., but hurry.

6
A. Oh, I'm sorry.
B. How could you?
C. Wait a minute.

MP3 **2-25**

7
A. Oh, good. We still have time.
B. The game is over now.
C. Where are we going?

8
A. Don't hurry.
B. Don't go anywhere.
C. Come here, please.

9
A. How fast do you run?
B. Let's go then.
C. Wait here.

10
A. Don't worry.
B. Don't take too long.
C. I'm late for the bus.

主題 26 拒 絕

聽力練習 每題請聆聽錄音機播出的英文句子之後,再從試題冊上的選項 A 、B 、C 三個選項中,選出一個與題意最相符的答案。(每題只播一次,請仔細聽。) ☞ (答案請見 **P.287**)

答題時間 約 **15** 秒/題

MP3 **2-26**

1
A. No way.
B. That's nothing.
C. That's not true.

2
A. No, sorry about that.
B. Sorry to bother you.
C. It's all the same to me.

3
A. We need to get help.
B. No way.
C. No, but thank you anyway.

4
A. What a waste!
B. Do you need anything help?
C. Any questions?

5
A. Thanks. I'd love to.
B. Not really.
C. No, I won't.

6

A. Not for me, thanks.
B. Not me. I didn't.
C. It's not mine.

MP3 **2-26**

7

A. That's not possible.
B. See you tomorrow.
C. I haven't finished it.

8

A. No way.
B. No, you may not.
C. Yes, you may.

9

A. No, that's all for now.
B. I'm tired now.
C. Excuse me.

10

A. I saw her washing her car.
B. No, thank you. It's OK.
C. I'd like to buy a new car.

主題 27　道　謝

聽力練習 每題請聆聽錄音機播出的英文句子之後，再從試題冊上的選項 A、B、C 三個選項中，選出一個與題意最相符的答案。（每題只播一次，請仔細聽。）☛（答案請見 P.290）

答題時間 約 **15** 秒/題

MP3 **2-27**

1
A. Not much.
B. You're welcome.
C. We have some.

2
A. Don't mention it.
B. Sure. You are right.
C. It's for sure.

3
A. I'm happy.
B. Thank you very much.
C. It's good for you.

4
A. Any time.
B. I'm glad to hear that.
C. No, I didn't do anything.

5
A. It's my pleasure.
B. As you pleased.
C. You are wonderful.

6
A. That's OK.
B. It's fine with me.
C. Thank you very much.

MP3 2-27

7
A. Yes, thank you.
B. Yes, I will. Thanks.
C. I'm very well.

8
A. What do you like to play?
B. I'm glad to hear that.
C. I'm so glad for you.

9
A. It's just what I want. Thank you.
B. I will do what I can.
C. It was nothing like that.

10
A. Don't worry. I will help you.
B. Sit down, please.
C. Thanks. You're very kind.

主題 28 讚 美

Hint 快速上手句

important sentences

讚歎語

1. Good job! 對! 就是這樣!

2. (Very) well done! 對! 就是這樣!

3. Way to go! 你好極了! 你好棒! 你好厲害!

4. Nice going! 對! 就是這樣!

5. Looking good! 對! 就是這樣!

6. That'll do it! 對! 就是這樣!

Way to go!!

答題時間 約 **15** 秒/題

MP3 **2-28**

1
A. That's nice.
B. You're nice.
C. It's a nice boat.

2
A. Look. How is it?
B. Thank you.
C. You're cool.

3
A. Guess what!
B. Take a guess.
C. You're smart.

4
A. Good for you!
B. Great. Let's do together.
C. OK, that's all.

5
A. Congratulations!
B. You did a good job.
C. You look great today.

6
A. What a beautiful day.
B. Wow, you're so beautiful.
C. Wow, what a beauty.

7
A. Umn, it smells good.
B. I'm dying for a drink.
C. What would you like for dinner?

MP3 **2-28**

主題 **28** 強調短句 v 讚美

8
A. Oh, no. Not at all.
B. Oh, no!
C. Good heaven!

9
A. Just look at what you've done.
B. Take it or leave it.
C. It's delicious!

10
A. Really? You are?
B. Well done.
C. Cheer up!

道 歉

🎵🎵🎵🎵 **聽力練習** 每題請聆聽錄音機播出的英文句子之後，再從試題冊上的選項 A、B、C 三個選項中，選出一個與題意最相符的答案。（每題只播一次，請仔細聽。）☞（答案請見 **P.294**）

答題時間 約 **15** 秒/題

MP3 **2-29**

1
A. You'll be sorry.
B. What kept you so long?
C. What for?

2
A. I'm sorry.
B. Excuse me.
C. I don't know.

3
A. OK, see you tomorrow.
B. I had better go by myself.
C. I'm out of here.

4
A. It's no trouble.
B. Leave it to me.
C. Take your time.

5
A. Sorry. It's my fault.
B. You can't do that.
C. Hi, how are you?

6
A. Oh, my mistake.
B. Who knows where Jim is?
C. You are?

MP3 **2-29**

7
A. Never mind.
B. It's a terrible story.
C. Pardon me.

8
A. I'll give you a call.
B. What do you call it?
C. OK, put it through.

9
A. Let me think about it.
B. Forget it.
C. Never.

10
A. I will do my best.
B. Sorry. Let me treat you a coffee.
C. You got it.

主題
29
強調短句 v 道歉

安撫與鼓勵

important sentences

鼓勵語氣

1. Have a try! 試試看！

2. Have a go! 試試看！

3. Try again! 再試試看！

4. Go for it! 儘管放手一試！

5. You can do it (if you try)!
   試試看，你可以做到的！

6. Trust me! You can make it!
   相信我，你可以做到的！

You can do it!

每題請聆聽錄音機播出的英文句子之後，再從試題冊上的選項 A、B、C 三個選項中，選出一個與題意最相符的答案。（每題只播一次，請仔細聽。）☛（答案請見 P.296）

答題時間
約 **15** 秒/題

MP3 **2-30**

主題 **30**

強調短句 v 安撫與鼓勵

1
A. I hope so.
B. Let's write to Alex.
C. Do you mean it?

2
A. That's good news.
B. Did he agree?
C. I'm fine.

3
A. Did you miss me?
B. Don't worry about it.
C. Don't be mad at me.

4
A. That's OK. Did you get hurt?
B. Please don't hurt me!
C. The cup is broken.

5
A. Surly you will.
B. Come on this way.
C. Come on. Give it a try.

6
A. Don't give up.
B. Yes, the egg is too hard.
C. Don't do that.

7
A. Guess what!
B. Why didn't you?
C. Why not?

MP3 2-30

8
A. Not really. It's a big horse.
B. It's your home.
C. But it's nice.

9
A. Go ahead. Don't worry about me.
B. Sure. Take a chance.
C. You'll never know until you do it.

10
A. Better late than never.
B. Hurry up.
C. What's this for?

主題 31　表示不介意

聽力練習　每題請聆聽錄音機播出的英文句子之後，再從試題冊上的選項 A、B、C 三個選項中，選出一個與題意最相符的答案。（每題只播一次，請仔細聽。）☞（答案請見 **P.298**）

答題時間 約 **15** 秒/題

MP3 **2-31**

1
A. I don't mind.
B. Please say it again.
C. You're welcome.

2
A. See you later.
B. So soon?
C. It doesn't matter.

3
A. Never mind.
B. What would you like?
C. Don't talk to me.

4
A. Forget it.
B. I say what I mean.
C. Have you forgotten what I said?

5
A. It happens.
B. I'm doing fine.
C. It's nothing important, really.

6
A. Don't say so much.
B. It's not important.
C. No, go ahead.

MP3 **2-31**

7
A. Let me get you some tea.
B. You can decide it.
C. I'd love some.

8
A. We'd better hurry.
B. I don't care.
C. Did he?

9
A. Who cares!
B. I'll take care of it.
C. What do you think about it?

10
A. Oh, that's no problem.
B. I just want to help.
C. I have no idea.

主題 32　　　猜　測

聽力練習 每題請聆聽錄音機播出的英文句子之後，再從試題冊上的選項 A、B、C 三個選項中，選出一個與題意最相符的答案。（每題只播一次，請仔細聽。） ☞（答案請見 **P.300**）

答題時間 約 **15** 秒/題

MP3 **2-32**

1
A. It's all done.
B. I guess so.
C. I'll write it down.

2
A. We'll get there by a taxi.
B. As usual.
C. I guess not.

3
A. It's possible.
B. That's easy!
C. We'd better tell the teacher.

4
A. Pass me the ball, please.
B. It's better.
C. I don't know.

5
A. That all depends on what it is.
B. You're welcome.
C. I'm fine.

6

A. Not this summer.
B. Not last winter.
C. Do I?

MP3 2-32

7

A. He's at home.
B. Maybe not.
C. He may not.

8

A. There's only half an hour left.
B. Sooner or later.
C. I guess "forever".

9

A. I just want to help people.
B. Well, I did get an A.
C. I will cheer for you!

10

A. We should work hard everyday.
B. I don't go to work on weekends.
C. No, but maybe the teacher won't ask for it.

主題 33 尋求認同

聽力練習 每題請聆聽錄音機播出的英文句子之後,再從試題冊上的選項 A、B、C 三個選項中,選出一個與題意最相符的答案。(每題只播一次,請仔細聽。)☛(答案請見 P.302)

答題時間 約 **15** 秒/題

MP3 **2-33**

1
A. Yes, I like it.
B. Yes, he's nice.
C. No problem.

2
A. No problem.
B. That's right.
C. That's all.

3
A. That's you, not me.
B. Yes, we share everything.
C. Yes, it's all right.

4
A. Yes, it's a bed.
B. Yes, it's a bat.
C. I'm afraid so.

5
A. I can't believe it, either.
B. But it's true.
C. But we are leaving.

6
A. You did a great job.
B. May I take a picture of you?
C. I'd like some more, please.

MP3 2-33

7
A. Oh, we're sorry.
B. No, no way.
C. Not too bad.

8
A. Yes, go ahead.
B. Do you play golf?
C. It's better than nothing.

9
A. Sure. He's our friend.
B. I'm sorry.
C. It's terrible.

10
A. Do you think I'm stupid?
B. What is wrong with you!?
C. Of course you can.

主題 34　表達認同

聽力練習　每題請聆聽錄音機播出的英文句子之後，再從試題冊上的選項 A、B、C 三個選項中，選出一個與題意最相符的答案。（每題只播一次，請仔細聽。）☛（答案請見 P.304）

答題時間 約 **15** 秒/題

MP3 **2-34**

1
A. Yes, it's novel.
B. I like to read a book on weekend.
C. You're right.

2
A. It sure is.
B. How is it?
C. What is it?

3
A. It was great.
B. Yeah, I went.
C. What a great idea.

4
A. Right, we'll ride a bike.
B. That sounds nice.
C. Have a nice trip.

5
A. Yeah, it's my plan.
B. It seems great!

C. I agree.

6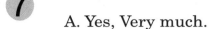

A. Yes, I'm.

B. There's nothing I can say.

C. Yes, I'm just like you.

7

A. Yes, Very much.

B. Yes, it's very noisy.

C. Yes, we're alike.

8

A. Sounds good.

B. I'm sorry to hear that.

C. I can't agree more.

9

A. Yes, Luke won the first place in the game.

B. Yes, she has a warm heart.

C. Yes, I think so too.

10

A. So do I.

B. So am I.

C. Nor do I.

主題 35 不完全肯定

聽力練習 每題請聆聽錄音機播出的英文句子之後，再從試題冊上的選項 A 、B 、C 三個選項中，選出一個與題意最相符的答案。（每題只播一次，請仔細聽。）☛（答案請見 **P.307**）

答題時間 約 **15** 秒/題

MP3 **2-35**

1
A. Really?
B. Isn't it delicious?
C. Is she?

2
A. Is it?
B. No, I have no idea.
C. That' too bad.

3
A. Will he?
B. Are you sure?
C. Has he?

4
A. I don't know she's divorced.
B. Is she getting better?
C. Is that true?

5
A. Really? He's a waiter?
B. Is that so?
C. Isn't he famous?

6
A. Thanks. Don't bother.
B. I'm not myself today.
C. Do you think so?

MP3 2-35

7
A. Yes, we'll be there.
B. I hope so.
C. Are you sure?

8
A. Not always.
B. I enjoyed it.
C. Let me guess.

9
A. I like Seattle best.
B. Oh, I've been to lots of countries.
C. It's hard to say. Each country is different.

10
A. It seemed that way at first.
B. Are they?
C. I'm not Chinese.

主題 36 不認同

Hint 快速上手句

important sentences

不認同對方的看法

1. I can't go along with what you say.
   我無法同意你所說的。

2. I don't agree with your point.
   我不同意你的論點。

3. I don't think so.
   我不這麼認為。

4. I don't see it that way.
   我不這麼想。

5. I'm not sure.
   我不確定。

I don't agree with you.

聽力練習 每題請聆聽錄音機播出的英文句子之後，再從試題冊上的選項 A、B、C 三個選項中，選出一個與題意最相符的答案。（每題只播一次，請仔細聽。）☞（答案請見 **P.309**）

答題時間 約 **15** 秒/題

MP3 **2-36**

1
A. No, math is harder than English.
B. You did it wrong.
C. I don't think so.

2
A. Don't you?
B. No, I don't.
C. I believe so.

3
A. Not really.
B. Do they play badly?
C. They don't pray at all.

4
A. Me, too.
B. Not only two.
C. No, it's not.

5
A. Of course we can.
B. Trust me, you can make it.
C. Believe it or not.

6
A. No, you may not.
B. It's no use. He won't listen to you.
C. He kept on smoking all the time.

7
A. It's too late.
B. See you later.
C. What did you see?

MP3 2-36

主題
36
強調短句 v 不認同

8
A. It's the right time.
B. She will never sell her car.
C. It's impossible.

9
A. Sorry to let you down.
B. No, I don't have a fax machine.
C. I believe in you.

10
A. Never think about it.
B. OK, I'll give it a try.
C. I can't forgive you.

提供或尋求協助

提供協助

- Do you need any help? 你需要幫忙嗎？
- How can I help you? 我可以怎麼幫你？
- Would you like me to... 你要我……嗎？
- Let me... 讓我……。

接受

- I'd appreciate it. 我很感激。
- Would (could) you? 可以……嗎？

回絕

- It's OK, I can do it. 沒問題，我自己來。
- No, but thank you just the same.
  不用了，不過還是要謝謝你。
- I'd rather / I'd better do it myself.
  我寧可/最好自己來做。
- Thanks, I can manage.
  謝謝，我可以應付。

每題請聆聽錄音機播出的英文句子之後，再從試題冊上的選項 A、B、C 三個選項中，選出一個與題意最相符的答案。（每題只播一次，請仔細聽。）☞（答案請見 P.311）

答題時間 約 **15** 秒/題

MP3 **2-37**

主題 **37** 強調短句 ∨ 提供或尋求協助

1
A. Sure thing.
B. I did it.
C. Go ahead.

2
A. With pleasure.
B. Yes, it's for you.
C. It will do.

3
A. No, do it yourself.
B. This will help.
C. There's no hope for me.

4
A. Let me think it over.
B. Sorry, I don't have a watch.
C. I've got plenty of time.

5
A. Can you show me an example?
B. I'll try it on.
C. I can hardly hear you.

6
A. What's wrong?
B. Could you tell me how to do?
C. Excuse me.

7
A. Who are you?
B. You can't.
C. No thanks, I'm just looking.

MP3 2-37

8
A. No, don't bother.
B. Turn right here.
C. You have no right.

9
A. Yes, please. That would be very kind of you.
B. We need to get help.
C. This is difficult.

10
A . It's not the answer.
B. I'll help you.
C. If you wouldn't mind.

主題 38 請求許可與允諾

聽力練習 每題請聆聽錄音機播出的英文句子之後,再從試題冊上的選項 A、B、C 三個選項中,選出一個與題意最相符的答案。(每題只播一次,請仔細聽。)☛(答案請見 **P.313**)

約 **15** 秒/題

MP3 **2-38**

1
A. It's tea time.
B. It depends on you.
C. Make yourself home.

2
A. Sure. Take it.
B. I'm sure you borrowed it.
C. Lend it to me, please.

3
A. Get me some, please.
B. I'd love some. Thanks.
C. Please help yourself.

4
A. Stay there.
B. I'll be right back.
C. Come on in.

5
A. Sure. Come follow me.
B. Oh, I can't believe you're saying this.
C. We don't have enough money.

6
A. You should study hard.
B. Yes, read it aloud.
C. You're the class leader.

MP3 2-38

7
A. That's OK with me.
B. I'm OK.
C. This is going nowhere.

8
A. Of course you may.
B. You won these?
C. You're welcome.

9
A. No, go ahead.
B. Save it!
C. I didn't mean to do it.

10
A. Try me.
B. It fitted you very well.
C. Why don't you?

主題 39　　建　議

聽力練習 每題請聆聽錄音機播出的英文句子之後，再從試題冊上的選項 A 、 B 、 C 三個選項中，選出一個與題意最相符的答案。（每題只播一次，請仔細聽。）☞（答案請見 **P.315**）

答題時間 約 **15** 秒/題

MP3 **2-39**

1
A. We'll have dinner at 7:00.
B. How about watching a movie?
C. How about eating out?

2
A. Keep in mind.
B. What about this?
C. I can't make up my mind.

3
A. You may take a taxi.
B. You should go back.
C. You can get it.

4
A. Come out and play!
B. I'll buy the tickets.
C. That's a good idea.

5
A. Why don't you learn?
B. You knew it.
C. How did you know?

6
A . Bring an umbrella.
B. I don't like this.
C. You might try this.

MP3 2-39

7
A. Yes, I'll go.
B. No. It's only a three-minute walk.
C. You should take the chance.

8
A. Thank you for asking.
B. I'll write you a check for the car.
C. Okay. Thank you very much.

9
A. You should drink more water.
B. Where did you get the flute?
C. Here's some fruit you want.

10
A. I wish I could.
B. Have you been to the doctor?
C. Get ready for bed.

主題 40 確 認

聽力練習 每題請聆聽錄音機播出的英文句子之後,再從試題冊上的選項 A、B、C 三個選項中,選出一個與題意最相符的答案。(每題只播一次,請仔細聽。)☞(答案請見 P.318)

答題時間 約 **15** 秒/題

MP3 **2-40**

1
A. He didn't say.
B. He'll be back.
C. I happened to overhear what he said.

2
A. Yes, it's difficult.
B. Yes, that's easy!
C. Yes. Learn it by heart.

3
A. You don't know me?
B. Jimmy Taylor is absent.
C. I understand it now.

4
A. I'll start right away.
B. No chance at all.
C. How many?

5
A. Who do you think you are (talking to)?
B. Can you order one for me?
C. No more excuses.

6

A. I mean it's expensive.

B. I know what you mean.

C. I really mean it.

MP3 2-40

7

A. How can you tell?

B. For sure?

C. This is the answer.

8

A. Is that all?

B. What did you say?

C. What have happened to you?

9

A. Will she come?

B. Don't give me your excuses.

C. Did she say why?

10

A. How was your show?

B. Can't you see me?

C. Yeah? Tell me more about it.

11

A. What's the difference?

B. This one is more expensive.

C. Yes, how about this one?

全民英檢聽力測驗

簡短對話

作答提示

▶ 每題請聆聽錄音機播出的一段對話和相關問題之後，再從試題冊上[A][B][C]三個選項中，選出一個與題意最相符的答案。

（每題只播出一次，請仔細聽）

簡短對話

聽力
練習
每題請聆聽錄音機播出的一段對話和相關問題後，再從試題冊上
A、B、C三個選項中，選出一個與題意最相符的答案。（每題只
播一次，請仔細聽。）☞（答案請見 **P.322**）

Conversation 1.
A. Taipei Train Station.
B. The taxi stand.
C. The bus station.

答題時間
約 **15** 秒/題

MP3 **3-1**

Conversation 2.
A. At Cindy's home.
B. At his home.
C. At the park.

Conversation 3.
A. Paris.
B. Beijing.
C. She hasn't decided where to go yet.

Conversation 4.
A. In Taiwan.
B. In London.
C. In America.

主題 2　問 > 什麼人

每題請聆聽錄音機播出的一段對話和相關問題後，再從試題冊上 A、B、C 三個選項中，選出一個與題意最相符的答案。（每題只播一次，請仔細聽。）☞（答案請見 **P.324**）

聽力練習

答題時間
約 **15** 秒/題

MP3 **3-2**

Conversation 1.

A. Jenny.

B. The library.

C. Ted.

Conversation 2.

A. The man.

B. The woman.

C. Neither of them.

Conversation 3.

A. The woman.

B. The man.

C. Both of them.

Conversation 4.

A. Both of them like it.

B. Neither of them liked it.

C. His mother liked it, but his father didn't.

問 > 什麼種類

每題請聆聽錄音機播出的一段對話和相關問題後，再從試題冊上
A、B、C三個選項中，選出一個與題意最相符的答案。（每題只
播一次，請仔細聽。）☞（答案請見 **P.326**）

Conversation 1.

A. Math.

B. A novel.

C. A test paper.

MP3 **3-3**

Conversation 2.

A. Soda.

B. Milk.

C. Fruit juice.

Conversation 3.

A. She is good at English spelling.

B. The spelling contest.

C. Betty is nervous.

Conversation 4.

A. To a video shop.

B. To a CD shop.

C. To buy some CD's

主題 4 問 > 做什麼

聽力練習 每題請聆聽錄音機播出的一段對話和相關問題後，再從試題冊上 A、B、C 三個選項中，選出一個與題意最相符的答案。（每題只播一次，請仔細聽。）☛（答案請見 **P.328**）

Conversation 1.

A. Go to the movie theater.

B. Watch TV.

C. Play the volleyball.

答題時間 約 **15** 秒/題

MP3 **3-4**

Conversation 2.

A. He had dinner with Ann.

B. He went to Ann's party.

C. He threw a birthday party.

Conversation 3.

A. To go shopping with her.

B. To get more money.

C. To buy some fruit.

Conversation 4.

A. To help him to get some food.

B. To have some more food.

C. To drink some tea.

聽力練習 每題請聆聽錄音機播出的一段對話和相關問題後，再從試題冊上 A、B、C 三個選項中，選出一個與題意最相符的答案。（每題只播一次，請仔細聽。）☛（答案請見 **P.330**）

Conversation 1.
A. At 5:45.
B. At 5:35.
C. At 5:30.

答題時間 約 **15** 秒/題

Conversation 2.
A. It's ten o'clock.
B. It's a quarter past ten.
C. It's a quarter to ten.

MP3 **3-5**

Conversation 3.
A. At 10:00 P.M.
B. At 9:00 A.M.
C. At 9:00 P.M.

Conversation 4.
A. 9:00 a.m. to 6:00 p.m.
B. 9:00 a.m. to 12:00 a.m.
C. It is closed.

主題 6　問 > 日期

聽力練習　每題請聆聽錄音機播出的一段對話和相關問題後，再從試題冊上 A、B、C 三個選項中，選出一個與題意最相符的答案。（每題只播一次，請仔細聽。）☞（答案請見 P.332）

Conversation 1.
 A. It's Monday.
 B. It's Sunday.
 C. It's Saturday.

答題時間 約 **15** 秒/題

MP3 **3-6**

Conversation 2.
 A. Today.
 B. Not Friday.
 C. On Friday.

Conversation 3.
 A. On Wednesday.
 B. Any day.
 C. Next week.

Conversation 4.
 A. In March.
 B. In April.
 C. On March 4.

每題請聆聽錄音機播出的一段對話和相關問題後，再從試題冊上 A、B、C 三個選項中，選出一個與題意最相符的答案。（每題只播一次，請仔細聽。）☛（答案請見 **P.334**）

Conversation 1.

A. Spring and summer.

B. Spring.

C. Summer.

答題時間 約 **15** 秒/題

MP3 **3-7**

Conversation 2.

A. It's freezing and rainy.

B. It's sunny and hot.

C. It's freezing but sunny.

Conversation 3.

A. December.

B. January.

C. February.

Conversation 4.

A. January.

B. February.

C. November.

主題 8 問 > 數字與計算問題

聽力練習 每題請聆聽錄音機播出的一段對話和相關問題後，再從試題冊上 A、B、C 三個選項中，選出一個與題意最相符的答案。（每題只播一次，請仔細聽。）☛（答案請見 P.336）

Conversation 1.

A. 3218-5467.
B. 3218-6574.
C. 3281-6547.

答題時間 約 **15** 秒/題

MP3 **3-8**

Conversation 2.

A. She is fifteen years old.
B. She is 3 years younger than Tim.
C. She is 3 years older than Tim.

Conversation 3.

A. $200.
B. $300.
C. $150.

Conversation 4.

A. Seven thirty.
B. Seven twenty-three.
C. Seven thirty-seven.

比　較

🎧 聽力
練習

每題請聆聽錄音機播出的一段對話和相關問題後，再從試題冊上 A、B、C 三個選項中，選出一個與題意最相符的答案。（每題只播一次，請仔細聽。）☛（答案請見 **P.338**）

Conversation 1.

    A. Ben is younger.

    B. Mary is younger.

    C. They're of the same age.

答題時間
約 **15** 秒/題

MP3 **3-9**

Conversation 2.

    A. Jane.

    B. Mary.

    C. Rebecca.

Conversation 3.

    A. He wants a sheep.

    B. He wants a bigger sheet of paper.

    C. He wants a smaller sheet of paper.

Conversation 4.

    A. The dress.

    B. The blouse.

    C. The handbag.

主題 10　Yes-No 問題

聽力練習　每題請聆聽錄音機播出的一段對話和相關問題後，再從試題冊上 A、B、C 三個選項中，選出一個與題意最相符的答案。（每題只播一次，請仔細聽。）☞（答案請見 P.341）

Conversation 1.

A. Yes, he did.
B. No, he didn't.
C. We don't know.

答題時間 約 **15** 秒/題

MP3 3-10

Conversation 2.

A. No, she didn't.
B. Yes, she did.
C. Yes, she worked in a library for three months.

Conversation 3.

A. No, she doesn't like working.
B. Yes, she has to work.
C. No, she has to work.

Conversation 4.

A. He can't find his mother.
B. Yes, he can.
C. No, he can't.

混淆音

聽力
練習

每題請聆聽錄音機播出的一段對話和相關問題後，再從試題冊上 A、B、C 三個選項中，選出一個與題意最相符的答案。（每題只播一次，請仔細聽。）☞（答案請見 P.343）

Conversation 1.
    A. Stephen.
    B. Ms. Smith.
    C. Sandy.

答題時間
約 **15** 秒/題

MP3 **3-11**

Conversation 2.
    A. Blake.
    B. Frank.
    C. Eric.

Conversation 3.
    A. A dog.
    B. A coat.
    D. A cat.

Conversation 4.
    A. A recorder.
    B. A pair of shoes.
    C. We don't know.

主題 12 推測

聽力練習 每題請聆聽錄音機播出的一段對話和相關問題後，再從試題冊上 A、B、C 三個選項中，選出一個與題意最相符的答案。（每題只播一次，請仔細聽。）☞（答案請見 P.345）

Conversation 1.

A. In a restaurant.
B. In a toy shop.
C. In a shoe store.

答題時間 約 **15** 秒/題

MP3 **3-12**

Conversation 2.

A. He will open the door.
B. He will answer the door.
C. He will close the door.

Conversation 3.

A. She's a student.
B. She's a teacher.
C. She studies English.

Conversation 4.

A. She works at midnight.
B. She works at home.
C. She works as a writer.

聽力練習 每題請聆聽錄音機播出的一段對話和相關問題後，再從試題冊上 A、B、C三個選項中，選出一個與題意最相符的答案。（每題只播一次，請仔細聽。）☛（答案請見 **P.347**）

Conversation 1.

A. He's bad.
B. He's a doctor.
C. He got a stomachache.

答題時間 約 **15** 秒/題

Conversation 2.

A. She is sick.
B. She is wrong.
C. She is not home.

MP3 **3-13**

Conversation 3.

A. The man.
B. The woman.
C. The man's mother.

Conversation 4.

A. Father and daughter.
B. Doctor and patient.
C. Teacher and student.

主題 14 會面與道別

聽力練習 每題請聆聽錄音機播出的一段對話和相關問題後,再從試題冊上 A、B、C 三個選項中,選出一個與題意最相符的答案。(每題只播一次,請仔細聽。)☛(答案請見 **P.350**)

答題時間 約 **15** 秒/題

MP3 **3-14**

Conversation 1.

A. Clair.
B. Lisa.
C. Holly.

Conversation 2.

A. At Julie's home.
B. At the party.
C. In Joe's car.

Conversation 3.

A. He's saying goodbye.
B. He's driving.
C. He is going to stay longer.

Conversation 4.

A. She will be leaving by 3 o'clock.
B. She has a piano class.
C. She has a piano.

用餐

每題請聆聽錄音機播出的一段對話和相關問題後，再從試題冊上 A、B、C 三個選項中，選出一個與題意最相符的答案。（每題只 播一次，請仔細聽。）☛（答案請見 **P.353**）

Conversation 1.

A. Some bread and water.
B. Some cakes and coffee.
C. Some cakes and water.

答題時間
約 **15** 秒/題

Conversation 2.

A. She feels hungry.
B. She feels like eating some dessert.
C. She feels full.

MP3 **3-15**

Conversation 3.

A. Pizza and spaghetti.
B. Fried chicken and soda.
C. Rice and fish.

Conversation 4.

A. Cola and coffee.
B. Coffee and cake.
C. Pancake and sandwiches.

| 主題 **16** | 購物 |

聽力練習 每題請聆聽錄音機播出的一段對話和相關問題後，再從試題冊上 A、B、C 三個選項中，選出一個與題意最相符的答案。（每題只播一次，請仔細聽。）☛（答案請見 **P.355**）

Conversation 1.
  A. A shirt.
  B. A jacket.
  C. A coat.

答題時間 約 **15** 秒/題

MP3 **3-16**

Conversation 2.
  A. He's police officer.
  B. He's a shop salesman.
  C. He's a fashion designer.

Conversation 3.
  A. He doesn't look good on them.
  B. They are too big.
  C. They are too small.

Conversation 4.
  A. In a book shop.
  B. In a library.
  C. In a VCD shop.

主題 17　約定・預約

聽力練習　每題請聆聽錄音機播出的一段對話和相關問題後，再從試題冊上 A、B、C 三個選項中，選出一個與題意最相符的答案。（每題只播一次，請仔細聽。）☛（答案請見 **P.358**）

Conversation 1.
A. She is Miss Yu.
B. She is the man's Miss Right.
C. We don't know.

答題時間
約 **15** 秒/題

MP3 **3-17**

Conversation 2.
A. Mr. Ford.
B. No. 4.
C. The dentist.

Conversation 3.
A. The day after tomorrow.
B. Tomorrow.
C. Today.

Conversation 4.
A. On June 6.
B. By plane.
C. Ride a train.

主題 18 學 校

每題請聆聽錄音機播出的一段對話和相關問題後，再從試題冊上
A、B、C三個選項中，選出一個與題意最相符的答案。（每題只
播一次，請仔細聽。）☛（答案請見 P.360）

Conversation 1.

A. Neither English nor math is interesting.
B. Math.
C. English.

MP3 **3-18**

Conversation 2.

A. She begins to learn Japanese.
B. She has learned Japanese for two years.
C. She met a very good Japanese teacher.

Conversation 3.

A. To the English teachers' office.
B. To the third floor.
C. To the Chinese teachers' office.

Conversation 4.

A. It was 95.
B. It was less than 95.
C. It was 98.

聽力 練習 每題請聆聽錄音機播出的一段對話和相關問題後，再從試題冊上A、B、C三個選項中，選出一個與題意最相符的答案。（每題只播一次，請仔細聽。）☛（答案請見 **P.363**）

Conversation 1.

A. She is nurse.

B. She is looking for a job.

C. She is a housewife.

Conversation 2.

A. He has a meeting on Tuesday.

B. He is unhappy with the meeting.

C. The manager is angry.

MP3 **3-19**

Conversation 3.

A. About finding a job.

B. About hopes.

C. About running a company.

Conversation 4.

A. An artist.

B. Pianist.

C. We don't know.

主題 20　　　　社　交

聽力練習　每題請聆聽錄音機播出的一段對話和相關問題後，再從試題冊上
A、B、C 三個選項中，選出一個與題意最相符的答案。（每題只
播一次，請仔細聽。）☛（答案請見 P.365）

Conversation 1.
    A. Cookies and cake.
    B. Some drinks.
    C. Something that can eat.

答題時間 約 **15** 秒/題

MP3 **3-20**

Conversation 2.
    A. To help him to get some food.
    B. To have some more food.
    C. To leave some food.

Conversation 3.
    A. She doesn't like dancing.
    B. She doesn't like people in there.
    C. She doesn't like people smoking in there.

Conversation 4.
    A. Singer and audience.
    B. Shop owner and customer.
    C. Host and guest.

短文聽解

作答提示

▶ 每題請聆聽錄音機播出的英文內容之後，再從試題冊上的選項 [A] [B] [C] 三張圖片中，選出一個最適當的答案。

（每題只播出一次，請仔細聽）

短文聽解

第一類 廣播

主題 1　交通工具上

課前暖身

以下是這類題型的經典問句。請先瀏覽一次，對稍後的聽力訓練會有很大的幫助喔！

經典問句

問法1 Where does the talk take place?

　　　單字補充 take place 進行

聽力練習

每題請聆聽錄音機播出的英文內容之後，再從試題冊上的選項 A 、B 、 C 三張圖片中，選出一個最適當的答案。（答案請見 **p.368**）

答題時間
約 **15** 秒/題

Q1

MP3 **4-1**

（每題只播一次，請仔細聽。）

A.　　　　　　B.　　　　　　C.

Q2

MP3 **4-1**

（每題只播一次，請仔細聽。）

A.　　　　　　B.　　　　　　C.

Q3

MP3 **4-1**

（每題只播一次，請仔細聽。）

A.　　　　　　B.　　　　　　C.

電台

以下是這類題型的經典問句。請先瀏覽一次,對稍後的聽力訓練會有很大的幫助喔!

經典問句

問法 **1** Where can you hear this talk?

問法 **2** What might be the background?

單字補充 background 背景

聽力練習

每題請聆聽錄音機播出的英文內容之後,再從試題冊上的選項 A 、 B 、 C 三張圖片中,選出一個最適當的答案。(答案請見 **p.371**)

答題時間
約 **15** 秒/題

Q1

MP3 **4-2**

（每題只播一次，請仔細聽。）

A.
B.
C.

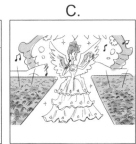

主題
2
廣播 ∨ 電台

Q2

MP3 **4-2**

（每題只播一次，請仔細聽。）

A.
B.
C.

Q3

MP3 **4-2**

（每題只播一次，請仔細聽。）

A.
B.
C.

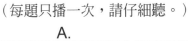

百貨公司 · 賣場

課前暖身

以下是這類題型的經典問句。請先瀏覽一次，對稍後的聽力訓練會有很大的幫助喔！

經典問句

問法① Where will you most probably hear this announcement?

單字補充 probably 大概，可能

問法② At what place might you hear this announcement?

單字補充 announcement 宣佈，公佈

聽力練習

每題請聆聽錄音機播出的英文內容之後，再從試題冊上的選項 A、B、C 三張圖片中，選出一個最適當的答案。（答案請見 **p.374**）

主題
3
廣播 ∨ 百貨公司 · 賣場

（每題只播一次，請仔細聽。）

Q1

MP3 **4-3**

A.　　　　　B.　　　　　C.

  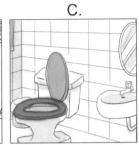

（每題只播一次，請仔細聽。）

Q2

MP3 **4-3**

A.　　　　　B.　　　　　C.

（每題只播一次，請仔細聽。）

Q3

MP3 **4-3**

A.　　　　　B.　　　　　C.

第二類 留言

主題 4 親友間

課前暖身　以下是這類題型的經典問句。請先瀏覽一次，對稍後的聽力訓練會有很大的幫助喔！

經典問句

問法 ① What will (someone) probably do?

問法 ② What might (someone) do next?

聽力練習　每題請聆聽錄音機播出的英文內容之後，再從試題冊上的選項 A、B、C 三張圖片中，選出一個最適當的答案。（答案請見 **p.377**）

Q1

MP3 4-4

（每題只播一次，請仔細聽。）

A. 　B. 　C.

Q2

MP3 4-4

（每題只播一次，請仔細聽。）

A. 　B. 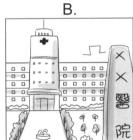　C.

Q3

MP3 4-4

（每題只播一次，請仔細聽。）

A. 　B. 　C.

| 主題 **5** | 公事 |

課前暖身

以下是這類題型的經典問句。請先瀏覽一次,對稍後的聽力訓練會有很大的幫助喔!

經典問句

問法**1** How is (someone) going to do?

聽力練習

每題請聆聽錄音機播出的英文內容之後,再從試題冊上的選項 A、B、C 三張圖片中,選出一個最適當的答案。(答案請見 **p.380**)

主題
5
留言 ∨ 公事

Q1

MP3 4-5

（每題只播一次，請仔細聽。）

A.  B.  C.

Q2

MP3 4-5

（每題只播一次，請仔細聽。）

A.  B.  C.

Q3

MP3 4-5

（每題只播一次，請仔細聽。）

A.  B.  C.

主題 **6**　　　　　　　　提醒

以下是這類題型的經典問句。請先瀏覽一次,對稍後的聽力訓練會有很大的幫助喔!

經典問句

問法 **1** What is suggested?

問法 **2** What is reminded?

聽力練習

每題請聆聽錄音機播出的英文內容之後,再從試題冊上的選項 A、B、C 三張圖片中,選出一個最適當的答案。(答案請見 **p.383**)

答題時間
約 **15** 秒/題

（每題只播一次，請仔細聽。）

Q1

MP3 **4-6**

A.　　　　　　　B.　　　　　　　C.

（每題只播一次，請仔細聽。）

Q2

MP3 **4-6**

A.　　　　　　　B.　　　　　　　C.

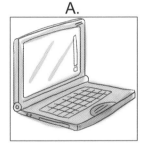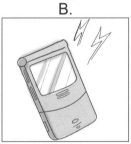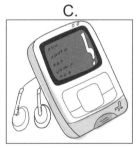

（每題只播一次，請仔細聽。）

Q3

MP3 **4-6**

A.　　　　　　　B.　　　　　　　C.

第三類 簡短談話

課前暖身 以下是這類題型的經典問句。請先瀏覽一次，對稍後的聽力訓練會有很大的幫助喔！

經典問句

問法① Where is probably mentioned?

　　單字補充 mention 提及，說及

問法② What might be the place?

問法③ Which place suits the description best?

　　單字補充 suit 符合，適合

　　　　　　 description 描述

聽力練習 每題請聆聽錄音機播出的英文內容之後，再從試題冊上的選項 A、B、C 三張圖片中，選出一個最適當的答案。（答案請見 **p.386**）

答題時間
約 **15** 秒/題

Q1

MP3 **4-7**

（每題只播一次，請仔細聽。）

A.  B.  C.

主題 **7** 簡短談話 ∨ 問「什麼地方」

Q2

MP3 **4-7**

（每題只播一次，請仔細聽。）

A. B. C.

 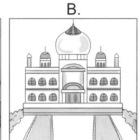 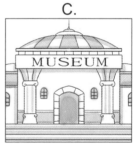

Q3

MP3 **4-7**

（每題只播一次，請仔細聽。）

A. B. C.

問「做什麼」

課前暖身
以下是這類題型的經典問句。請先瀏覽一次,對稍後的聽力訓練會
有很大的幫助喔!

 經典問句

問法**❶** What will (someone) do later?

問法**❷** What did (someone) do yesterday / last week?

問法**❸** What might (someone) plan to do?

聽力練習
每題請聆聽錄音機播出的英文內容之後,再從試題冊上的選項 A、
B 、 C 三張圖片中,選出一個最適當的答案。(答案請見 **p.389**)

答題時間
約 **15** 秒/題

Q1

MP3 **4-8**

（每題只播一次，請仔細聽。）

A. 　B.　C.

Q2

MP3 **4-8**

（每題只播一次，請仔細聽。）

A. 　B. 　C.

Q3

MP3 **4-8**

（每題只播一次，請仔細聽。）

A. 　B. 　C.

📋 **課前 暖身**

以下是這類題型的經典問句。請先瀏覽一次，對稍後的聽力訓練會有很大的幫助喔！

 經典問句

問法 ❶ What can be expected from (someone)?

問法 ❷ What can be told from the short talk?

📋 **聽力 練習**

每題請聆聽錄音機播出的英文內容之後，再從試題冊上的選項 A 、 B 、 C 三張圖片中，選出一個最適當的答案。（答案請見 **p.392**）

答題時間
約 **15** 秒/題

Q1

MP3 **4-9**

（每題只播一次，請仔細聽。）

A.　　　　B.　　　　C.

Q2

MP3 **4-9**

（每題只播一次，請仔細聽。）

A.　　　　B.　　　　C.

 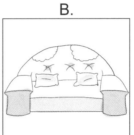 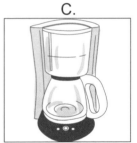

Q3

MP3 **4-9**

（每題只播一次，請仔細聽。）

A.　　　　B.　　　　C.

主題 10 綜合問題

課前暖身 以下是無法歸類在上述幾項的其他經典問句。請先瀏覽一次,對稍後的聽力訓練會有很大的幫助喔!

 經典問句

問法① Which one is _____?

問法② Which picture matches the talk?

問法③ Which picture is the best match?

單字補充 match 符合

聽力練習 每題請聆聽錄音機播出的英文內容之後,再從試題冊上的選項 A、B、C 三張圖片中,選出一個最適當的答案。(答案請見 **p.395**)

答題時間
約 **15** 秒/題

主題
10
綜合問題

Q1

MP3 **4-10**

（每題只播一次，請仔細聽。）

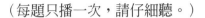

A.　　　　B.　　　　C.

Q2

MP3 **4-10**

（每題只播一次，請仔細聽。）

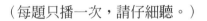

A.　　　　B.　　　　C.

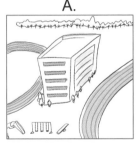  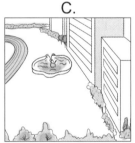

Q3

MP3 **4-10**

（每題只播一次，請仔細聽。）

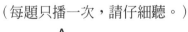

A.　　　　B.　　　　C.

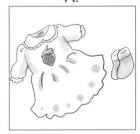  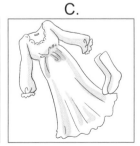

解答　看圖辨義

主題 **1** **物品・動物** Article ・ Animals

Q1 What is this?　這是什麼？

A:＿＿＿＿＿＿＿＿＿＿＿＿＿＿＿＿＿

A. It's a book. 一本書。
B. This is a sheet of paper. 這是一張紙。
C. It's a sheep. 一隻羊。

解答 B

※〔註〕選項 B.中 a sheet of（一張）的 sheet 和選項 C.的 sheep（羊）發音容易混淆，是聽力常考重點。

Q2 What are these?　這些是什麼東西？

A:＿＿＿＿＿＿＿＿＿＿＿＿＿＿＿＿＿

A. They are chairs. 是椅子。
B. They are furniture. 是家具。
C. These are beds and desks. 是床和桌子。

解答 B

※〔註〕畫面中 chair（椅子）、bed（床）和 desk（書桌）都出現了，這些都是 furniture（家具），所以答案要選 B.。

Q3 What can people find in here?

人們可以在這裡發現什麼？

A:＿＿＿＿＿＿＿＿＿＿＿＿＿＿＿＿＿

A. Zoo animals. 動物園裡的動物。
B. Sea animals. 海底動物。
C. Pets. 寵物。

解答 B

※〔註〕在「海洋世界」常見 seal（海獅）和 whale（鯨魚）表演，這些都是 sea animals（海底動物），因此答案為 B.。

集合名詞 Collective Nouns

物品	furniture 家具 stationery 文具 clothes 衣服 footwear 鞋子	food 食物 fruit 水果 vegetables 蔬菜
生物	animals 動物 pets 寵物	plants 植物 insects 昆蟲

主題 **2**　　　　**活動** Activities

Q1 What is he doing?　他在做什麼？

A:＿＿＿＿＿＿＿＿＿＿＿＿＿＿＿＿

A: He is sleeping. 他在睡覺。
B: He is taking a bath. 他在泡澡。
C: He is washing his face. 他在洗臉。

解答 B

※〔註〕場景是在「浴池」裡面，男子在這裡泡澡，即為美語的 taking a bath（泡澡）。 taking a shower 則為「淋浴」之意。

如何描述進行中的動作

身體清潔	taking a shower 淋浴 washing his hair 洗頭髮 brushing his teeth 刷牙

Q2 What's happening here? 這裡發生了什麼事？

A: _____

A: People are watching a game. 大家在看比賽。
B: They are playing basketball. 他們在打籃球。
C: Students are playing the musical instruments.
　 學生在彈奏樂器。

解答 A

※〔註〕這些人在 watching a game（看比賽），電視畫面轉播的是 football game（足球比賽）。

Column
加分必背

watching + 節目

watching TV 看電視
watching a movie 電影
watching a game 比賽
watching a show 表演

playing + 運動

playing baseball 打棒球
playing basketball 打籃球
playing soccer 踢足球
playing volleyball 打排球
playing tennis 打網球
playing badminton 打羽球
playing ping-pong 打乒乓球

playing + the + 樂器

playing the piano 彈鋼琴
playing the violin 拉小提琴
playing the drums 打鼓
playing the flute 吹笛子

Q3 What is she going to do? 她將要做什麼？
A: _____

A. She is going to cook. 她將要煮飯。
B. She is going to go shopping. 她將要去購物。
C. She is going to go swimming. 她將要去游泳。

解答 B

※〔註〕由畫面中的女子提著 bag（包包），推測她正在前往某處，打算去 shopping（購物）的可能性最高。

Column

加分必背

"go V-ing" 表示去做某事

go shopping 去購物
go swimming 去游泳
go surfing 去衝浪
go fishing 去釣魚
go jogging 去慢跑
go hiking 去健行
go bowling 去打保齡球
go picnicking 去野餐

Q1 What is this place?　這是什麼地方？

A: _____

A. This is a museum. 這是博物館。
B. This is a library. 這是圖書館。
C. This is an office. 這是辦公室。

解答 B

※〔註〕從構圖很容易看出，這個地方是 library（圖書館），只要對單字熟悉，就很容易可以選對。

Column 加分必背

參觀地點

museum 博物館
art gallery 美術館
zoo 動物園
aquarium 水族館

學術地點

library 圖書館
school 學校
classroom 教室
auditorium 禮堂

工作地點

company 公司
office 辦公室
conference room 會議室
factory 工廠

主題
3
地點 Place

Q2 # Where are these two girls?

這兩個女孩在哪裡？

A: _____

A. They're in a restaurant. 她們在餐廳裡。
B. They're in a supermarket. 她們在超市裡。
C. They're in a stadium. 她們在體育場。

解答 C

※〔註〕題目用 Where 這個疑問詞問的問題，答案要選的是地點，因此只有選項 C.正確。

購物地點

supermarket 超市
mall 大賣場
grocery store 雜貨店
department store 百貨公司
shoe store 鞋店
flower store 花店
stationery store 文具店
book shop 書店
toy shop 玩具店
sport goods store 運動用品店

restaurant 餐廳
fast food restaurant 速食餐廳
cafeteria 自助餐廳
cafe 咖啡廳
bakery 麵包店

休閒地點

stadium 體育場
gym 健身房
park 公園
amusement park 遊樂園
movie theater 電影院
theater 劇院

Q3 # Where are they probably going?

他們有可能是要去哪裡？

A: _____

A. They are probably going to the airport.
   他們可能是要去機場。
B. They are probably going to the hospital.
   他們可能是要去醫院。
C. They are probably going to the barbershop.
   他們可能是要去理髮店。

解答 B

※〔註〕這題必須從圖中主角的情況判斷，由於大肚子的婦人似乎要生產了，而要生產最可能前往的地點當然是 hospital（醫院）。

Column

加分
必背

搭乘運輸交通地點

airport 機場
port 港口
train station 火車站
MRT station 捷運站
bus stop 公車站牌
taxi stand 計程車招呼站

醫療相關地點

hospital 醫院
clinic 診所
drug store 藥局

美容健康地點

barbershop 理髮店
hair salon 美髮店
beauty salon 美容院
fitness center 健身中心
spa 水療溫泉；三溫暖

Q1 What is the time? 現在是什麼時間？

A: ＿＿＿＿＿＿＿＿＿＿＿＿＿＿＿＿＿＿

A. It's six-o-five. 現在是六點零五分。
B. It's six o'clock. 現在是六點鐘。
C. It's five-o-six. 現在是五點零六分。

解答 C

※〔註〕注意！當問題問到"what time"，回答應該是一個時間點，而非一段時間。根據畫面中的數字 5:06 即可選出正確的答案。

6:00 ～ 6:30 英文怎麼說？

◆六點鐘
(6:00) six o'clock.

◆六點零一分～六點零九分
(6:01 ～ 6:09) six-o-one ～ six-o-nine

◆六點十分～六點十九分
(6:10 ～ 6:19) six ten ～ six nineteen

◆六點二十分～六點二十九分
(6:20 ～ 6:29) six twenty ～ six twenty-nine

◆六點三十分
(6:30) six thirty

Q2 Look at the clock on the wall. What time is it? 請看牆上的時鐘，現在是幾點？

A: _____

A. It's a quarter to three. 差一刻三點。
B. It's half past two. 兩點半。
C. It's a quarter after two. 兩點十五分。

解答 A

時刻的表示法

- ◆ a quarter（一刻鐘）
    = 15 minutes（15 分鐘）
- ◆ half（半點鐘）= 30 minutes（30 分鐘）
- ◆ a quarter to three
    = a quarter before three
    = 2:45
- ◆ half past two = half before three = 2:30
- ◆ a quarter past two
    = a quarter after two
    = 2:15

Q3 When does the show start?

表演什麼時候開始？

A: _____

A. It starts at 6:30 p.m. 下午 6:30 開始。
B. It starts at noon. 正午開始。
C. It starts at 6:00 p.m. 下午 6:00 開始。

解答 C

※〔註〕p.m.是拉丁文 after noon（正午以後）的意思，由插圖可知表演是在「下午六點鐘」開始的。
※補充： a.m.(拉丁文 Ante Meridiem) =before noon 正午前

加分必背

午別：上午、下午、晚上

(1) a.m.（拉丁文 Ante Meridiem）
  = before noon 正午前
  p.m.（拉丁文 Post Meridiem）
  = after noon 午後

※ "a.m." 和 " p.m." 常出現在時間數字之後。
如：(x) p.m. 6:00 ==> (o) 6:00 p.m.。

(2) noon = 12:00 a.m.
  midnight = 12:00 p.m.

※注意： noon / midnight 之後不可以再加 a.m.
或 p.m.。

主題 **5** **情緒・外表** Feelings ・ Looks

Q1 How is the girl feeling? 這個女孩覺得怎樣？

A: _____

A. She is happy. 她很開心。
B. She's worried. 她很擔心。
C. She's angry. 她很生氣。

解答 B

※〔註〕從不理想的成績單和小女生的表情來判斷，她應該是
worried（擔心）父母看到會不高興，這個答案才合理。

關於情緒的常用表現

1. 情緒問法：
How do you feel? / How are you feeling? /
How are you? 你覺得如何？
2. 情緒回答：
I feel sad. / I'm feeling sad. / I am sad.
我很傷心。

Q2 How does the man look?

這名男子看起來怎樣？

A: _____

A. She looks tired. 她看起來很累。
B. He looks excited. 他看起來很興奮。
C. They are bored. 他們很無聊。

解答 B

※〔註〕題目問的是 "the man"（男子），單數，答案的主詞應該是 he（他）才正確。此外，他的表情看起來應該是 excited（興奮的）。

人的分類

man 男人
woman 女人
kid 小孩
baby 嬰兒
elder 老人
youth 青年
adult 成年人

angry 生氣的
nervous 緊張的
bored 無聊的
sad 傷心的
worried 擔心的
tired 累的
sleepy 睏的
happy 開心的
excited 興奮的

Q3 ## What does the girl look like?

這個女生看起來如何？

A: _____

A. She is short and fat. 她又矮又胖。
B. She has a thin face. 她有張瘦瘦的臉蛋。
C. She looks heavy. 她看起來胖胖的。

解答 B

※〔註〕畫面中的女生體型瘦瘦的（thin），一點也不胖（fat / heavy），答案很容易選。

Column

加分
必背

身材的形容詞

tall 高的
short 矮的
thin / skinny 瘦的
fat / heavy 胖的
slim / slender 苗條的

關於外型的其他回答方式

◆ She / He has＿＿＿＿＿＿.

替換字： long legs 長腿
　　　　big ears 大耳朵
　　　　short curly hair 短的捲髮
　　　　brown eye 棕色眼睛

※注意：我們常說東方人有「黑眼睛」，但是在英語裡他們卻說 "brown eyes"。

主題 6 疾病‧不適症狀 Disease‧Illness

Q1 What happened to the boy?

這個男孩發生了什麼事？

A: ＿＿＿＿＿＿＿＿＿＿＿＿＿＿＿＿

A. He hurt his toes. 他傷了腳趾頭。
B. He heard bad news. 他聽到了一個壞消息。
C. He happened to pass by. 他碰巧經過。

解答 A

※〔註〕畫面中可看出男孩 hurt his toes（傷了腳趾頭）。要注意是選項 B.的動詞 heard（聽到）和正確選項 hurt 的發音很像，這種混淆音的考法是聽力測驗的常見題型。

Q2 Why is Kyle here? 凱爾為什麼在這裡？

A: ＿＿＿＿＿＿＿＿＿＿＿＿＿＿＿＿＿

A. He has hurt his nose. 他傷了鼻子。
B. He is sick. 他生病了。
C. He hurt his leg. 他的腿受傷了。

解答 C

※〔註〕選項 B.不可選，因為男子是腿受傷，並不是生病（sick / ill）。

加分必背

「～受傷」的說法

He (has) hurt his _____.
= He got hurt in his _____.
= His _____ was / got hurt.

Q3 ## What is wrong with the boy?

這個男孩怎麼了？

A: _____

A. He has a toothache. 他牙痛。
B. He hurt his finger. 他傷了手指。
C. He has a cold. 他感冒了。

解答 A

※〔註〕畫面中的男孩是在看牙醫，所以研判他是「牙痛」。

Column

加分必背

感冒常見症狀與用法

a cold 感冒
a flu 流行感冒
a cough 咳嗽
a sore throat 喉嚨痛發炎
a runny nose 流鼻水
a stuffy nose 鼻塞

※〔註〕感冒 = have a cold / flu
　　　　　　 caught a cold / flu

一般疼痛

a toothache 牙痛
an earache 耳朵痛
a stomachache 肚子痛
a sore eye 眼睛酸痛發炎

主題 **7**　食物 Food

Q1 ## What is the girl eating?　這個女孩正在吃什麼？
A: ＿＿＿＿＿＿＿＿＿＿＿＿＿＿＿＿

A. She is eating a lunch box. 她正在吃便當。
B. He is having fried chicken. 他正在吃炸雞腿。
C. She is eating fast food. 她正在吃速食。

解答 C

※〔註〕再次提醒，當題目問的主角是 the girl，選項中主詞是 he 的就千萬不可選。由插圖可知正確選項應該是 C。

Column
加分
必背

速食 fast food

◆have = eat / drink
"have" 這個字可以表示「吃」或「喝」。

速食 fast food	
	fried chicken 炸雞
	French fries 薯條
	hamburger 漢堡
	chicken nuggets 雞塊
	orange juice 柳橙汁
	milk shake 奶昔
	coke 可樂

Q2 What does the daughter want to have?

這個女兒想要吃什麼？

A: _____

A. She wants to have some rice. 她想要吃飯。
B. She wants to have some bread. 她想要吃麵包。
C. She wants some noodles. 她想要吃麵。

解答 B

家庭成員

mother 媽媽	brother 兄；弟
father 爸爸	sister 姐；妹
son 兒子	cousin 堂、表兄弟姐妹
daughter 女兒	uncle 伯、叔、舅、姑父
grandfather 祖父	aunt 嬸、伯、姨、姑母
grandmother 祖母	
parents 雙親	

中式&西式主食

rice 米飯
noodles 麵
cereal 麥片
oatmeal 燕麥粥
rice porridge 稀飯
bread 麵包
dumpling(s) 水餃
spaghetti 義大利麵
pizza 披薩

Q3 # What would the man like?

這個男子想要點什麼？

A: _____

A. He would like a cup of coffee with cream and sugar. 他點一杯加糖和奶精的咖啡。
B. He would like a piece of cake and a glass of juice. 他要點蛋糕和果汁。
C. He would like a cup of black coffee.
他要點一杯黑咖啡。

主題
7
食
物
Food

解答 C

※〔註〕問「某人想吃什麼」，回答方式有：「主詞 would like ＋食物」、「主詞 want ＋食物」、「主詞 want to have ＋食物」。

咖啡 coffee

black coffee 黑咖啡（不加奶精或糖）
cream 奶精　　　sugar 糖

計量詞 + 不可數名詞

a cup of 一杯 　coffee 咖啡 　tea 茶 a glass of 一杯 　juice 果汁 　milk 牛奶 　water 水 a cup / glass of 一杯 　wine 葡萄酒	whisky 威士忌 a spoonful of 一匙 　cream 奶精 　salt 鹽 　sugar 糖 a piece of 一片 　cake 蛋糕 　apple pie 蘋果派

※〔註〕點餐的時候，通常省略計量詞，直接說： "a coffee", "two coffees"...等。

Q1 What's the man wearing?

這名男子穿著什麼？

A: _____

A. He's wearing shorts. 他穿著短褲。
B. He's wearing jeans. 他穿著牛仔褲。
C. He's wearing a jacket. 他穿著夾克。

解答 A

※〔註〕本題的男子身上穿著 shirt（男式襯衫）和 shorts（短褲），因此答案應選 A.。

Column 加分必背

服裝 clothing	
全身	a suit 套裝 sportswear / sweat suit 運動服 a jacket 夾克 a coat 厚外套
上半身	a shirt 襯衫 a T-shirt T 恤 a sweater 毛衣
下半身	shorts 短褲 / pants 長褲 jeans 牛仔褲 a skirt 裙子

※〔註〕所有的褲子都以「複數形態」出現，因為人皆有一雙腿。

purse 女皮包   wallet 男皮包

Q2 What is the third person in line carry-ing?

隊伍裡的第三個人拿著什麼東西？

A: _____

A. He is wearing a necktie. 他打著領帶。
B. He is carrying a suitcase. 他拿著一個公事包。
C. He is carrying a book bag. 他拿著一個書包。

解答 B

※〔註〕A. C.都是描寫排隊在等公車的第一個人，但正確符合題意的，只有選項 B.。

皮包類

suitcase / briefcase 公事包

book bag 書包

handbag 手提包

backpack 背包

wallet 皮夾

pouch 化妝包

服裝配件

a necktie --> neckties 領帶

a scarf --> scarves 圍巾

a handkerchief --> handkerchiefs 手帕

a pair of glasses 一副眼鏡

a belt 皮帶

glove(s) 手套

sock(s) 短襪

stockings 長襪

Q3 **What is she going to buy?** 她要買什麼？

A: _____

A. They are wearing shoes. 她們穿著鞋子。
B. She is going to buy shoes. 她要買鞋子。
C. They are going to buy glasses. 她們要買眼鏡。

解答 B

※〔註〕問句的主詞是 She，所以答句的主詞也應為 She，所以答案選 B。

鞋子種類	
shoes 鞋子	sandal 涼鞋
sneakers 布鞋	slipper 室內拖鞋
high heels 高跟鞋	mule 無後跟的拖鞋
boots 靴子	pump 淺口女鞋

主題 **9** **個人資料** Personal Data

Q1 **How old is the child?** 這個小孩幾歲？

A: _____

A. He is seventy years old. 他七十歲。
B. He is seven years old. 他七歲。
C. She is seventeen years old. 她十七歲。

解答 B

※〔註〕這題主要是要測驗考生對數字的熟悉度，尤其是-teen（thirteen 到 nineteen）和-ty（thirty 到 ninety）的發音很多人相當容易混淆，要多聽、多說，才能一聽就明白。由插圖中的 7 根蠟燭可知：答案應該選 B。

主題 **9** 個人資料 Personal Data

另一種年齡問法

◆ What is his / her age?
她 / 他的年齡多大？

◆ She / He is _____ year(s) of age.
她 / 他是～歲大。

Q2 How heavy is the woman? 這個女人多重？
A: _____

A. She is fifty-six kilograms. 她有五十六公斤。
B. She is heavy. 她很重／胖。
C. She is a woman. 她是女人。

解答 A

另一種體重問法

◆ What is her / his weight?
她 / 他體重多少？

◆ She / He weights _____kg.
她 / 他重達～公斤。

◆ She / He is _____kg in weight.
她 / 他的體重有～公斤。

※〔註〕國外提到重量時大都是用 "pound 英磅"。

Q3 How tall is the boy? 這個男孩多高？

A: _____

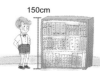

A. He is one meter tall. 他有一公尺高。
B. He is one hundred and fifteen centimeters.
   他有 115 公分。
C. He is one-point-five meters tall.
   他有 1.5 公尺高。

解答 C

公尺、公分的換算

◆ 1 M = one meter 一公尺 = 100 cm
   = one hundred centimeters 一百公分
◆ 1.5 M = one-point-five meters 一點五公
   尺 = 150 cm = one hundred and fifty
   centimeters

※〔註〕當回答身高有多高時，"tall" 說不說都可以。例如：He is one meter (tall).。

另一種身高、體重的問法

◆ What is her / his weight?
   她 / 他體重多少？
◆ She / He is _____ cm in height.
   她 / 他的身高有～公分。

※〔註〕國外提到長度時大都是用 "foot（feet）英呎"、"inch（inches）英吋"。

主題 10 季節・月份 Seasons ・ Months

Q1 What season is it? 這是什麼季節？

A: _____

A. It is windy. 風很大。
B. It is winter. 冬天。
C. It is a cold day. 很冷的一天。

解答 **B**

※〔註〕問 What season（什麼季節），就一定要回答四季之一，也就是 spring（春）、summer（夏）、fall/autumn（秋）或 winter（冬）。

Q2 What month is it? 這是幾月份？

A: _____

A. It is April. 這是四月。
B. It is not April. 這不是四月。
C. It is raining. 正在下雨。

解答 **A**

※〔註〕問 What month（什麼月份），就應該回答十二個月份之一，把以下的韻文背下來，就可以記熟十二個月份的說法了。

Column

加分必背

月份

Months of the Year
一年十二個月
January, February, March, and April,
一月、二月、三月和四月，
May, June, July, and August,
五月、六月、七月和八月，
September, October, November, December,
九月、十月、十一月、十二月，
Twelve months make a year.
十二個月就是一年。

Q3 What time of year is it?

這是一年中的什麼時候？

A: _____

A. It is New Year's Day. 這是新年。
B. It is a new day. 這是新的一天。
C. It is a new year. 這是新的一年。

解答 C

※〔註〕問 what time of the year（一年中的什麼時候），可以回答某個季節、某個月份，或某一天。這題只有 A.明確道出是 New Year's Day（新年）這一天，其他兩個選項都不對。

美國重要節慶		
日期	節日英文	節日中文
1 月 1 日	New Year's Day	新年
2 月 14 日	Valentine's Day	情人節
3 月中旬	St. Patrick's Day	聖派翠克節
7 月 4 日	Independence Day	獨立紀念日 美國國慶
10 月 31 日	Halloween	萬聖節
11 月第 4 個 禮拜四	Thanksgiving Day	感恩節
12 月 25 日	Christmas	聖誕節

台灣農曆重要節慶

日期	節日中文	節日英文
1月1日	農曆春節	Chinese New Year's Day
1月15日	元宵節	the Lantern Festival
5月5日	端午節	the Dragon-Boat Festival
7月7日	七夕情人節	Chinese Lovers' Day
7月15日	中元節	the Ghost Festival
8月15日	中秋節	the Moon Festival
9月9日	重陽節	the Chrysanthe-mum Festival
10月15日	下元節	the Water God Festival

※〔註〕新曆 (solar) calendar
　　　農曆 lunar calendar

Q1 What day is today? 今天星期幾？

A: _____

A. It is Tuesday. 星期二。
B. Today is Thursday. 今天星期四。
C. Today is Saturday. 今天星期六。

解答 B

※〔註〕圖中的小女孩在跳舞，由牆上的課程表找到跳舞課是禮拜四，故答案選 B.。

Calendar Song 日曆頌

There are 7 days, there are 7 days,

有七天，有七天，

There are 7 days in a week.

一星期有七天

Sunday, Monday, Tuesday, Wednesday.

星期日、星期一、星期二、星期三

Thursday, Friday, Saturday.

星期四、星期五、星期六

Q2 What is the date today? 今天是幾月幾日？

A: _____

A. It is the girl's birthday.
今天是這個女生的生日。
B. Today is Sunday. 今天是星期日。
C. It is February 2. 今天是二月二日。

解答 C

※〔註〕問 What is the date today?，回答一定要是明確的日期。如果這題題目問的是 What day is today?，則選項 A. 和 C. 就都是正確的答案了。

Q3 When is Terry's birthday?

泰瑞的生日在什麼時候？

A: _____

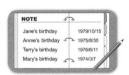

A. It is on April 14th. 是在四月十四日。
B. On June 11th. 在六月十一日。
C. Her birthday is August 30th.
她的生日是八月三十日。

解答 B

※〔註〕講一個人的生日或某個節日，可以直接說出月份和日期（如選項 C.），或在這之前加上一個介系詞 on（如選項 A.或 B.）。由通訊錄找到 Terry 的生日是六月十一日（June 11th）。

主題 **12**　　位置 Positions

Q1 Where is bus 220? 「220 公車」在哪裡？

A: _____

A. It's between a car and a motorbike.
在一輛轎車和一輛摩托車中間。
B. It's in front of a car. 在一輛轎車前面。
C. It's behind a motorbike. 在一輛摩托車後面。

解答 B

※〔註〕要能回答這題，一定得熟悉道路交通工具，更得知道相關位置的說法。

道路交通工具

bus 巴士
car 轎車
taxi 計程車
van 箱型車
motorbike / motorcycle 摩托車
scooter 小輪摩托車
bike / bicycle 腳踏車

Q2 # Where does Peter live? 彼得住在哪裡？

A: _____

A. He lives in the school. 他住在學校裡。
B. He lives next to the theater. 他住在戲院隔壁。
C. He lives across from the school.
他住在學校對面。

解答 C

※〔註〕題目是要考生找出彼得家和社區內其他建築的相對位置，選項 A. 回答的是 Peter 這個人住在哪裡，並非他的家在哪裡；而且圖中並沒看到 theater（戲院），因此選項 B. 也錯；答案是 C.。

社區建築

school 學校
library 圖書館
swimming pool 游泳池
bank 銀行
post office 郵局
police office 警察局
fire station 消防局

Q3 What is under the chair?

椅子下面是什麼東西？

A: _____

A. The breakfast is under the table.
早餐在桌子下面。
B. The cat is under the chair. 貓在椅子下面。
C. The toy is on the table. 玩具在桌子上面。

解答 B

※〔註〕很多人 under 和 on 這兩個介系詞乍聽之下，常會混淆，要特別小心。"under the chair"的有 cat（貓）；"on the table"有 breakfast（早餐）和 newspaper（報紙）。

主題 13 　數量 Quantity

Q1 What number is it? 號碼是幾號？

A: _____

A. It is number thirty. 30 號。
B. Thirty-one. 31 號。
C. Thirteen. 13 號。

解答 B

※〔註〕這題考的就是 thirteen 和 thirty 的發音，是常出的聽力陷阱。

Q2 How many children are there?

這裡有幾個小孩？

A: _____

A. They are on the beach. 他們在沙灘上。
B. There are two children. 有兩個小孩。
C. They are wearing swimming suits.
他們穿著泳衣。

解答 B

※〔註〕問 How many（幾個）就一定要回答出一個明確的數字，選項 B.回答了"two" children（兩個小孩），所以是正確答案。

Q3 Who is first? 誰是第一名？

A: _____

A. Sally is running. 莎莉在跑步。
B. Emily is second. 艾蜜莉第二。
C. Sally is first. 莎莉第一。

解答 C

※〔註〕題目不是問誰第二，是問誰第一，因此 C. "Sally is first"才是正確答案。

序數（1～20）

1st = first	11th = eleventh
2nd = second	12th = twelfth
3rd = third	13th = thirteenth
4th = fourth	14th = fourteenth
5th = fifth	15th = fifteenth
6th = sixth	16th = sixteenth
7th = seventh	17th = seventeenth
8th = eighth	18th = eighteenth
9th = ninth	19th = nineteenth
10th = tenth	20th = twentieth

※〔註〕序數 4 到 20 的唸法都是基數後面加上 "th"，但是字尾拼法有些必須稍作改變。

主題 14　價錢 Prices

Q1 How much is the ticket to Taichung?

到台中的票多少錢？

A: _____

Ticket Fare	
To Tainan	$ 856
To Taichung	$ 412
To Keelung	$ 165

A. NT. 412. 四百一十二元。
B. NT. 865. 八百六十五元。
C. NT. 165. 一百六十五元。

解答 A

※〔註〕問 How much（多少錢），一定要回答出明確的價錢，所以答案是 A.。

Q2 How much does a watermelon cost?

一粒西瓜多少錢？

A: _____

A. Six for ninety-nine dollars. 六粒九十九元。
B. One hundred and eighty-nine dollars.
　一百八十九元。
C. A kilo of grapes costs forty-five dollars.
　葡萄一公斤四十五元。

解答 B

※〔註〕這題其實很簡單，西瓜一粒賣 $189 元。

Q3 How much did she spend?

她花費了多少錢？

A: _____

A. $ 50. 五十元。
B. She bought 5 toys. 她買了五個玩具。
C. She spent $ 200. 她花了兩百元。

解答 C

※〔註〕由標示可知每件玩具是 50 元，小女孩買了 4 個，所以總共是 200 元。

加分必背

花費金錢的用法

※〔註〕動詞三態 cost / cost / cost
spend / spent / spent

◆物 + cost + 錢

ex: The toy costs two hundred dollars.
這個玩具要兩百元。

◆物 + cost + 人 + 錢

ex: The toy cost me two hundred dollars.
這個玩具花了我兩百元。

※〔註〕cost 爲過去式。

◆人 + spend + 錢 + on + 物

ex: I spent two hundred dollars on this
toy. 我花了兩百元買這個玩具。

※〔註〕spent 爲過去式。

主題 **15**　　　　天氣 Weather

 How's the weather? 天氣如何？

A: _____

A. It's cold and windy. 又冷又起風。
B. It's hot and sunny. 又熱又出太陽。
C. It's cool and rainy. 又涼又下雨。

解答 A

※〔註〕題目問的是天氣，通常都是用 It 當代名詞。而畫面中看得出來天氣十分寒冷（cold）而且有風，故選 A.。

Q2 What will the weather be like on Thursday?

星期四天氣會如何？

A: _____

A. More rain will come. 又會下雨了。
B. It will be cloudy. 多雲。
C. We'll have clear skies. 萬里無雲。

解答 B

※〔註〕從氣象預報圖看到，Thursday（星期四）應該是陰天(cloudy)，而選項 C.的 clear sky（萬里無雲）就是晴天的另一種說法，而且通常以第一人稱複數"We"當主詞。

Q3 What's the temperature in Tainan?

台南的溫度是多少？

A: _____

A. The temperature is 34.5 ℃.
   溫度是攝氏三十四點五度。
B. It is 36 ℃. 攝氏三十六度。
C. It is hot. 天氣很熱。

解答 A

※〔註〕正確溫度是 34.5 ℃（thirty-four point five Celsius degree）。所以答案是 A.。

溫度的說法

◆ Celsius 攝氏；Fahrenheit 華氏
35.5 ℃/℉唸做 "thirty-five point five degree Celsius[`sɛlsɪəs] / Fahrenheit[`færən͵haɪt]"。
※〔註〕"degree" 後面不可以加複數 "-s"。

Q1 ## What is the woman?
這個女人是做什麼的？

A: _____

A. She is a woman. 她是個女人。
B. He's a policeman. 他是個警察。
C. She's a police officer. 她是個警察。

解答 C

※〔註〕穿著制服的女子正在指揮交通（direct traffic），但問句的意思等於"What is the woman's job?"，問的是這名女子的職業，故選 C。

不同職業的新、舊名稱

舊職業名	新職業名
police man 警察	police officer 警員
fireman 救火員	firefighter 消防隊員
mail man 郵差	mail carrier 郵務士
sales man 推銷員	salesperson 銷售員
businessman 生意人	business person 生意人

※〔註〕以上這些職業不再被稱為 "～ man" 或 "～ woman" 是為了要避免性別歧視。

Q2 What does Andrew do? 安德魯是做什麼工作的？

A: _____

A. It is an automatic teller machine.
這是一部自動提款機。
B. He works as a teller. 他做的是銀行出納員。
C. He is a banker. 他是個銀行家。

解答 B

※〔註〕bank teller 和 banker 的定義很多人容易混淆，其實 bank teller（銀行出納員）是受雇的員工，而 banker（銀行家）是投資者，千萬要弄明白。

銀行相關用語

◆ automatic teller machine
= ATM 自動提款機
◆ teller = bank teller 銀行出納員
◆ banker 銀行家
◆ name of account 帳戶名稱存款人

Q3 Whom should people call for help?

人們應該打電話向誰求救？

A: _____

A. They should call a reporter.
他們應該打電話給記者。
B. Call 119. 打 119 電話。
C. Call the library. 打電話到圖書館。

解答 B

※〔註〕由圖中的火災可知當時應該打 119 電話求救。

加分必背

	watching + 節目	
求救電話	求救單位	求救對象
110 警察局	police station 警察局	the police 警方
119 消防局	fire station 消防局	the firefighters 消防隊員
	hospital 醫院	the ambulance (crew) 救護車組員

※〔註〕請記得！在美國消防隊的求救電話是 "911"。

主題 17　　比較 Comparisons

Q1　What is more expensive? 什麼東西比較貴？

A: _____

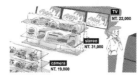

A. The stereo is more expensive. 音響比較貴。
B. The TV is more expensive than the stereo.
電視比音響貴。
C. The stereo is less expensive. 音響比較不貴。

解答 A

※〔註〕形容詞比較級 more 表示「更多」，less 表示「更少」，我們知道 stereo set（音響）比 TV set（電視）貴，所以答案為 A。

主題 17 比較 Comparisons

形容詞比較級

more expensive = less cheaper

less expensive = cheaper

相反詞

expensive 貴 ↔ cheap 便宜

fast / quick 快 ↔ slow 慢

tall 高 ↔ short 矮

high 高 ↔ low 低

thick 厚 ↔ thin 薄

strong 強 ↔ weak 弱

hot 熱 ↔ cold 冷

big 大 ↔ small / little 小

young 年輕 ↔ old 老

new 新 ↔ old 舊

wide 寬 ↔ narrow 窄

Q2 What is the cheapest way to Kaohsiung?

到高雄去什麼交通工具最便宜？

A: _____

3 Ways to Kaohsiung	
By Plane	$ 2000
By Train	$ 600
By Bus	$ 550

A. By train. 搭火車。
B. Take the plane. 搭飛機。
C. By bus. 搭巴士。

解答 C

※〔註〕「by＋交通工具」＝「take the＋交通工具」，要到高雄搭巴士（by bus）最便宜，所以答案為 C.。

運輸方式

1. by + 交通工具 = take the + 交通工具
2. by sea = by boat 船運

   by air = by plane 空運

   by land 陸運

Q3 Who should pay the most? 誰要付最多錢？

A: ＿＿＿＿＿＿＿＿＿＿＿＿＿＿＿＿＿＿

A. The old man should pay. 老人要付。

B. The woman. 女人。

D. The kid should pay the most. 小孩要付最多錢。

解答 B

※〔註〕但 kid（小孩）和 old man/woman（老人）的票價比較便宜。 woman 票價 $80 元，是最貴的，所以答案為 B.。

the + 形容詞最高級→最～的

the most 最多

the least 最少

the best 最好

the worst 最差

主題18	**人際關係** Daily Relationships

Q1 Who's the person behind Maria?

在瑪莉亞後面的人是誰？

A: _____

A. She is Lily. 是莉莉。
B. He is Philip. 是菲力浦。
C. Maria is between Mark and Rosa.
　 瑪莉亞是在馬克和羅莎之間。

解答 **B**

※〔註〕behind 是「在……之後」的意思。在 Maria 後面的是 Philip，故答案是 B。

Q2 Who is the man in a black tie?

打著黑色領帶的男子是誰？

A: _____

A. He is probably the woman's doctor.
　 他可能是這位女士的醫生。
B. He is probably the boss. 他可能是老闆。
C. He is probably the woman's classmate.
　 他可能是這位女士的同學。

解答 **B**

※〔註〕聽到問句 "Who is + 主詞"，應該回答這個主角的「身分」，或與配角的「關係」。本場景是在辦公室，故選 B。

Q3 What is their relationship? 他們是什麼關係？

A: _____

A. They're a rider and a passenger.
　 他們是騎士和乘客。
B. They're strangers to each other.
　 他們彼此是陌生人。
C. They're a family. 他們是一家人。

解答 **B**

※〔註〕問到彼此間 relationship（關係），可能是一個名詞如：family（家人），但此時的名詞前面都不加冠詞 a / an 或 the。

常見的人際關係

family 家人
relative 親戚
classmate 同學
roommate 室友
housemate 住同屋但不同房的朋友
friend 朋友
co-worker / colleague 同事
rival 競爭對手

相對應的人際關係

parents 父母 ↔ children 子女
teacher 老師 ↔ student 學生
coach 教練 ↔ athlete 運動員
director 導演 ↔ actor 男演員
　　　　　　　　actress 女演員
conductor 指揮家 ↔ player 演奏家
taxi / bus driver 計程車 / 公車司機
↔ passenger 乘客
doctor 醫生 ↔ patient 病人
store clerk 店員 ↔ customer 顧客

主題 **19** 日常用品 (1) Articles for Daily Use (1)

Q1 ## Where can you probably find these things?

你可能會在哪裡發現這些東西？

A: _____

A. In a pencil box. 在鉛筆盒裡。
B. In a closet. 在壁櫥裡。
C. In a refrigerator. 在冰箱裡。

解答 A

※〔註〕畫面中這些物品是文具，可以找到文具最合理的地方就是 pencil box（=pencil case「鉛筆盒」）裡了。

Q2 ## Where should these things be put?

這些東西應該放哪裡？

A: _____

A. They should be put away. 這些東西必須收好。
B. They should be put in the office.
　　這些東西應該放在辦公室裡。
C. They should be put in the bathroom.
　　這些東西應該放在浴室裡。

解答 C

Column 加分必背

房屋格局

bathroom 浴室	dining room 餐廳
bedroom 臥室	study 書房
living room 客廳	balcony 陽台
kitchen 廚房	storeroom 儲藏室

Q3 What goes with this machine?
這個機器要配上什麼東西？

A: _____

A. A vase. 花瓶。
B. A computer. 電腦。
C. A pair of shoes. 一雙鞋子。

解答 B

※〔註〕這台 machine（機器）正確的名稱是 printer（印表機），必須搭配 computer（電腦）才能使用，故選 B.。

電腦配備

monitor 螢幕	printer 印表機
keyboard 鍵盤	modem 數據機
disk 磁碟機	mouse 滑鼠

主題 20 日常用品 (2) Articles for Daily Use (2)

Q1 What does the man need most?
這名男子最需要什麼？

A: _____

A. A public phone. 公共電話。
B. He needs a pay card. 他需要一張電話卡。
C. He needs to pay. 他必須付錢。

解答 B

※〔註〕pay card 儲值卡 =phone card 電話卡，才是畫面中站在公共電話前的男子所需要的。

各類電話

phone / telephone 電話
cell / mobile phone 手機
car phone 汽車電話
pay / public phone 公共電話
intercom 室內對講機
walkie-talkie 行動對講機

Q2 Who needs these tools most?

誰最需要這些工具？

A: _____

A. A hair dresser needs them most.
美髮師最需要它們。
B. This is a school. 這是一所學校。
C. These tools are for musicians.
是音樂家的工具。

解答 A

※〔註〕問 who 就要回答出「人物」，所以只有 A. 是正確答案。

Q3 What's the boy's trouble?

小男孩遇上了什麼麻煩？

A: _____

A. He can't get down to the ground.
他無法回到地面上。
B. He can't fly. 他無法飛。
C. He can climb the tree. 他會爬樹。

解答 A

※〔註〕由畫面中的表情及處境可判斷：小男孩應該是被困在樹上了，故答案選 A。

問答

第一類 招呼與問候

主題 1 見面

Q1 Hey! How are you?

嗨，你好嗎？

A. How are you? 你好嗎？
正解 ► B. Fine. And you? 很好，你呢？
C. It's fine. 這樣好。

Q2 How are you doing?

你好嗎？

A. How do you do it? 你會怎麼做？
正解 ► B. I am doing well. 我很好。
C. I am doing my homework. 我正在做功課。

※〔註〕這題的問句等於 "How are you?"，答案選 B.。A.的問句應為 "What do you do it (to keep fit)? (你都是靠做些什麼來（維持身材）？)" "C.的問句應為 "What are you doing? (你在做什麼？)"

Q3 Hi, Tom. How have you been?

嗨，湯姆。您近況好嗎？

正解 ► A. Well, about the same. 嗯，差不多一樣。
B. They are the same. 他們一樣。
C. I don't know what I'm doing. 我不知道我在做什麼。

※〔註〕這個問句是一段時間沒見面之後的常見問候語，答案 A. 的意思是和平常沒兩樣，沒什麼特殊的事發生。C. 的問句應為 "What are you doing now? (你在做什麼？)"。

Q4 Hi, good to see you again.

嗨，能再見到你真好。

正解 ► A. Yeah, how have you been? 是啊，您最近好嗎？
B. It's good to meet you. 真高興認識你。
C. I'm O.K. 我還不錯。

Q5 Hello, Sue.

哈囉，蘇。

A. I'm Sue. 我是蘇。
B. How do you do? 你好嗎？
正解 ► C. Hi, Jack. What a surprise. 嗨，傑克。真想不到！

※〔註〕這個開場也是「再度」見面時的問候語，雙方應該是彼此認識的，所以答案選 C.。選項 A. 和 B. 是與對方「第一次」認識時的自我介紹和客套話。

Q6 Mark, is that really you?

馬克，真的是你嗎？

A. It's yours. 這是你的。
正解 ► B. Yes, Sam. It's me. 是的，山姆。是我。
C. Yes, it's mine. 是的，這是我的。

Q7 Did you have a good holiday?

假期愉快嗎？

正解 ► A. It was wonderful. 很棒。
B. Wish you a happy holiday. 祝你佳節愉快。
C. No, it's good. 不，這很好。

Q8 Hi, I'm Johnson. Are you Maria?

嗨，我是強生。妳是瑪莉亞嗎？

A. Maria is a good girl. 瑪莉亞是位好女孩。
B. Hello, Maria. How do you do? 哈囉，瑪莉亞，妳好。
正解 ► C. Yes, that's right. Hello Johnson. 是，沒錯。你好，強生。

※〔註〕這裡的情形應該是 Johnson 和 Maria 相約第一次碰面，如果 Johnson 問的這個女生不是 Maria，她應該要回答 "No, I'm not Maria."選項中的答案應為 Yes 或 No 開頭。

主題 **1** 招呼與問候 v 見面

Q9 You must be Dr. Evans. Let me introduce myself. I'm Betty Davis.

你一定是伊凡斯醫生，請容我自我介紹，我是貝蒂・戴維斯。

正解 A. How do you do, Ms. Davis? 妳好嗎？戴維斯小姐。
B. Who is Betty Davis? 誰是貝蒂・戴維斯？
C. Do you know her? 妳認識她嗎？

※〔註〕當你要自我介紹時，一定會說出自己的名字，這位向 Dr. Evans 自我介紹的人叫 Betty Davis，是位女士，不知道已婚或未婚，所以 Dr. Evans 問候她時稱她為 "Ms. Davis"。

Q10 Frank, this is Rose, my classmate.

法蘭克，這位是羅絲，我的同學。

A. Goodbye, Rose. 再見，羅絲。
正解 B. Hi, Rose. It's nice to meet you. 嗨，羅絲。很高興認識妳。
C. It's nice of you, Rose. 妳人真好，羅絲。

主題 **2** 道 別

Q1 Goodbye, Jill.

再見，吉兒。

正解 A. Bye. Take care. 再見，保重。
B. What did you buy? 你買了什麼？
C. By train. 搭火車。

Q2 Come over again.

有空再來。

A. Go away. 走開。
B. I come here sometimes. 我有時會來這裡。
正解 C. Thanks, I will. 謝謝，我會的。

Q3 Have a nice trip.
旅程愉快！

正解 A. Thank you. 謝謝。
B. We're going on a trip. 我們要去旅行。
C. Yes, we had a nice trip. 是，我們的旅程很愉快。

Q4 I'm going to a party now.
我要去舞會了。

A. Happy birthday. 生日快樂。
正解 B. Enjoy yourself. 好好地玩啊！
C. Who is coming? 誰來了？

※〔註〕正確答案為 B.，意思是希望對方能在派對中玩得盡興。

Q5 Have a nice day.
祝你有美好的一天。

正解 A. You, too. 你也是。
B. It's a nice day, isn't it? 天氣很好，不是嗎？
C. Hi, I'm back. 嗨，我回來了。

※〔註〕如果有人比你早說出這句話，那你也要趕快回應 "You, too."，祝對方一整天都順遂。至於 B. 和 C. 兩個選項的錯誤在於談論的主題有異，原本應該是談「一天的心情」，但 B. 談的卻是「天氣」，C. 談的則是「人」。

Q6 Will I see you tonight?
我今晚會見到你嗎？

正解 A. Yes. Bye. 會的，再見。
B. Yes, you can see it too. 對，你也會看到。
C. Oh, I see. 喔，我懂了。

Q7 Give me a call when you get there, okay?
你到的時候打個電話給我，好嗎？

正解 A. Sure thing. 一定會的。
B. Here you are. 給你。
C. I will get there by three. 三點以前我會到。

※〔註〕正確答案 "Sure thing." 等於 "Sure. / Certainly. / OK."的意思。選項 B. 應該是你要拿東西給對方時的說法，選項 C. 則是回答對方問你 "When will you get there?"。

Q8 I will miss you.

我會想你的。

正解 A. Same here. 我也是。

B. I missed the bus. 我錯過了巴士。

C. Did I miss anything? 我錯過了什麼嗎？

※〔註〕正確答案 "Same here." 的意思等於 "I will miss you, too."。這裡的 miss 是「思念」之意，而選項 B. 和 C. 則都是「錯過」的意思。

Q9 Good night, Daddy.

晚安，爹地！

A. Yes, it's a good knife. 是的，這是一支好刀。

正解 B. Have a sweet dream. 祝你有個美夢。

C. Have some sweet. 來些甜點。

※〔註〕knife [naɪf] 刀；小刀

Q10 Do you really have to go?

你真的得走嗎？

A. You go first. 你先。

B. Yes, I will go. 是，我會去。

正解 C. Yes. I'm sorry. 是的，對不起。

※〔註〕問句的 go 等於 "leave" 的意思，說話者捨不得你離開，這時候如果你執意要走可能會讓對方很傷心，因此你會說 "I'm sorry." 向他道歉。

主題 **3** 邀約與招待

Q1 Can you come?

你可以來嗎？

正解 A. Sorry, I don't have time. 對不起，我沒有時間。

B. Of course I can count. 我當然會算。

C. Yes, I am Ken. 是，我是肯恩。

※〔註〕有人向你邀約，你卻必須拒絕時，除了要說 "sorry." 對不起之外，最好能明確地說出理由，例如 "I don't have time. I have to work late tonight. (我沒有時間，我今晚得工作到很晚。)"

Q2 Come over sometime.
有空常來。

A. I don't have enough time. 我沒足夠的時間。
正解 ▶ B. Thanks. I will. 謝謝，我會的。
C. We will make good use of our time. 我們會善用我們的時間。

Q3 Will you come with us?
你要和我們一起來嗎？

正解 ▶ A. Not this time. 下次吧！
B. I won't be late. 我不會遲到。
C. You first. 你先請。

Q4 Would you like to have lunch together?
要一起吃午餐嗎？

正解 ▶ A. I'd love to. 好啊！〔我很樂意。〕
B. I am with you. 我同意你說的。
C. We are together. 我們同在一起。

Q5 Come on in.
進來吧！

A. What for? 為什麼？
B. I'd love to come. 我很樂意。
正解 ▶ C. Thank you. 謝謝。

※〔註〕主人邀請你進入屋內時，說句 "Thank you."，然後就趕快進屋吧。這時候你應該已經在門口了，所以不可能還問 "What for?"。

Q6 How are you doing?
你還好嗎？

正解 ▶ A. I'm having a good time. 我很開心。
B. I'm doing my homework. 我在做功課。
C. I'm twenty years old. 我二十歲。

※〔註〕在聚會的場合，主人最在意客人是否盡興盡歡，當他關心地問你 "How are you doing?"時，你應該給予肯定的答覆 "I'm having a good time."，讓他放心。B.的原問句應為 "What are you doing?（你在做什麼？）"。

主題
3
招呼與問候 v 邀約與招待

Q7 Would you care for something to drink?

你要不要喝點什麼？

A. I like drinking tea. 我喜歡喝茶。
正解 B. No, thanks. I'm fine for now. 不用了，謝謝。我現在還好。
C. Be careful with what you eat. 小心你吃的東西。

Q8 Please make yourself at home.

請不要拘束。

A. I can make it home. 我有辦法到家。
正解 B. Thanks, I will. 謝謝，我會的。
C. Nobody's home. 沒人在家。

※〔註〕"Please make yourself at home."是主人希望來訪的客人當成在自己的家一樣，不要拘束，這時候客人回答 "Thanks, I will."，感謝主人的體貼，並且要對方放心，自己一定會放輕鬆的。

Q9 Why don't you have a seat?

坐下來吧！

A. Best wishes. 誠摯的祝福。
正解 B. Thank you. 謝謝。
C. Because I have no money. 因為我沒有錢。

Q10 It's too bad that you have to go.

真遺憾你要走了。

A. Let me see you out. 我送你出去。
B. Welcome. Please come in. 歡迎，請進。
正解 C. Thanks very much. It was a great party! 非常感謝！這次聚會好極了！

※〔註〕在聚會還沒結束，卻有人必須先離開時，主人會想挽留他，如果無法挽留，就會惋惜地說 "It's too bad that you have to go."，所以這句話是「主人」說的。接下來就應該是要離開的「客人」回應，但三個選項中只有 C. 正確，選項A.、B. 都是「主人」的台詞，所以不可選。

主題 4 祝賀與道喜

Q1 Merry Christmas!

聖誕快樂！

A. Mary and Chris are happy. 瑪莉和克里斯很幸福。

正解 ▶ B. Merry Christmas to you, too. 也祝你聖誕快樂！

C. Happy New Year! 新年快樂！

Q2 Happy birthday! This is for you.

生日快樂！這個送你。

A. Happy birthday! 生日快樂！

B. How are you? 你好嗎？

正解 ▶ C. Oh! How nice. 喔，真好！

※〔註〕壽星聽到別人的祝福，又收到禮物，一定很開心，覺得對方真好，選項 C. "How nice." 的完整意思就是"How nice of you for giving me this present."。

Q3 Congratulations! It's a girl.

恭喜，是個女孩。

A. Thank you, girl. 謝謝你，小女孩。

B. Wonderful! I'm graduated. 太棒了，我畢業了！

正解 ▶ C. Great! I have a daughter! 太好了，我有個女兒！

※〔註〕特別注意 congratulation 字尾一定要加上 -s，如果要指出值得恭喜的事，則加上介詞 "on"，例如：Congratulations on your marriage.「恭喜你結婚。」

Q4 I'm getting married next month.

我下個月要結婚了。

正解 ▶ A. You are? Congratulations! 真的？恭喜！

B. You are married? 你結婚了？

C. Molly is a good girl. 莫莉是個好女孩。

Q5 See you in a week.

下星期見。

正解 ▶ A. Have a nice trip. 玩得愉快！

B. Did you see that? 你有看到嗎？

C. I see. 我懂了。

Q6 We have a big game tomorrow.
我們明天有一場大賽。

A. Good day. 你好。
正解▶ B. Good luck. 祝你們好運！
C. I can't wait to play the TV game. 我等不及要打電動玩具了。

Q7 I've had this cough for a week now.
我這樣咳嗽已經一週了。

A. Why were you off for a week? 你為什麼離開了一週？
B. Have a nice trip. 旅程愉快。
正解▶ C. That's too bad. I hope you get well soon. 那真是太糟糕了！祝你早日康復。

Q8 I hope you will pass the exam.
希望你通過考試。

正解▶ A. That's very kind of you to say so. 謝謝你這麼說。
B. Can I get past, please? 麻煩借我過！
C. I'm afraid not. 恐怕不行。

※〔註〕選項 B. 的用句是當別人擋住了你的去路時所說的慣用語，通常前面會加上 "Excuse me.（對不起。）" 而選項 C.的使用時機應該是：在你覺得對方的意見不可行的時候的一種較委婉的說法，例如：
A: Can I get a discount?（可以給我打個折扣嗎？）
B: I'm afraid not.（恐怕不行耶。）

Q9 I can't believe my luck.
我不敢相信我的好運。

A. What do you believe? 你相信什麼？
B. I hope we have the key to this lock. 我希望我們有這個鎖的鑰匙。
正解▶ C. Honey, I'm so happy for you. 親愛的，我真為你高興！

※〔註〕"I can't believe..." 通常是根本不預期的事竟然發生了，有「震驚」或「驚喜」的情緒，當 luck「好運」降臨在你身上，你的親人或朋友當然也會為你高興 "happy for you"。選項 A. 的 believe 意思卻是「信任」、「信仰」，選項 B. 則利用類音字 luck / lock 的陷阱來混淆你的判斷。

Q10 Happy New Year.
新年快樂。

正解 A. Same to you. 你也是。
B. I saw the news. 我看過那則新聞。
C. How are you? 你好嗎?

※〔註〕只要有人祝你佳節愉快,無論是"Happy New Year." 或是 "Merry Christmas." 你都可以回答同樣的話 "Same to you."

主題 5 健康狀況

Q1 Are you all right?
你還好嗎?

A. It's nothing. 沒什麼〔別客氣!〕。
B. You look kind of pale. 你看起來有點蒼白。
正解 C. I'm not feeling well. 我覺得不太舒服。

Q2 Well, what's the trouble?
喔,有什麼問題?

A. It doesn't matter. 沒關係。
B. I'm in trouble. 我有麻煩了。
正解 C. I have a headache. 我頭痛。

※〔註〕看到一個人悶悶不樂或遭受病痛所折磨,通常可以問他 What's the trouble?,這也是醫生常會對來看診的病患說的開場白。(B) 的回答不夠明確,(A) 則應該是回應 "I'm sorry."的慣用句。

Q3 What's wrong? You look pale.
怎麼了? 你看起來很蒼白。

A. You have the wrong number. 你打錯(電話)了。
B. It's not correct. 這不對。
正解 C. I broke my tooth. 我把牙齒撞斷了。

※〔註〕"What's wrong?"一般情況都是在「關心」對方發生了什麼「不好」的事。 pale [pel] 蒼白的;灰白的。

Q4 How often do I take the medicine?

多久要服用一次藥？

A. It will take you three days. 會花你三天的時間。

正解► B. Three times a day; after meal, please. 每天三次，請餐後服用。

C. I have three meals a day. 我一天吃三餐。

Q5 You don't look well.

你看起來不太好。

A. We have to get to a hospital. 我們得要去醫院。

B. So that's what happened! 原來如此！

正解► C. Well, I couldn't sleep well. 嗯，我沒睡好。

※〔註〕一個人 not look well 表示臉色不好，可能是身體不好或心情不好。因此回答造成的原因是 not sleep well，因為沒睡好可能精神不好，所以臉色不好。

Q6 Do you have some medicine for a stomachache?

你有沒有胃痛的藥？

A. I have a cold. 我感冒了。

B. What can go wrong? 不可能出錯的。

正解► C. You'd better see a doctor. 你最好去看醫生。

Q7 I have a fever, so I didn't go to school.

我發燒了，所以沒去上學。

A. Ouch! It hurts. 啊！會痛。

正解► B. Did you see a doctor? 你有看醫生嗎？

C. What's your favorite subject? 你最喜歡哪個科目？

※〔註〕A. 是在受傷的時候、別人踩到你的腳、不小心打到你的時候會做出的立即反應，中文驚呼語是：「哦～！」，英文則會說 "Ouch! [`aʊtʃ]"。選項 C. 則是用相似音 favorite（最喜歡的）、fever（發燒）故意造成混淆。

Q8 My tooth hurts when I eat.
我吃東西的時候牙齒就痛。

正解 ▶ A. Too bad. 真慘。

B. You need to blow your nose. 你需要擤個鼻涕。

C. You have bad teeth. 你牙齒很差。

※〔註〕別人向你抱怨，但是原因不在你，就可以用同理心回應他 "Too bad."，這句話實質上並不會改善對方的處境，但是卻可以稍微有心理上的安慰。

【補充】常用感冒症狀
a running nose 流鼻水
a caugh 咳嗽
a headache 頭痛
a sore throat 喉嚨痛

Q9 How do you feel now?
你現在覺得怎樣？

正解 ▶ A. Oh, I'm getting better. 喔，我覺得比較好了。

B. I've been feeling sick all week. 我已經不舒服一整個星期了。

C. Yes, it's the cold. 是啊，都是因為感冒的關係。

Q10 Does it hurt when I press it here?
我按這裡會不會痛？

A. My nose is running. 我在流鼻涕。

正解 ▶ B. Not much. 不太會。

C. Please call an ambulance. 請叫救護車。

※〔註〕ambulance [ˋæmbjələns] 救護車。

主題 5 招呼與問候 v 健康狀況

電話用語

Q1 Hello, is Grace there?

喂，葛蕾絲在嗎？

A. I'm here. 我在這裡。

正解 ▶ B. This is Grace. 我就是。

C. Hi, how are you? 嗨，你好嗎？

※〔註〕在對方無法看見自己的時候，比如說在電話上，不能直接以 I am... 回答，必須說 This is....，加上自己的名字，或用受格代名詞 her, him, me 。在門口按鈴的情形也是一樣的，例：

A: Who is it? 是誰？
B: It's me. 是我。

Q2 Is this Erin Price?

是艾琳·普萊斯嗎？

正解 ▶ A. Yes, it is. Who's this? 是的，您是哪位？

B. What's the price? 價錢多少？

C. No, I'm Erin. 不，我是艾琳。

Q3 Hello. Can I talk to Sharon, please?

喂，請找雪倫聽電話？

正解 ▶ A. I'll get her. Hold on, please. 我去叫她，請等一下。

B. Sharon is talking. 雪倫在講話。

C. Yes, you can talk. 是，你可以說。

Q4 May I speak to Tom, please?

可以請湯姆聽電話嗎？

A. Hello, May. 你好，梅。

B. I'm pleased. 我很高興。

正解 ▶ C. I'm sorry, but he is out. 對不起，他出去了。

※〔註〕打電話來的人不能確定是 May ，故不可選 A.，問句裡的 May 是助動詞， A. 裡的則是人名，屬「同音異義字」。 B.同樣也出現「同形異義字」pleased ，原句的 please 是副詞用法，表示「請…」； be pleased 則是動詞（被動）用法，表示「（被）取悅」，因為是被動，有字典或文法書也稱之為形容詞。

Q5 Sorry. He's not here. Please call back.

對不起，他不在。請你再打來吧！

A. I'll be right back. 我馬上回來。

正解 → B. Thank you. I'll call back later. 謝謝，我等一下再打來。

C. OK, tell me later. 好，等一下告訴我。

Q6 Who's calling, please?

請問哪裡找？

正解 → A. This is her friend, Lily. 我是她的朋友，莉莉。

B. This is her. 我就是〔你要找的她〕。

C. I'll call you. 我會打電話給你。

※〔註〕注意！(A) 是來電者的回應，(B) 則是受話者的回應。

Q7 Can I take a message?

需要留言嗎？

正解 → A. Yes, please. 好的，謝謝。

B. Yes, take it. 是，拿去。

C. No, you can't. 不，你不可以。

※〔註〕"leave a message" 是來電者要求要留言，動詞改成 "take"，就是受話者問需不需要幫忙留言，例如：I'm sorry, he's out. Can I take a message for you? (對不起，他出去了。您要我幫你留言嗎？)

Q8 May I leave a message?

可以幫我留言嗎？

A. Hold on, I can't take it any more. 等一下，我再也受不了。

正解 → B. Hold on, let me get a pen and paper. 等一下，我去拿筆和紙。

C. Hold it still, please. 請握著別動。

Q9 I'm afraid you have the wrong number.

恐怕您打錯號碼了！

A. Don't be afraid. 別害怕

正解 → B. I'm terribly sorry. 非常抱歉！

C. You look terrible. 你看起來真糟。

主題 **6** 招呼與問候 ∨ 電話用語

Q10 What number are you calling?

你撥幾號？

A. What do you call him? 你叫他什麼？
B. I'm number 23. 我是 23 號。

正解 — C. Is this 2222-3333? 這裡是 2222-3333 嗎？

※〔註〕當你判斷來電者打錯電話時，可以直接說 "I'm afraid you've got a wrong number." 或問清楚他撥的號碼正不正確 "What number are you calling?"。

第二類 稱謂與關係

主題 7 名字、人名與職業

Q1 What's the actor's name?

那個演員叫什麼名字？

A. He's a famous actor. 他是著名的演員。

正解 — B. He's Gray Davis. 他叫葛雷‧戴維斯。

C. He's a super star. 他是個超級巨星。

※〔註〕(A) 和 (C) 的問句應為 "Who is he?"（他是誰？）。

Q2 May I have your name, please?

請問您的大名是？

A. Nice to meet you. 很高興認識你。
B. The Chen's. 陳〔姓〕家。

正解 — C. Helen Chen, C-H-E-N, Chen. 陳海倫，C-H-E-N 陳。

Q3 Do you remember the name of the restaurant?

你記得那家餐廳的名字嗎？

A. I can't, either. 我也不行。

正解 — B. No, I don't. 不，我不〔記得〕。

Q4 C. So do I. 我也是。

Mr. Shade is my teacher this year.

正解 ► 雪德先生是我這學年的老師。

A. Mine, too. 我的〔老師〕也是〔雪德先生〕。
B. I am, too. 我〔自己〕也是。
C. Who's your teacher? 你的老師是誰？

Q5

What do you call your dog?

你怎麼叫你的狗？〔你的狗叫什麼名字？〕

正解 ► A. It's a lucky dog. 這是一隻幸運狗。
B. We call him "Lucky." 我們叫他 "Lucky"。
C. My father gave him a name. 我爸給他取了個名字。

Q6

How do you say this in English?

這個東西的英文怎麼說？

正解 ► A. It's name is "Micky." 牠叫「米奇」。
B. It's a "mouse." 是叫 "mouse〔老鼠 → 滑鼠〕"。
C. I don't like it. 我不喜歡這個。

Q7

What do you do?

你是做什麼的？

A. I'm fine. Thank you. 我很好，謝謝。
正解 ► B. How do you do? 你好。〔初次見面的問候語〕
C. I'm a computer engineer. 我是電腦工程師。

Q8

Are you a doctor or a dentist?

正解 ► 你是醫生還是牙醫？

A. Neither, I'm a vet. 都不是，我是獸醫。
B. Either a doctor or a dentist. 不是醫生，就是牙醫。
C. Both of them. 他們兩個都是。

※〔註〕問「X or Y」，回答時就一定要回答其中一個，當然不可以又回答兩個，故 (B)、(C) 皆錯。如果兩者都不是，就回答 "Neither"，然後說出第三個選擇。

主題

7

稱謂與關係 V 名字、人名與職業

Q9 What do you want to be when you grow up?

長大後你想當什麼？

A. I am a firefighter. 我是消防隊員。

正解 ► B. I want to be a teacher. 我想當老師。

C. I want to grow up. 我想長大。

※〔註〕"What do you want to be?" 可以在玩扮家家酒時用，意思是「你要當什麼（角色）？」。這句話後面加上了副詞子句 "when you grow up" 表示的是「未來」的事，(A)、(C) 表示的都是「現在」，故不可選。

Q10 Do you like your job?

你喜歡你的工作嗎？

A. No, I don't want to be. 不，我不想當。

B. No, I won't be a doctor. 不，我不會當醫生。

正解 ► C. No, I want to be a reporter. 不，我想當名記者。

※〔註〕(A)、(B) 的答案都是指「未來」的可能性，原句問的則是「現在」你喜不喜歡的問題，故選 (C)。

主題 **8**　　　　　　　　　**所有格關係**

Q1 Is that your dog?

那是你的狗嗎？

正解 ► A. That's right. 沒錯。

B. That is a dog. 那是一隻狗。

C. No, it's not yours. 不，那不是你的。

Q2 Is that our new teacher?

那是我們的新老師嗎？

A. Yes, it's new. 是，這是新的。

B. We have a few. 我們有一些。

正解 ► C. I think so. 我想是吧！

※〔註〕Yes-No 問句的回答除了直接以 Yes 或 No 回答之外，也可能是不確定的回答，例如 "I think so."、"I'm not sure.（我不確定）"、"Maybe.（也許吧）"。

Q3 Is this Jim's?

這是吉姆的嗎？

A. Yes, this is Jim. 是，這位是吉姆。

正解► B. I don't know. 我不知道。

C. I didn't know it's James'. 我不知道這是詹姆士的。

※〔註〕(A) 不對，原句是問「誰的～」，這裡回答的卻是「誰」。(C) 不對，因為 Jim 的所有格是 Jim's，而 James 的所有格是 James' 發音類似，極有可能會聽錯，要小心！

Q4 Which one is yours?

哪一個是你的？

正解► A. The red one. 紅色那個。

B. I want this one. 我要這個。

C. Watch.〔你〕看。

Q5 Use mine.

用我的吧！

正解► A. Which one? 哪一個？

B. Never think about it. 想都別想。

C. It's no use. 沒用的。

※〔註〕這樣的對話情況可能是甲大方地要借東西給乙，但是乙看到了好幾個東西，不確定是哪一個，所以要向甲確認清楚。另外，(C) 出現的同音異義字 use，原句是動詞「使用」的意思，這裡則是當名詞「用途」的意思。

Q6 Which is which?

哪個是哪個？

正解► A. This is mine; that is yours. 這個是我的；那個是你的。

B. I don't know when. 我不知道何時。

C. Two for each. 每人兩個。

Q7 Is that Michael?

那是麥可嗎？

正解► A. Who? 誰？

B. Wait for my call. 等我電話。

C. Give me a call. 打電話給我。

※〔註〕相似音 "Michael [ˋmaɪk!] / my call [maɪ kɔl]"。

Q8 Who's that?

那個人是誰？

A. This is mine. 這是我的。
正解 → B. That's my sister. 那是我妹妹。
C. She's not my sister. 她不是我妹妹。

Q9 Do you know him?

你認識他嗎？

正解 → A. Yes, very well. 認識，很熟呢！
B. No, he doesn't. 不，他沒有。
C. I know what you mean. 我懂你的意思。

Q10 Is she his girlfriend?

她是他的女朋友嗎？

正解 → A. No. Wife. 不，是老婆。
B. It's him. 就是他。
C. Not me. 不是我。

※〔註〕B. 和 C. 談論的對象都不符合題意，原句談論的是 she，這裡卻是 he (him) 或 I (me)。

| 主題 **9** | 自 己 |

Q1 Whose is this?

這是誰的？

正解 → A. It's mine. 是我的。
B. It's me. 是我。
C. I am. 我是。

Q2 Who is it?

是誰？

正解 → A. It's me. 是我。
B. This is mine. 這是我的。

248

Q3 C. Here I am. 我在這裡。

Who's there?
誰在那裡？

A. I'm not. 我不是。
正解 B. This is Bryan calling. 我是布萊恩。〔電話中〕
C. It's me, Bryan. 是我，布萊恩。

※〔註〕突然發現有人在周圍，卻不知道是誰，就可以說 Who's there?。對方如果是你熟悉的人，只要你聽到聲音就知道是誰的人，通常就會回應你 "It's me."。

Q4

Who knows the answer?
誰知道答案？

A. Answer me, please. 請回答我。
正解 B. I know Ann, sir. 我認識安，長官。
C. I do. 我知道。

Q5

Let's see who's here. Cathy?
我們來看看誰來了。凱西？

正解 A. Yes, I see. 是，我懂了。
B. Here I am. 是我〔在這兒〕。
C. I heard from Cathy yesterday. 昨天凱西跟我聯絡了。

Q6

Oh, you're Alexander Stone.
正解 喔，你是亞歷山大‧史東。

A. Just call me Alex. 叫我亞歷士就好。
B. Stop calling me. 別叫我了。
C. What a shame. 真丟臉！

Q7

Dana! Is it really you?
正解 戴娜，真的是妳嗎？

A. Hi, Jane. Yes, it's really me. 嗨，珍。沒錯，真的是我。
B. You're really a good friend. 你真是好朋友。
C. It is really dark. 真暗。

※〔註〕be 動詞開頭的問句，在回答時應有 Yes 或 No，所以答案選 A.。

Q8 Who broke the window?
誰打破的窗戶？

A. I will. 我會。
正解► B. I did. Sorry. 是我！對不起。
C. I brought it. 我帶來的。

※〔註〕相似音有 "broke [brok] / brought [brɔt]"。

Q9 Did you do this all by yourself?
這全是你自己做的嗎？

A. Help yourself, please. 請自己動手吧！
正解► B. Yes, I did. 沒錯，我自己做的。
C. Didn't you? 你沒有嗎？

※〔註〕問話者問的是「過去」發生的事，(A)的時間點不對；(C)主詞則錯了，應改成 I。

Q10 Is there anyone else at home?
還有其他人在家嗎？

A. What else? 還有什麼？
正解► B. No, I'm the only one. 沒有，只有我在家。
C. Yes, I need glasses. 是，我需要眼鏡。

※〔註〕發問者問的是「人」，選項 (A)、(C)回答的則都是「物」，故不可選。

主題 **10** 　　　　個人資料

Q1 Do you speak Chinese?
你會說中文嗎？

A. I'm from China. 我來自中國。
B. Yes, I'm a Chinese. 是，我是中國人。
正解► C. Just a little. 只會一點點。

Q2 Do you live with your family?
你和家人同住嗎？

正解 ► A. No, I live alone in Taipei. 不，我自己住在台北。
B. We live in Taipei. 我們住在台北。
C. Yes, I love my family. 是，我愛我的家人。

※〔註〕主題問的是「住」的問題，不是「愛不愛」的問題，(C)與主題不符。問「與誰」住，而不是問住「哪裡」，故 (B) 也不對。

Q3 Are you an only child?
你是家裡唯一的孩子嗎？

A. Yes, I'm Charlie. 是，我是查理。
B. No, I'm not your son. 不，我不是你兒子。
正解 ► C. No, but I'm an only son. 不是，不過我是獨子。

Q4 I have a large family.
我有個大家庭。

正解 ► A. Oh? How many are there? 哦？你家有多少人？
B. We are family. 我們是一家人。
C. Now you have a new family. 現在你有個新家庭。

Q5 I go to elementary school.
我上小學。〔我是小學生。〕

正解 ► A. What grade are you in? 你是幾年級？
B. Really? An elephant school? 真的嗎？大象學校？
C. What time do you go to school? 你幾點去上學？

※〔註 1〕在台灣小學有六年，要問對方讀幾年級就可以 "What grade are you in?"，故選 (A)。(B) 則是類似音 elementary / elephant 的陷阱，不可選。

※〔註 2〕相似音 "elementary [ˌɛlə`mɛntərɪ] / elephant [`ɛləfənt]"。

Q6 Does your mother work?
你的母親在工作嗎？

A. No, my mother works. 不，我媽媽有工作。
正解 ► B. Yes, she's a teacher. 是，她是一位老師。
C. No, she's a factory worker. 不，她是個工人。

主題 **10** 稱謂與關係 v 個人資料

Q7 Are you married?

你結婚了嗎？

正解 ► A. Yes, with two children. 是的，還有兩個小孩。

B. Yes, I'm Marian. 是，我是瑪利安。

C. No, I'm not single. 不，我不是單身。

※〔註〕(B) 與主題不符，是類音字 married ／ Marian 的陷阱。(C) 則與發問者唱反調，不可選。答案為 (A)，不但結了婚，而且有孩子了。

Q8 I walk to the office.

我走路到辦公室。

正解 ► A. So it's near your house? 所以辦公室離你家很近囉？

B. So you're going for a walk? 所以你要去散步囉？

C. So you're off now? 所以你要走囉？

※〔註〕go for a walk = take a walk = have a walk 散步
be off = be leaving = go 離開

Q9 What do you think of computer games?

你對電腦遊戲有什麼看法？

A. I want to have a computer. 我想要有一部電腦。

B. I love surfing the net. 我喜歡上網瀏覽。

正解 ► C. I think it's wasting time. 我認為那是在浪費時間。

※〔註〕surf 衝浪；surf the net 上網

Q10 Can you swim?

你會游泳嗎？

A. Why not me? 為什麼不是我？

正解 ► B. Sure. I'm a good swimmer. 當然，我還游得很好呢！

C. Yes, she's sweet. 是的，她很甜美。

※〔註〕類似音組 "swim [swɪm] / sweet [swit]"。
※〔註〕swim 游泳；swimmer 游泳者；go swimming 去游泳；swimming pool 游泳池；swimming suit 游泳衣 = bathing suit

第三類 情境

主題 11　餐廳

Q1 How many persons, sir?

先生，請問幾位？

正解 ► A. Three, please. 三位。
B. Yes, sir. 是，長官。
C. Are you sure? 你確定嗎？

Q2 Do you want to order now?

現在想點餐了嗎？

A. I like May. 我喜歡五月。
正解 ► B. I'd like to see the menu, please. 我想看看菜單。
C. Put these things in order, please. 請把這些東西排好。

※〔註〕"order" 當動詞用法，有「點菜；點選」的意思；片語 "in order" 意思是「照順序」，這裡的 "order" 是名詞。

Q3 May I take your order now?

現在可以為您點餐嗎？

正解 ► A. Yes, I'll have a Sirloin steak. 可以。我要一客沙朗牛排。
B. No, you may not. 不，你不行。
C. Here, take it. 這裡，拿去。

Q4 How would you like your steak, sir?

您牛排要幾分熟？

A. Medium level. 中級。
B. In the medium. 在中間。
正解 ► C. Medium rare, please. 三分熟。

※〔註〕五分熟說 medium，全熟說 well-done，幾分熟的說法是一種慣用法，只能這麼用，熟記就對了。

補充：

牛排熟度	牛排醬料	可樂／比薩	咖啡	用餐地點
rare 生的 （一分熟）	black pepper 黑胡椒	small 小	black 純／黑咖啡	To go. / Take out. 外帶
medium rare 三分熟	mushroom 蘑菇	regular 中	with cream / milk 加奶精	For here. / Eat in. 內用
medium 五分熟		large 大		
with sugar 加糖				
medium well-done 七分熟				
well-done 全熟				

Q5 Which sauce would you want?

您要哪一種醬料？

正解 ▶ A. Well, I like black pepper. 嗯，我喜歡黑胡椒。

B. I like sausages. 我喜歡香腸。

C. Yes, I sold it. 是，我把它賣了。

※〔註〕sauce / sausage / sold 三個字的發音相當類似，但是 (B)、(C) 主題都偏離了，正確答案為 (A)。

Q6 Would you like anything to drink?

想要喝點什麼嗎？

A. Never mind. 別在意。

B. Nothing else. 沒別的了。

正解 ▶ C. I'll have coffee, please. 我要咖啡，謝謝。

※〔註〕答案 (A) 通常回應 I'm sorry.，答案 (B) 則回應 Anything else...?，皆不符合主題，故正確答案為 (C)。

Q7 Now or later?

現在還是等一下（再上飲料）？

正解 A. After the meal, please. 請餐後再送。
B. It's a letter. 這是一封信。
C. Get me a ladder, please. 幫我拿個梯子。

※〔註〕later, letter, ladder 是類似音，但與主題都不符，(B)、(C) 皆錯。答案為 (A)，這通常是在餐廳裡的侍者與食客間的對話。

Q8 Next, please.

下一位。

A. Who is it? 是誰？
B. I'd like just one. 我只想要一個。
正解 C. One cheeseburger, to go. 一個起司漢堡，外帶。

Q9 Anything else?

還要別的嗎？

正解 A. That's enough. 這樣就夠了。
B. Nothing special. 沒什麼特別的。
C. What a thing it is! 了不起的東西！

Q10 This is Room 1103 here. Can I order something to eat?

這是 1103 號房。我可以點餐嗎？

A. What did you eat? 你吃了什麼？
正解 B. Certainly, what would you like? 沒問題，您要點什麼？
C. What's your phone number? 你的電話幾號？

主題 **11** 情境 v 餐廳

外表打扮

Q1 How tall is your boyfriend?

妳男朋友多高？

A. He's 23 years old. 他二十三歲。
B. He's very fat. 他很胖。
正解 C. He's 172 cm. 他一百七十二公分。

Q2 I'm too heavy.

我太重了。

正解 A. What's your weight? 你的體重多少？
B. Who is heavier? 誰比較重？
C. How do you like it? 你喜歡嗎？

※〔註〕正確答案為 (A)，另一種問法是用動詞 weigh：How much do you weigh?

Q3 Which is your brother, the tall one or the short one?

哪個是你哥哥？是高的、還是矮的那個？

A. My brother is taller than me. 我哥哥比我高。
B. He is as tall as me. 他和我一樣高。
正解 C. The tall one. 高的那個。

※〔註〕這是一個二選一的問題，一定要從中選出一個，而且比較高矮的人並非你和你哥哥，而是某個和你哥哥站在一起的人，故答案為 (C)。

Q4 What does he look like?

他長什麼樣子？

A. He likes sports. 他喜歡運動。
正解 B. He is a tall young man with long hair. 他是個高大的年輕人，留著一頭長髮。
C. He is fine. 他很好。

Q5 How ugly she is!

她長得真醜！

A. No, she's not beautiful. 不，她不漂亮。

正解 ▶ B. No, she's not. 不，她不〔醜〕。

C. She did pretty well. 她做得還不錯。

Q6 What did the woman wear?

那名女子如何打扮？

A. A purse. 皮包。

正解 ▶ B. A dress. 洋裝。

C. Luggage. 行李。

※〔註〕若是描述手提的東西則要使用動詞 "carry"。"purse [pɝs]、luggage [`lʌgɪdʒ]"。

Q7 My pants are way too big.

我的長褲太大了。

A. You're gown up. 你長大了。

正解 ▶ B. Go to get a belt. 去拿條皮帶。

C. You should wear a tie. 你該繫條領帶。

※〔註〕題目中 are way too big 中的 way 是表示「程度」之意。此句為美語慣用會話。

Q8 My feet are cold.

我的腳好冷。

A. Put on a hat. 戴上帽子。

B. Get dressed. 穿上衣服。

正解 ▶ C. Socks will keep them warm. 襪子可以保暖。

※〔註〕襪子 (socks) 被穿在腳上 (feet)，所以選 (C)。

Q9 How often do you shampoo your hair?

你多久洗一次頭？

A. A little. 一點點。

B. Yesterday. 昨天。

正解 ▶ C. Every day. 每天。

※〔註〕問句關鍵字 How often...，回答必須說出「一段時間」，而不是一個時間點，故不可選 (B)，答案為 (C)。

Q10 I have nothing to wear to the party.
我沒有適合舞會穿的衣服。

A. Do I? 我有嗎？

正解 B. Don't you? 你沒有嗎？

C. Do you? 你有嗎？

主題 13　　　　　　結　帳

Q1 Let me pay this time.
這次我來付。

正解 A. Oh, no. Let me get it. 不，我來付。

B. Got it? 懂了嗎？拿到了嗎？

C. You'll pay for it. 你會付出代價的。

Q2 It's my treat.
我請客。

正解 A. Oh, thank you. I'll get the next one. 謝謝，下次我付。

B. You can't cheat. 你不能作弊。

C. Oh, no. It's too bad. 喔，不。真是太糟了。

※〔註〕問句和答案 B.為類音字組 treat / cheat，只有字首的音不同，但 (B) 與題意不符。(C) 通常回應「糟糕」的情況，亦不合理。

Q3 Check, please.
買單。

正解 A. One moment. 馬上來。

B. Is the money right? 金額對嗎？

C. I'll pay by check. 我要用支票付款。

※〔註〕(C) 出現「同字異義」字 check，但題目之意為「帳單」，此為「支票」。(B) 則應該是顧客拿了帳單付了錢才會說，目的是在確認找的零錢對不對。

258

Q4 Credit card or cash?
信用卡或現金？

A. It's a credit card. 這是一張信用卡。
B. I'm in a rush. 我趕時間。
正解 ― C. Cash. 現金。

※〔註〕類音字組 "cash [kæʃ] / rush [rʌʃ]"。

Q5 OK. That's $ 36.79, please.
好的，總共是 $ 36.79 元，謝謝。

正解 ― A. I want to pay with a credit card. 我要刷卡。
B. How much is it? 多少錢？
C. Money isn't everything. 金錢不是萬能的。

※〔註〕(B) 的時間點不對，應該是在發話者之前的提問。

Q6 Twenty dollars sixty cents.
二十元六十分。

A. How much do you charge? 怎麼收費？
B. What's wrong? 怎麼回事？
正解 ― C. Oh, it's too expensive. 喔，太貴了！

Q7 How much do I owe you?
我要付多少錢？

A. You're 3 years older than me. 你大我三歲。
B. I own it. 是我的。
正解 ― C. That'll be fifty-five dollars and twenty cents. 一共五十五元二十分。

※〔註〕類音字組 "owe [o]"、"own [on]"、"old [old]"。

Q8 How much will it be altogether?
總共多少錢？

正解 ― A. It'll be $120. 一共是一百二十元。
B. It's $120 each. 每個一百二十元。
C. We'll get 120 altogether. 總共會有一百二十個。

主題 **13** 情境 v 結帳

Q9 Here is your change.

這是您的零錢。

A. I don't want to change it. 我不想換。

正解 B. Oh, keep the change. 零錢不用找了。

C. Catch the chance. 抓住機會。

※〔註〕(A) 出現「同字異義」，發問者說的 change 是「零錢」的意思，在此則為動詞「改變」的意思。(C) 則是類音字 change / chance，字尾發音不同。

Q10 Is the service charge included?

這有包含服務費嗎？

正解 A. Yes, it is. 是，有包含。

B. I got a flu. 我得了流行感冒。

C. We have good service. 我們的服務很完善。

| 主題 **14** | 個人好惡 |

Q1 Is it a good movie?

那是一部好片嗎？

A. Yes, a movie. 是，一部電影。

正解 B. I like it. 我喜歡。

C. I like the movie theater. 我喜歡那家電影院。

Q2 How do you like these pictures?

你有多喜歡這些照片？

A. Yes, I like them. 是，我喜歡。

B. I have a camera. 我有一台相機。

正解 C. Very much. 非常喜歡。

Q3 Do you like this sport?

你喜歡這項運動嗎？

正解 A. Yes, it's my favorite. 喜歡，這是我的最愛。

B. Yes, I love doing sports. 是，我喜歡做運動。

C. I like jogging, swimming and skating. 我喜歡慢跑、游泳和溜冰。

Q4 I'm interested in music.

我對音樂很感興趣。

正解 → A. What kind? 哪一種音樂？

B. What do you like? 你喜歡什麼？

C. Are you interested in music? 你對音樂有興趣嗎？

Q5 How's that song?

那首歌如何？

正解 → A. Not so good. 不怎麼好聽。

B. Right on! I'm going to buy some new CDs. 正好！我正要去買唱片。

C. I can't sing. 我不會唱。

※〔註〕How's...? 的句型是問好或不好，喜歡不喜歡，只有 (A) 是合理的回應。(B) 如果改成 I'm going to buy this CD.，表示喜歡，而且會去買這片 CD，那這個選項就可以選。

Q6 What kind of juice do you want?

你想要喝什麼果汁？

A. I'd rather wear jeans than a dress. 我寧可穿長褲也不穿裙子。

正解 → B. Do we have a choice? 我們還有別的〔可以選擇〕嗎？

C. Be my guest. 我請客。

※〔註〕(A) 利用類音字組 juice / jeans，主題不符，不可選。(C) 同樣也是身為「提議者」會說的話，角色不對。(B) 才是接受提議者的合理回應。

Q7 Would she like this style?

她會喜歡這種款式嗎？

A. I'm afraid she would. 我擔心她會。

B. She didn't tell me. 她沒告訴我。

正解 → C. No, I don't think so. 不會，我不認為她會喜歡。

Q8 How do you like the university?

你覺得大學如何？

正解 → A. I love it very much. 我很愛大學生活。

B. This university is famous. 這所大學很著名。

C. You're unlike me. 你不像我。

※〔註〕問你喜歡或不喜歡，故只有 (A) 為合理回應。注意 (C) 的 unlike 是形容詞，意思為「不相像的」，相反詞為 like「相像的」；發問者的 like 用法則是動詞，意思是「喜歡」。

主題 **14** 情境 V 個人好惡

Q9 How would you like it cut?

你想要怎麼剪？

A. Just a haircut. 只要剪個頭髮就可以了。

正解 ► B. Cut it short all over. 整個剪短。

C. I'd like a shampoo. 我想洗頭。

※〔註〕發問者可能是美髮師，已經知道顧客是要剪髮，(A)、(C) 的說法應該都是在發問者問這句話之前的開場，時間上錯誤，故選 (B)。

Q10 Don't you want to visit New York some-time?

你不會想要偶爾去參觀紐約嗎？

正解 ► A. Yes, I do. I'll go there one day. 會，我想。我有一天一定要去。

B. I'll be there in a second. 我馬上就會到了。

C. I visited the city several times. 我參觀過那座城市幾次。

※〔註〕發問者問 Don't you want to... sometime? 問的是「未來」你想不想，(C)的時間點是「過去」，不對。(B) 的時間點雖是未來，但是距離時間太近了，無法旅行到另一個城市，甚至是國家，也不對。正確答案為 (A)，one day 表示「未來有一天…」。

第四類 數字

主題 15 詢 價

Q1 How much is the room rate?

房間價錢怎麼算？

正解 ► A. It's about $ 1,200 for one night. 一晚大約一千兩百元。

B. We'll stay for 3 nights. 我們要待三天。

C. This is for rent. 這是要出租的。

※〔註〕費用 rate [ret] / 出租 rent [rɛnt]。

Q2 How much is the round-trip fare?

來回票價多少？

正解 ─ A. It's $ 70. 七十元。

B. It's $ 70 per hour. 每小時七十元。

C. It's fair. 這很公平。

※〔註〕票價 fare [fɛr] / 公平的 fair [fɛr]。

Q3 Are they free?

這些都是免費嗎？

正解 ─ A. Yes, they are. 是的。

B. You are free. 你自由了！

C. Yes, there are four. 對，有四個。

※〔註〕免費、自由都寫做 free [fri]。

Q4 Are the meals included in the rent?

房租裡包括膳食費嗎？

A. Three meals a day. 一天三餐。

B. $100 a meal. 一餐一百元。

正解 ─ C. No, they aren't. 不包括。

Q5 How much are you asking?

你的預算多少？

正解 ─ A. US$ 10.00 a day. 一天美金十元。

B. US dollars. 美金。

C. Nothing. 沒有。

Q6 What do you charge?

怎麼收費？

A. Can I change to another room? 我可以換房間嗎？

B. I have a 25-cent coin. 我有一個 25 分的硬幣。

正解 ─ C. US$ 25.00 a week. 一個星期美金 25 元。

※〔註〕What do you charge? 是問一些服務的收費情形，例如住宿、乾洗店、修車廠…等，一般回答都有一些收費標準，例如：一天（星期）多少錢、一件襯衫多少錢，或換一個零件多少錢…等，故 (C) 為正確答案。

Q7 How much should I pay you?

我要付你多少錢？

正解 ─ A. Oh, it's free. 哦，這是免費的。

B. Oh, you have to pay in cash. 喔！你必須付現金。

C. Should I? 我應該要嗎？

※〔註〕How much...? 是問該付「多少」錢，不是「如何」付錢，不可選 (B)。而選項中的內容只有重複問句裡的某個片語通常是錯誤的答案，所以 (C) 不可選，因為角色也混淆了，這句話應該也是發話者的台詞。

Q8 It must have cost you a lot.

這一定花了你很多錢。

正解 ─ A. You're worth it. 你值得。

B. I have a lot of it. 我有很多。

C. Yes, I bought you a coat. 對，我幫你買了一件外套。

※〔註〕發話者的情況應該是收到了一份禮物，客氣地對送禮者表示感謝，(A) 是送禮人合理的回應。而 (B) 當中的 a lot 是形容詞，與原句副詞用法不同。(C) 則應該也是送禮者這個角色的台詞，而且出現了類音字 cost / coat 的陷阱。

Q9 How do you pay for it?

你怎麼付得起？

正解 ─ A. I won't pay for it. 我是不會付的。

B. I pray before going to bed. 我在睡前做禱告。

C. It's too much. 太多了。

※〔註〕購物者一定是想買一件不便宜的東西，超出他的能力範圍外的，結果是購物者根本沒有自己付錢，故選 (A)。而 (B) 則是出現了類音字 pay/pray。如果選項 (C) 是 It's not much. = It doesn't cost much. 那就可以選，表示這件東西根本不貴。

Q10 Can I get it cheaper?

可以算便宜一點嗎？

A. This is a country. 這是一個國家。

B. Please count it. 請算一下。

正解 ─ C. I'm sorry, but not. 對不起，不行。

主題 16 例行時間

Q1 What time do you get up?

你幾點起床？

A. Why did you get up so early? 你怎麼這麼早起床？
B. It's time to go to bed. 睡覺時間到了。
正解 C. I usually get up at six thirty. 我通常都六點半起床。

Q2 At what time does the store open?

幾點開始營業？

A. At the store. 在店裡。
正解 B. At ten o'clock, sir. 十點，先生。
C. The store is open. 商店營業中。

Q3 What time does the class start?

課幾點開始？

A. It's time to start the class. 上課囉！
B. He's a big star. 他是大明星。
正解 C. It starts at three thirty in the afternoon. 下午三點半開始。

※〔註〕(A)、(B) 出現了類音字 start / star，但是與主題不符，不可選。

Q4 What are your working hours?

你的上班時間是什麼時候？

A. Keep early hours. 早睡早起。
正解 B. It is 9:00 a.m. to 5:30 p.m. 早上九點到下午五點半。
C. I worked from 9:00 a.m. to 5:30 p.m. yesterday. 我昨天從早
上九點工作到下午五點半。

Q5 When does the sun go down there?

那裡的太陽什麼時候下山？

正解 A. Sundown is about 8:30 p.m. here.
這裡的日落大概在下午八點半。
B. My son came at 8:30. 我兒子八點半來的。

Q6 C. The sun goes down in the west. 太陽從西邊落下。

When does the train for Los Angeles leave?

正解 往洛杉磯的火車什麼時候開？

A. 9:25 on Track 12. 九點廿五分，在第十二月台。

B. It takes 9 hours by train. 坐火車要九個小時。

C. We will leave Los Angeles by 9 o'clock. 我們九點前離開洛杉磯。

Q7

When does the plane arrive?

飛機什麼時候會抵達？

A. We plan to leave at 11:45. 我們計畫在十一點四十五分離開。

正解 B. It should be close at 11:45. 應該十一點四十五分會關門。

C. It should be here at 11:45. 應該十一點四十五分會到。

※〔註〕三個選項雖然都提到了時間點，但應該發生的事件卻只有 (C) 正確，be here = arrive。

Q8

What time do I have to be at the airport?

正解 我必須幾點到機場？

A. Check-in time is 11:00 a.m. 十一點辦理登機手續。

B. Please check out before 11:00 a.m. 請在早上十一點前退房。

C. We'll check the plane at 11:00 a.m. 我們將在早上十一點檢查飛機。

※〔註〕通常飛機起飛一至兩個小時前，乘客就必須到櫃檯 check in（登記），故選 (A)。 check in 的另一個情況是事先旅館訂房，住宿當天到旅館櫃檯登記；check out 則是辦理旅館退房，與搭機、下機都沒有關係，故 (B) 情境不對。(C) 當中的 check 又是另一個意思，表「檢查」，主題也不符。

Q9

What time is the show on?

節目幾點開始？

A. The show is good. 節目很好。

正解 B. She showed up on time. 她準時出現。

C. I have no idea. 我不知道。

※〔註〕問句關鍵詞 What time...? 是問一個時間點，不是問好不好，故 (A) 不對。發話者說的 show 意思是「表演、節目」；片語 "show up" 則是「出現」的意思，故 (B) 主題不符。

Q10 How long is the ride?

車程多久？

正解 A. About ten minutes. 大約十分鐘。
B. About ten meters. 大約十公尺。
C. About ten long ropes. 大約十條長繩。

※〔註〕the ride 意思是一段車程，問句關鍵詞 How long...? 在此是問「多久」的時間，故選 (A)。

主題 17 時間約定

Q1 Joe. Get up.

喬，起床了。

正解 A. Is it seven o'clock already? 已經七點了嗎？
B. It's seven o'clock. 七點了。
C. I get up at seven o'clock. 我七點起床。

※〔註〕(B) 應是回應 "What time is it?"。(C) 回應 "When do you get up?"。只有 (A) 為合理答案，顯然 Joe 是睡過頭了。

Q2 Would 9:00 tomorrow be all right?

明天九點可以嗎？

A. At 9:00 last night. 昨晚九點。
B. Nothing is right. 沒有一件事是對的。
正解 C. I'm afraid not. 恐怕不行。

Q3 How would 12:45 be?

十二點四十五分如何？

A. The house is made out of wood. 這房子是木造的。
正解 B. Just a second. I'll have to check. 等一下，我要查看看。
C. O.K. I'll check the house. 好，我會檢查房子。

※〔註〕發話者是在提議一個會面時間，所以只有 (B) 為合理答案。

Q4 We'll be on time, won't we?

我們會準時到達的，對嗎？

A. What is the time? 幾點了？

正解 — B. I hope so. 我希望如此。

C. Yes, you are here on time. 對，你們準時到了。

Q5 Will you be here at nine o'clock tomorrow?

你明天九點鐘會到這兒嗎？

正解 — A. Okay, I will. 好的，我會。

B. Will you come tonight? 今晚你會來嗎？

C. Yes, I can hear. 是，我聽得到。

※〔註〕同音異字 "here [hɪr] / hear [hɪr]"；類音組 "nine [naɪn] / tonight [təˋnaɪt]" 都會造成混淆。

Q6 When are you leaving?

你什麼時候離開？

正解 — A. At one o'clock in the afternoon. 下午一點。

B. Winnie's not leaving. 溫妮不離開。

C. I don't know why. 我不知道為什麼。

Q7 I want to try to catch a 6:00 train.

我要趕六點的火車。

正解 — A. I think you'll make it. 我想你可以趕上。

B. When does the train leave? 火車什麼時後離開？

C. Try to catch me. 來抓我啊！

※〔註〕發話者已經說出火車時刻，所以 (B) 不對。(C) 則是同形異義字的陷阱，catch 原意是「趕上」，在此是「抓」。正確答案為 (A)，You can make it. 表示對方可以做得到，也就是說對方要趕上火車是沒問題的。

Q8 The flight is late.

飛機誤點。

A. Turn on the light. 把燈打開。

B. It's getting late. 越來越晚了。

正解 — C. For how long? 會多久？

※〔註〕flight [flaɪt] 表「飛機航班」，與選項 A.的 light [laɪt] 表示「燈；光」發音只差字首 "f"，聽力上容易造成意義的混淆。

Q9 See you in the evening at home.

晚上家裡見。

正解── A. Ok, bye. 好，再見。

B. I come home at 5:00 in the evening. 我傍晚五點回家。

C. Did you see? 你看到了嗎？

※〔註〕(B)、(C) 語意皆與題意不符，故選 (A)。這段對話應該是早上要出門時，對家人常說的道別語。

Q10 What time?

什麼時間？

正解── A. You name the time. 你決定。

B. Ten times. 十次。

C. In old time. 古時候。

※〔註〕三個選項所出現的 time 的意思都不相同，依序為「時間」、「次數」、「時代」，因此 (A) 為正確答案。 name 在此是動詞用法，表示「指定」之意。

主題 **18** 數字 ∨ 詢問時間

主題 **18** 詢問時間

Q1 What time is it now?

現在幾點？

A. It's the time. 是時候了。

B. See you next time. 下次見面。

正解── C. It's half past eight. 八點半。

※〔註〕time 的意思有不可數名詞「時間」和可數名詞的「次數」。

Q2 Can you tell me what time it is?

您可以告訴我現在幾點嗎？

正解── A. It's one o'clock sharp. 現在是一點整。

B. Don't touch. It's sharp. 別摸，這很銳利。

C. Don't ask. 別問。

※〔註〕選項 A.中的 sharp 是指「～點整」。

Q3 Can you tell me the time, please?

您可以告訴我現在幾點嗎？

A. Can't you? 你不行嗎？
B. Are you sure? 你確定嗎？
正解 ► C. Sure. It's twenty to nine. 沒問題，現在是八點四十分。

Q4 Do you know what time it is?

你知道現在幾點嗎？

正解 ► A. Yes, it's a quarter to seven. 知道，六點四十五分。
B. Please be quite. 請安靜。
C. Show me. 給我看。

Q5 Please tell me the time.

請告訴我時間。

A. I won't tell Tom. 我不會告訴湯姆的。
B. It's not for Tom. 這不是給湯姆的。
正解 ► C. It's four o'clock. 四點了。

Q6 Excuse me, sir. Do you have the time?

對不起，先生。你知道現在幾點嗎？

A. It's two hundred and twenty. 兩百二十。
正解 ► B. It's two twenty. 兩點二十分。
C. Two times twenty is forty. 二乘二十等於四十。

※〔註〕time 的另一個意思是數學裡的「乘法」，單數動詞的字尾一定要加 "-s"；方程式裡的「等於」可以用 is 或 equals 表示，還是以單數動詞表示。
〔例〕2 × 20 = 40 → Two times twenty equals forty.

Q7 Have you got the time?

你知道幾點了嗎？

A. Time flies. 時光飛逝。
B. It's fifteen minutes fast. 快了十五分鐘。
正解 ► C. It's fifteen minutes past seven. 七點十五分。

※〔註〕這一題要能得對的關鍵就在聽懂問句，問的是現在的時刻，故合理答案為 (C)。注意！(A) 的 time 表示的是「時光」，但題目問的是「幾點鐘」。

Q8 I wonder what time it is.

不知道現在幾點了。

正解 A. I don't think it is five o'clock yet. 我想現在還不到五點。

B. I don't think so. 我不這麼認為。

C. No wonder. 難怪！

※〔註〕這題的情境應該是對話雙方都沒戴手錶，放眼過去也找不到可以指示時間的來源，所以兩人的用語 I wonder... 與 I don't think... 都表示相當不確定眞正的時間。

Q9 What time do you have?

你的錶幾點了？

正解 A. My watch says two o'clock. 我的錶是兩點。

B. Watch what you say. 小心你的措詞。

C. Watch out. 小心。

※〔註〕(B)、(C) 當中的 watch 當動詞有「小心」的意思，與詢問時間的主題完全不符。注意！正確答案 (A) My watch **says**...的動詞 **says** 爲一固定用法，中文通常無法直接翻譯出來。

Q10 May I have the time?

可以告訴我時間嗎？

A. I'm sorry, I have no money. 對不起，我沒有錢。

正解 B. I'm sorry, I have no watch. 對不起，我沒有錶。

C. I'm sorry, I have no change. 對不起，我沒有零錢。

※〔註〕問話者所談的主題是 time，但(A)、(C) 所談論的主題各爲 money 與 change，故皆爲錯的答案。

Q11 What o'clock is it?

現在是幾點？

正解 A. It has struck one. 剛過一點。

B. It's a clock. 這是一個時鐘。

C. Good luck. 祝你好運。

※〔註〕"strike / struck / struck" 表「敲擊」，這裡指「時鐘敲響報時」。
《棒球術語》Strike! 表示「三振出局」。

第五類 慣用句型

主題 19 詢問地點

Q1 Are you from America?
你來自美國嗎？

A. Yes, we're from Australia. 是，我們來自澳洲。
正解 ► B. No, I'm from Canada. 不是，我來自加拿大。
C. No, I'm an American. 不，我是美國人。

Q2 What city do you live in?
你住在哪個城市？

正解 ► A. I'm in Hualian. 我在花蓮。
B. I live in Korea. 我住在韓國。
C. I live in school housing. 我住校。

※〔註〕注意聽問句關鍵字是 What city...?，問的是一個城市，故選 (A)。

Q3 Where are you?
你在哪裡？

A. I'm fine. 我很好。
B. I'm a housewife. 我是個家庭主婦。
正解 ► C. I'm at home. 我在家。

Q4 Where are we?
我們在哪裡？（這是哪裡？）

A. We were not there. 我們不在那裡。
正解 ► B. We are lost. 我們迷路了。
C. You are losing it. 你瘋了！

※〔註〕(A)、(C) 時間點不對，而且主題不對。正確答案為 (B)。

Q5 Where is he going?

他要去哪裡？

正解 ▶ A. He's going to the library. 他要去圖書館。
B. Yes, he's going to the library. 是，他要去圖書館。
C. Yes, he's going. 是，他要去。

Q6 Have you decided where to go?

你決定要去哪裡了嗎？

A. Not me. 不是我。
正解 ▶ B. Not yet. 還沒。
C. I can't. 我不行。

※〔註〕Have you...? 問的是做了某事沒有，故選 (B)。

Q7 Where are we on this map?

我們在這張地圖的哪個位置？

A. We're on the bus. 我們在巴士上。
B. You're right. 你是對的。
正解 ▶ C. We're right here. 我們就在這裡。

※〔註〕問句中的 on this map 表示對話雙方都在看同一張地圖，必須指出在地圖上的位置說 "We're right here."，故選 (C)。

Q8 Where to?

去哪裡？

A. Don't go. 不要去。
B. It's in the airport. 在機場裡。
正解 ▶ C. The airport, please. 到機場，謝謝。

※〔註〕Where to 是一種非常簡潔的說法，聽不到動詞，完整的意思是 Where do you plan to go?，所以應回答一個確切的地點，答案爲 (C)。

Q9 Can you tell me a good place to eat?

你能告訴我哪裡有好吃的嗎？

正解 ▶ A. Do you like spaghetti? 你喜歡義大利麵嗎？
B. I know that place. 我知道那個地方。
C. How pretty! 好美！

主題 19 慣用句型 V 詢問地點

Q10 What country has the most people in the world?

世界上哪個國家有最多人？

A. People around the world know about it. 全世界的人都知道。
B. Canada has the most islands in the world. 加拿大擁有全世界最多的島嶼。
正解 C. Is it China? 是中國嗎？

主題 **20**　　　　　　　詢問方法

Q1 How do you go to school?

你怎麼到學校的？

A. Just take a chance. 就碰碰運氣。
正解 B. My father drives. 我父親開車送我。
C. Take it easy. 放輕鬆。

Q2 How can I get there?

我要怎麼到那裡？

A. Go ahead. 去吧！
B. I'll take it. 我拿這個〔這件〕。
正解 C. Take bus 202. 搭 202 號公車。

※〔註〕由問句中的 How 與 get there 可以知道，發問者在問的是一種「交通方式」，故選 (C)。

Q3 What is the easiest way to the zoo?

到動物園最簡單的方法是什麼？

正解 A. By MRT. 搭捷運。
B. It's by the zoo. 在動物園附近。
C. By heart. 憑記憶。

※〔註〕由 What...way...? 可知這也是一個問交通方式的題目，故答案為 (A)。

Q4 What should I do?

我該怎麼做？

正解 ▸ A. Easy. Just call her. 簡單，只要打電話給她就行了。
B. Easy come; easy go. 來得容易，去得也快。
C. On foot. 走路。

Q5 By which way would you like to pay?

你想要如何付款呢？

正解 ▸ A. Here is $2,000 cash. 這是兩千元的現金。
B. Here you come! 你來啦！
C. Here we are! 我們到了！

Q6 How did you know it was him?

你怎麼知道是他？

A. I looked it up in the dictionary. 我查了字典。
正解 ▸ B. I saw him. 我看到他了。
C. I didn't talk to him. 我沒和他說話。

※〔註〕問句關鍵字 How...? 表示問「方法」，(C) 並未說出方法，所以不對。(A) 說出方法，但是不合理，也不對。正確答案為 (B)。

Q7 How did you find me here?

你怎麼找到我在這裡的？

正解 ▸ A. Jason told me. 傑森告訴我的。
B. You're telling me. 還用你說！
C. Let me tell you why. 我來告訴你為什麼。

Q8 How can I help?

我該怎麼幫忙？

A. Help me, please. 請幫我。
正解 ▸ B. You can do the dishes. 你可以洗碗。
C. Why didn't you help me? 你怎麼沒幫我？

※〔註〕發話者已經表態要提供協助，受話者如果又再提出要求就不合理了，故 (A)、(C) 都不可選。

Q9 What can I do for you?

我能幫你什麼嗎？（我能為您服務嗎？）

A. You can leave now. 你現在可以走了。
B. I'm doing housework. 我正在做家事。
正解 C. I'd like to see the ties. 我想看看這些領帶。

Q10 What can I do to make you happy?

我要怎麼做妳才會開心？

正解 A. Just leave. 只要你離開。
B. Just a minute. 等一下。
C. I made a cake. 我做了蛋糕。

※〔註〕由發話者的問話知道，受話者的心情應該是不太好的，(A) 的回應表示他不想多談，只想獨處。

主題 21 **詢問原因**

Q1 I don't feel good.

我覺得不舒服。

正解 A. What's the matter? 怎麼一回事？
B. That's not good. 這樣不好哦！
C. It's a good idea. 好主意。

Q2 I have a fever.

我發燒了。

A. Excuse me. 對不起。
B. You'll be sorry. 你會後悔的。
正解 C. Did you catch a cold? 你感冒了嗎？

※〔註〕這題一定要先聽懂 fever（發燒），才能選出合理的回應。當你聽到對方發燒了，當然是關心他是不是感冒生病了，嚴不嚴重，看過醫生了沒，所以答案為 (C)。

Q3 What's wrong?

有什麼問題？

正解 A. I can't open this box. 我打不開這個盒子。

B. He's fine. 他很好。

C. Watch your mouth. 小心你說的話。

※〔註〕當發現對方被某事困擾著時，適時釋出你的關心，就可以問他 What's wrong?，這時候對方的合理回答應該就是像 (A) 一樣，告訴你什麼事出錯了。

Q4 What's up? You don't look yourself today.

怎麼了? 你看起來不太對勁。

A. I did it myself. 我自己做的。

B. That sounds great. 聽起來很不錯。

正解 C. Nothing. 沒事。

Q5 I'm happy today.

我今天很開心。

正解 A. Oh, are you? Why? 哦，是嗎？為什麼？

B. How can you say that? 你怎能這麼說？

C. Don't worry. 別擔心。

※〔註〕聽到對方心情很好，你當然也會為他開心，所以 (A) 是合理的回應，追問對方什麼事讓他這麼高興。

Q6 How come you didn't call me last night?

你昨晚怎麼沒打電話給我？

正解 A. I was ... busy. 我在……忙。

B. I came by a taxi. 我搭計程車來的。

C. Yeah, sure. 是啊，當然。

Q7 Cathy, can you help me with this?

凱西，你可以幫我一下嗎？

正解 A. Why me again? 為什麼又是我？

B. That's right. 沒錯。

C. Don't mention it. 別客氣。

主題 **21** 慣用句型 V 詢問原因

Q8 Wait a minute.

等一下。

A. You name it. 你來指定。
B. No, you don't understand. 不，你不了解。
正解 ─ C. Sure. What is it? 好。怎麼了？

Q9 Come here, John.

約翰，過來。

A. Yes, I'm. 是，我是。
正解 ─ B. What for? 什麼事？
C. Yes, I have. 是，我有。

※〔註〕這是一個命令句，當對方被下令作某事時，可能的反應是服從，另一個可能就是問為什麼，所以答案為 (B)。

Q10 I can't come tonight.

我今晚沒辦法過來。

A. It's cool! 太炫了！
B. Why not use a comb? 怎麼不用梳子？
正解 ─ C. Why not? 為什麼不行？

※〔註〕這裡的情形應該是雙方已經約定要前往某處，但臨時發話者卻無法赴會。(A)的回應太不合常理；(B) 出現了類似音 come / comb 的錯誤。(C) 為正確答案，追問對方原因。

主題 **22**　　　　　　　　　　**感官動詞**

Q1 Can you hear me?

你聽得到我嗎？

A. O.K. I'm here. 好，我在這裡。
正解 ─ B. Yes, very well. 可以，很清楚。
C. I'm pretty well, thank you. 我很好，謝謝。

※〔註〕(A) 為利用同音異字 hear / here 的錯誤；(C) 則故意與正確答案 very well 類似，但是這裡的 pretty well 其實是形容詞，相當於 I'm fine. 的意思。

Q2 How does it feel?

這感覺如何？

A. It's filled of water. 這裝滿了水。
B. He feels sick. 他覺得不舒服。
正解 C. It feels nice and soft. 感覺很柔軟、很舒服。

※〔註〕類音字組 feel [fil] / fill [fɪl]。

Q3 Do you like it?

你喜歡嗎？

A. Yes, I like you. 是，我喜歡你。
正解 B. Yes, it tastes good. 喜歡，嚐起來很棒。
C. No, it's not like that. 不，不是這樣的。

Q4 Dinner is ready.

晚餐煮好了。

A. Wow, beautiful lady. 哇，好美的小姐！
正解 B. Umm, it smells good. 嗯，聞起來好香。
C. I ate already. 我已經吃過了。

※〔註〕類音字組 "ready [`rɛdɪ] / lady [`ledɪ] / already [ɔl`rɛdɪ]"。

Q5 How do I look?

我看起來如何？

A. Can't you see? 你看不到嗎？
B. You're so nice. 你真好。
正解 C. Very handsome. 很帥！

Q6 What's the smell?

什麼味道？

A. I can't hear it. 我聽不到。
B. It smells good. 聞起來不錯。
正解 C. It smells like garbage. 聞起來像垃圾。

※〔註〕發問者是「聞到」某種味道，而不是「聽到」或「嚐到」東西。所以正確答案為 (C)，顯然這是不好聞的味道。

主題
22
慣用句型 ∨ 感官動詞

Q7 Why do you sound unhappy to see me?

為什麼你聽起來好像不高興見到我？

正解 ► A. Never. You just surprised me. 絕不會，只是你嚇了我一跳。

B. I'll never see you again. 我不想再見到你。

C. I have a sore throat. 我喉嚨痛。

※〔註〕這裡的情況是對話者已經見面了，所以 (B) 的時間點不對；選 (C) 的人則可能是把原文的 sound unhappy 聽成了 "sound bad（聽起來不對勁）"。

Q8 That sounds interesting.

那聽起來很有趣。

正解 ► A. So are you joining us? 所以你要加入我們嗎？

B. I was glad to talk with you. 和您談話很愉快。

C. You have a beautiful voice. 你的聲音很好聽。

Q9 This place feels like home.

這地方就像家一樣。

A. How does it feel? 說說你的感覺。

正解 ► B. Then why not stay longer? 那麼何不待久一點呢？

C. How do you feel? 你覺得如何？

※〔註〕發話者已經道出他的感覺，覺得像在家一樣自在，所以 (B) 回應顯然是主人，表示希望對方可以留下來。(A)、(C) 都是錯在說話的時間點，應該是在發話者之前，而不是之後。

Q10 It's freezing out here.

這裡外面很冷。

正解 ► A. Yeah, I can't feel my feet anymore. 是啊，我的腳都麻了。

B. It's not good for you. 這對你不是件好事。

C. I'm not feeling well. 我覺得不舒服。

※〔註〕(B)、(C) 都是利用類音字 freezing / feel / feet 的錯誤。正確答案為 (A)，呼應對方的說法，表示外頭冷到連腳都失去知覺了。

第六類 強調短句

主題 23 驚訝與驚喜

Q1 It's twelve already.
已經十二點了。

正解 ► A. Oh, no. Is it? 喔，不會吧？
B. How many? 幾個？
C. Do you have the time? 你知道時間嗎？

Q2 Time's up. It's time to leave.
時間到，請離開。

正解 ► A. Already? 已經到了嗎？
B. Here we are. 我們到了。
C. It' the wrong time. 時機不對。

Q3 This is for you.
這是給你的。

正解 ► A. What a surprise! 真是太意外了。
B. You can't do this. 你不能這麼做。
C. It's mine. 這是我了。

Q4 Oh, no! I don't believe it.
喔，天啊，我不相信！

正解 ► A. What's the matter? 怎麼了？
B. Do you believe it? 你相信嗎？
C. How can you do this? 你怎麼可以這麼做？

※〔註〕說話者已經明白的表現出震驚、不可置信的情緒，(A) 示出關心之情，為最佳答案。(B) 故意唱反調；(C) 完全離題。

Q5 Mark is late.
馬克遲到了。

正解 A. That's surprising. He's never late.
真讓人感到意外，他從不遲到的。
B. Why were you late? 你為什麼遲到？
C. Give me one second. 請等我一下。

※〔註〕談論的對象是 Mark，(B)、(C) 皆錯在對象的問題。(A) 回應者不敢相信這個人竟然會遲到，此為合理回應。

Q6 Joe is my friend.
喬是我的朋友。

正解 A. I can't believe it. 我不敢相信。
B. You won't believe it. 你不會相信的。
C. Believe it or not. 信不信由你。

Q7 No, she's not my sister. She's my mother.
不，她不是我姐姐，她是我媽媽。

正解 A. Are you joking? She looks so young.
你在開玩笑的吧? 她看起來這麼年輕。
B. No kidding? She's your sister? 沒開玩笑? 她是你姐姐？
C. Wow. What a good kid! 哇，好棒的孩子！

※〔註〕kid 的名詞用法是「孩子」的意思，動詞用法則是「開玩笑」的意思，就等於 joke [dʒok]，這個字當名詞就是「笑話」的意思，例如： It's a joke. 「這是個笑話（開玩笑的）！」。

Q8 Guess what! He's the boss.
猜得到嗎? 他是老闆。

A. Good guess. 猜得不錯。
B. They all laughed at him. 他們都嘲笑他。
正解 C. No kidding. 沒開玩笑吧？

Q9 It can't be true.
這不可能是真的。

正解 A. I'm afraid it is. 恐怕就是真的。
B. Yes, it's real. 是，這是真的〔東西〕。
C. For real this time? 這次是來真的？

※〔註〕true 是「真相、事實」，real 是「真實的」，兩者意義完全不同，故 (B)、(C) 皆錯。答案 (A)，告訴對方很不幸的真相就是如此。

Q10 Is it really you, Billy?

真的是你嗎？比利？

正解 ► A. Hi, long time no see. 嗨，好久不見。
B. It's not just you. 不只是你。
C. Yes, I'm really busy. 是，我真的很忙。

※〔註〕類音字組 "Billy [`bɪlɪ] / busy [`bɪzɪ]"。

主題 **24** 命令與警告

Q1 Be quiet. Don't talk.

安靜，別說話。

A. What are you talking about? 你在說什麼？
B. The teacher is speaking. 老師在講話。
正解 ► C. I'm sorry. 對不起。

Q2 Louder. I can't hear you.

大聲一點，我聽不到。

正解 ► A. All right. 好。
B. I'm all ears. 我洗耳恭聽。
C. We're in a library. 我們在圖書館。

※〔註〕典型的命令句，(A) 表示遵從，為合理答案。(B) 為角色錯誤，回應者必須是要說話的人，不是在聽的人。(C) 則為場合錯誤，在圖書館裡應該要小聲說話才對。

Q3 Now listen to me carefully.

現在仔細聽我說。

A. You're too careful. 你太過小心了。
B. I do care. 我真的關心。
正解 ► C. Yes. What is it? 好，什麼事？

Q4 Just leave me alone, will you?

你就別管我了，好嗎？

正解 ► A. OK. OK. 好，好！

B. Come on. Let's leave. 來，我們離開吧！

C. Go away. 走開。

※〔註〕基本上這是一個委婉的命令句，句子前半段明確說出要對方做的事，後半段的附加問句則使口氣緩和了一些。

Q5 Don't touch! Keep your hands off that vase.

別碰！別碰那個花瓶。

A. Would you hand me that vase? 你可以把那個花瓶拿給我嗎？

正解 ► B. Hey, take it easy. 嘿，別緊張。

C. It's easy as pie. 簡單得很〔小事一樁〕！

※〔註〕It's easy. = It's easy as pie. = It's a piece of cake.

Q6 Stop it, or I will....

停！否則我就……

A. Hey, I'm not stupid. 嘿，我不是笨蛋。

正解 ► B. You will what? 你就怎樣？

C. I'll see you out. 我送你出去。

※〔註〕類音字組有 "stop it [stɑp ɪt] / stupid [`stjupɪd]"。

Q7 Don't forget to brush your teeth.

別忘了刷牙。

正解 ► A. I won't. 我不會忘的。

B. I'm sorry. 對不起。

C. I forgot. 我忘了。

※〔註〕注意！命令者用的語法是 Don't...，但是回答時必須用未來式，絕不可以回答 I don't....，故 (A) 爲正確答案。(B)、(C) 都是時間點的錯誤。

Q8 Watch out for cars.

小心來車。

A. Are you O.K.? 你還好嗎？

B. I'm feeling better. 我覺得好多了。

正解 ► C. Thanks. 謝謝。

Q9 Watch your step!

小心走。

正解 A. Oh, thank you. 喔，謝謝你。
B. Better safe than sorry! 還是小心點好。
C. How are you? 你好嗎？

※〔註〕這個命令句實際上是個貼心提醒對方的用句，所以受話者等於是接受了對方的幫助，故正確答案 (A) 回以感謝之意。(B)、(C) 同樣應為提出警告者的話語，皆為角色混淆之錯誤。

Q10 Be careful, OK?

小心點，好嗎？

A. Please don't hurt me! 請不要傷害我！
正解 B. Don't worry. I will. 別擔心，我會的。
C. Ouch! It hurts. 唉喲，痛啊！

※〔註〕同上題，發話者的本意是提醒對方要注意，是善意的表現，所以 (A)、(C) 仇視性的回應是完全不合理的；(B) 則表示要對方放心，此為合理答案。

主題 25　催促與延緩

Q1 Hurry! We are late.

快一點，我們遲到了。

正解 A. OK, coming. 好，來了。
B. Gook luck! 祝你好運！
C. Take your time. 慢慢來。

Q2 Are you ready?

好了嗎？

正解 A. Just a minute. 再一會兒。
B. Help yourself. 請便〔別拘束〕。
C. Oh, that's all right. 喔，沒關係。

Q3 Will you wait for just one moment, please?

可以請你等我一下嗎？

正解 A. Sure. What is it? 好。怎麼了？
B. Slow down. 慢一點。
C. Don't push me. 別逼我。

Q4 I'll be right back.

我馬上回來。

A. Time's up. 時間到了。
正解 B. No problem. I'll wait. 沒問題，我會等。
C. Don't go away. 別走開。

※〔註〕此處的 right 是副詞，為「立刻、馬上」之意，這句話可以改換為 I'll be back very soon.，但是口語上用 right back 較為自然。

Q5 Hey, wait for me!

嘿，等等我！

A. What do you plan to do? 你打算做什麼？
B. Let's head out. 我們就走吧！
正解 C. O.K., but hurry. 好啊，可是快一點。

※〔註〕發話者只表示要對方等自己，沒有說出為什麼，因此 (A) 為合理的回應，表示願意等對方，並且催促他快一點。

Q6 Could you slow down, please?

你可以慢一點嗎？

正解 A. Oh, I'm sorry. 哦，對不起。
B. How could you? 妳怎麼可以這麼做？
C. Wait a minute. 等一下。

Q7 Don't rush. The game begins at 6:30.

別急，比賽六點半才開始。

正解 A. Oh, good. We still have time. 哦，好，我們還來得及。
B. The game is over now. 比賽結束了。
C. Where are we going? 我們要去哪裡？

※〔註〕說話者已經道出雙方又去參加或觀看一場 game，所以 (C) 明知故問了；而且說話者也表示比賽還未開始，所以 (B) 是故意唱反調，故答案為 (A)。

Q8 I'm coming now.

我馬上來了。

正解 A. Don't hurry. 不急。
B. Don't go anywhere. 那兒也別去。
C. Come here, please. 請過來。

Q9 I'm in a hurry.

我快來不及了。

A. How fast do you run? 你可以跑多快？
正解 B. Let's go then. 那我們就走吧！
C. Wait here. 在這兒等。

※〔註〕in a hurry 表示沒時間了，(A) 的話題變成了速度，不合理，(C) 的回應是故意在唱反調。正確答案為 (B)，回應者表示他可以配合對方，馬上就啟程。

Q10 Why all this hurry?

怎麼這麼趕？

A. Don't worry. 別擔心。
B. Don't take too long. 不要太久。
正解 C. I'm late for the bus. 我趕不上巴士了。

※〔註〕(A) 為類音字 hurry / worry 的錯誤，而且與 (B) 一樣都沒有回答出原因，無法回應發問者 Why...? 的問題。答案為 (C)，原因就是要趕搭巴士。

主題 26　　　　拒 絕

Q1 Can I borrow your dress for tonight's party?

我可以借妳的洋裝，參加今晚的派對嗎？

正解 A. No way. 別想！
B. That's nothing. 那沒什麼。
C. That's not true. 才不是呢！

Q2 Are you coming?
你會來嗎？

正解 A. No, sorry about that. 不會，對不起。
B. Sorry to bother you. 打擾了。
C. It's all the same to me. 隨便，怎麼樣都好。

Q3 Can I help you?
需要幫忙嗎？〔= 我能為你效勞嗎？〕

A. We need to get help. 我們要去找人幫忙。
B. No way. 絕對不可以。
正解 C. No, but thank you anyway. 不用，不過還是謝謝你。

Q4 Thanks, but I can't eat seafood.
謝謝，可是我不能吃海鮮。

正解 A. What a waste! 真可惜〔浪費〕。
B. Do you need anything help? 你需要幫忙嗎？
C. Any questions? 有什麼問題？

Q5 Do you want this?
你想要這個嗎？

A. Thanks. I'd love to. 謝謝，我願意。
正解 B. Not really. 不太想。
C. No, I won't. 不，我將不。

※〔註〕(A) I'd love to. 等於 I would love to.，與 (C) 一樣錯在助動詞不一致。
(B) 為正確答案，是簡化 I do not really want it. 的回答方式。

Q6 Who wants a drink?
誰要喝一杯？

正解 A. Not for me, thanks. 我不需要，謝謝。
B. Not me. I didn't. 不是我，我沒有。
C. It's not mine. 不是我的。

※〔註〕本句使用動詞 wants（現在式），所以助動詞不可以用 did，故 (B) 錯誤，如果你有需要，就可以回答 "I do."；不需要則說 "I don't." 或如 (A) Not for me.，最後記得還是要謝謝對方。

Q7 We have to finish it today.
我們今天必須完成。

正解 ► A. That's not possible. 那是不可能的。
B. See you tomorrow. 明天見。
C. I haven't finished it. 我們還沒做完。

Q8 Please lend me some money.
請借給我一些錢。

正解 ► A. No way. 想都別想！
B. No, you may not. 不，你不可以。
C. Yes, you may. 是，你可以。

※〔註〕(A) 為正確答案，是簡化 It's no way that I'll lend you some money. 的回答方式。

Q9 Do you want me to check the tires?
需要我為您檢查輪胎嗎？

正解 ► A. No, that's all for now. 不用，先這樣就好。
B. I'm tired now. 我現在累了。
C. Excuse me. 對不起〔打擾了〕。

※〔註〕(B) 出現了類音字組 tires / tired 的錯誤；(C) 則完全不相干。(A) 為正確答案，表示發問者先前已經為受話者做過一些服務，而受話者覺得不需要再麻煩他了。

Q10 Would you like your car washed?
你要把車洗一洗嗎？

A. I saw her washing her car. 我看見她在洗車。
正解 ► B. No, thank you. It's OK. 不，謝謝了。這樣可以了。
C. I'd like to buy a new car. 我想買部新車。

※〔註〕(A)、(C) 都重複了 car 這個字，但是卻都偏離主題了。正確答案應為 (B)，直接拒絕對方的提議，但補上一句 Thank you. 讓口氣仍然很委婉，如果少了這句話，口氣就完全不一樣了。

主題
26
強調短句 v 拒絕

道　謝

Q1

Thanks a lot.
多謝了。

A. Not much. 不多。
正解▶ B. You're welcome. 不客氣。
C. We have some. 我們有一些。

Q2

Thank you for helping me.
謝謝你幫我的忙。

正解▶ A. Don't mention it. 不用提了。
B. Sure. You are right. 是啊，沒錯。
C. It's for sure. 那是一定的。

Q3

I'll make you some coffee.
我幫你泡（煮）杯咖啡。

A. I'm happy. 我很高興。
正解▶ B. Thank you very much. 非常謝謝你。
C. It's good for you. 這對你有益。

※〔註〕當有人主動要幫你，最基本且最禮貌的回應當然就是謝謝對方，故答案為 (B)。

Q4

OK, I'll take it. Thank you for your help.
好，我拿這件。謝謝你的幫忙！

正解▶ A. Any time. 隨時都樂意。
B. I'm glad to hear that. 很高興聽到你這麼說。
C. No, I didn't do anything. 不，我沒做什麼事。

※〔註〕發言者是一位顧客，故回應者為店員，最合理之回應為 (A) Any time. = Anytime you need help, just come to me. （隨時需要幫忙就來找我。）

Q5 Thank you for coming to my birthday party.

謝謝您來參加我的生日派對。

正解 A. It's my pleasure. 這是我的榮幸。
B. As you pleased. 請隨意〔隨你高興〕。
C. You are wonderful. 你做得很好。

Q6 Here's your ticket and change.

這是您的票和找零。

A. That's OK. 還好。
B. It's fine with me. 沒關係。
正解 C. Thank you very much. 非常謝謝你。

Q7 Do you like it?

你喜歡嗎?

正解 A. Yes, thank you. 喜歡,謝謝。
B. Yes, I will. Thanks. 是,我會。謝謝。
C. I'm very well. 我很好。

Q8 Thank you. I had a lot of fun.

謝謝你,我玩得很開心。

A. What do you like to play? 你喜歡玩什麼?
正解 B. I'm glad to hear that. 很高興聽你這麼說。
C. I'm so glad for you. 我真為你高興。

Q9 Here's your birthday present. I hope you like this.

這是你的生日禮物,希望你會喜歡。

正解 A. It's just what I want. Thank you. 這就是我想要的,謝謝你。
B. I will do what I can. 我會盡我所能。
C. It was nothing like that. 根本不是這麼回事。

※〔註〕當你收到一份禮物時,當然要謝謝對方,(A) 除了表示感謝之外,更以 It's just what I want. 這句話表示自己「強烈」地喜歡對方所選的禮物,對方所選的禮物實在是太棒了!

主題 **27** 強調短句 v 道謝

Q10 Are you all right? Let me help you stand up.

你還好嗎？讓我來扶你站起來。

A. Don't worry. I will help you. 別擔心，我會幫你。
B. Sit down, please. 請坐下。
正解 ► C. Thanks. You're very kind. 謝謝。你人真好！

※〔註〕回應者應該是個接受協助的人，(A)、(B) 選項的回應都是一位提供者，所以是錯誤選項。答案為 (C)。

主題 28 讚 美

Q1 This is my new dress. I bought it yesterday.

這是我的新洋裝，我昨天買的。

正解 ► A. That's nice. 很不錯。
B. You're nice. 你真好。
C. It's a nice boat. 這是一艘好船。

※〔註〕向別人讚美穿著是一種增進人際關係很好的方法 (A) That's nice. 是一句非常好用的讚美。(B) 錯誤是討論的主角從「裙子」變成了「你」；(C) 則是利用類音字錯誤 bought / boat。

Q2 You look good in it.

你穿起來很好看。

A. Look. How is it? 你看，怎麼樣？
正解 ► B. Thank you. 謝謝。
C. You're cool. 你真酷〔很棒！〕。

Q3 I think the math test was easy.

我覺得數學考試很簡單。

A. Guess what! 你猜怎麼著？
B. Take a guess. 猜猜看！
正解 ► C. You're smart. 你很聰明。

※〔註〕一個人覺得考試簡單，一定是考前很用功，甚至本身資質就很優秀，這時候你就可以稱讚他一番 "You're smart."。(A)、(B)都在討論神秘的話題，與本題不符。

Q4 I still can't believe I made this all by myself.

我還是不敢相信這全是我自己做的。

正解 ▶ A. Good for you! 很棒喔！
B. Great. Let's do together. 太棒了，我們一起做。
C. OK, that's all. 好，就這樣。

Q5 What do you think of my painting?

你覺得我畫得如何？

A. Congratulations! 恭喜！
正解 ▶ B. You did a good job. 你做得很好。
C. You look great today. 你今天看來神采奕奕。

※〔註〕這又是一題對方希望受話者可以提供看法的題目，(C) You did a good job. 就等於 "That's nice."。(A) 使用時機不符。(C) 討論對象轉移，都是錯誤的選項。

Q6 Look. This is my girlfriend.

看，這是我女朋友。

A. What a beautiful day. 好棒的天氣！
B. Wow, you're so beautiful. 哇，妳真美！
正解 ▶ C. Wow, what a beauty. 哇，真是個美女！

Q7 Dinner's ready!

吃晚飯了。

正解 ▶ A. Umn, it smells good. 嗯，聞起來好香。
B. I'm dying for a drink. 我真渴望來杯飲料。
C. What would you like for dinner? 晚餐想吃什麼？

※〔註〕晚餐一定是剛準備好，還熱騰騰的，正散發出引人食欲的香味，所以回應者說 "It smells good."。

Q8 You are so nice.

你真好。

正解 ▶ A. Oh, no. Not at all. 哦，沒什麼啦！
B. Oh, no! 喔，不！
C. Good heaven! 我的天啊！

主題 **28** 強調短句 v 讚美

Q9 How do you like the cake?
蛋糕吃起來怎樣？（喜歡嗎？）

A. Just look at what you've done. 看你做了什麼。
B. Take it or leave it. 要就接受，不然拉倒。
正解 C. It's delicious! 很可口。

Q10 I'm proud of you.
我以你爲榮。

正解 A. Really? You are? 眞的？你眞的這麼認爲嗎？
B. Well done. 做得好。
C. Cheer up! 開心一點〔加油〕！

※〔註〕當對方做了一件令人佩服的事，例如成績優異、英勇救人等等，這時候就可對他說 "I'm proud of you."。回應者可能沒預期會受到讚美，所以不可置信地說 "Really? You are?"。

道 歉

Q1 Hey, Benny. Sorry, I'm late.
嗨，班尼。對不起，我遲到了。

A. You'll be sorry. 你會後悔的！
正解 B. What kept you so long? 你怎麼這麼久才來？
C. What for? 爲什麼？

Q2 Hey, this is mine. My name is on it.
嘿，這是我的，上面有我的名字。

正解 A. I'm sorry. 對不起。
B. Excuse me. 對不起〔打擾了〕。
C. I don't know. 我不知道。

Q3 Sorry, I have to go now.
對不起，我得走了。

正解 A.OK, see you tomorrow. 好，明天見。
B. I had better go by myself. 我最好親自去。
C. I'm out of here. 我要走啦！

Q4 Sorry for the trouble.
對不起給您添麻煩了。

正解 A. It's no trouble. 不麻煩。
B. Leave it to me. 交給我處理。
C. Take your time. 慢慢來。

Q5 This is a mistake.
這裡有個錯誤。

正解 A. Sorry. It's my fault. 對不起,這是我的錯。
B. You can't do that. 你不能這麼做。
C. Hi, how are you? 嗨,你好嗎?

※〔註〕fault [fɔlt] 過錯。

Q6 I'm not Jim.
我不是吉姆。

正解 A. Oh, my mistake. 喔,我認錯人了。
B. Who knows where Jim is? 誰知道吉姆在哪裡?
C. You are? 你是嗎?

※〔註〕這是一個認錯人的尷尬狀況,一旦犯了這樣的誤會,最合理的反應就是道歉,答案為 (A)。至於像 (B) 一樣故意轉移話題與注意力,或像 (C) 一樣還堅持對方是你要找的人,都是十分不禮貌與不合理的。

Q7 I'm terribly sorry.
我真的很抱歉!

正解 A. Never mind. 別在意。
B. It's a terrible story. 很差勁的故事。
C. Pardon me. 對不起。

※〔註〕當對方為某事向你道歉,而你對這件事情並不生氣時,就會說 "Never mind.",答案為 (A)。至於 (B) 則是類音字 sorry / story 的錯誤;(C) 完全不符合題意。

Q8 Excuse me. There's a call for you.
對不起,有您的電話。

A. I'll give you a call. 我會打電話給你。
B. What do you call it? 牠叫什麼名字?
正解 C. OK, put it through. 好,接過來。

主題
29
強調短句 v 道歉

Q9 Pardon me. Can you say it again?

對不起，您可以再說一次嗎？

A. Let me think about it. 讓我考慮一下。

正解→ B. Forget it. 算了。

C. Never. 絕不。

※〔註〕發話者可能在和對方說話時分心了，所以想請對方再說一次，但是對方不想再重述一次，所以回答 Forget it.

Q10 Well, you finally got here.

哎呀，你終於到了！

A. I will do my best. 我會盡全力的。

正解→ B. Sorry. Let me treat you a coffee. 對不起，我請你喝杯咖啡。

C. You got it. 你答對了！

主題 **30**　　安撫與鼓勵

Q1 Relax. It's all right.

放輕鬆，沒關係的。

正解→ A. I hope so. 希望如此。

B. Let's write to Alex. 我們來寫信給艾力克斯。

C. Do you mean it? 你是認真的嗎？

※〔註〕發話者試圖要安慰對方，這是一種善意的表現。(C) 反而充滿著敵意，實在不合理。(B) 則是利用類音字的錯誤 relex / Alex。正確答案為 (A)，受話者可能還是擔心事情不樂觀，所以才會說 "I hope so."。

Q2 David's O.K. now. He'll come to school tomorrow.

大衛已經好了，他明天會來上學。

正解→ A. That's good news. 那是個好消息。

B. Did he agree? 他答應了嗎？

C. I'm fine. 我很好。

※〔註〕聽得出來討論的對象 David 應該是生病或受傷了，現在好了，那真的是好消息，答案為 (A)。注意！news 字形看似可屬名詞的複數（字尾加上 -s），但其實是個不可數名詞，前面不可加任何冠詞。

Q3 I made a mistake.

我犯了一個錯。

A. Did you miss me? 你想我嗎？

正解 ─ B. Don't worry about it. 別擔心。

C. Don't be mad at me. 別對我生氣。

※〔註〕類音字組 "made [med] / mad [mæd]"。

Q4 Sorry, I broke your cup.

對不起，我打破了你的杯子。

正解 ─ A. That's OK. Did you get hurt? 沒關係，你有受傷嗎？

B. Please don't hurt me! 請不要傷害我！

C. The cup is broken. 杯子破了。

Q5 I'm not sure I can do it.

我不確定我做得到。

A. Surely you will. 你一定會〔去做〕。

B. Come on this way. 來，往這兒走。

正解 ─ C. Come on. Give it a try. 來吧！何妨一試。

※〔註〕當對方不確定自己有能力可完成某事，需要的就是別人的鼓勵，(C) 的意思就是要對方至少試一試，也許就成功了。(A) 的助動詞錯了，應改成 "Surely you can."。(B) 與主題完全不符。

Q6 This is so hard.

這好難喔！

正解 ─ A. Don't give up. 別放棄。

B. Yes, the egg is too hard. 對，這個蛋太硬了。

C. Don't do that. 別那麼做。

※〔註〕hard 除了表示「困難」，另外還有「堅硬」的意思。

Q7 Should I try to ask her again?

我應該再問她看看嗎？

A. Guess what! 你猜怎麼著。

B. Why didn't you? 你怎麼沒〔問〕呢？

正解 ─ C. Why not? 有何不可？

Q8 This is my house. It's small.

這是我的房子，很小。

A. Not really. It's a big horse. 才不是呢，這是一匹大馬。
B. It's your home. 這是你的家。
正解 C. But it's nice. 可是很棒。

※〔註〕類音字組 "house [haʊs] / horse [hɔrs]"。

Q9 I don't think I can make it.

我不認為我做得到。

A. Go ahead. Don't worry about me. 去吧，別擔心我。
B. Sure. Take a chance. 當然，碰碰運氣嘛。
正解 C. You'll never know until you do it. 你得做了才知道。

※〔註〕(A) 錯在討論的話題主旨從一件事情變成了一個人。(C) 才是正確答案。

Q10 It's too late to prepare for the exam.

來不及準備考試了。

正解 A. Better late than never. 遲做總比不做好。
〔喻〕亡羊補牢，猶未晚也！〕
B. Hurry up. 快一點。
C. What's this for? 這是做什麼用的？

主題 **31** 表示不介意

Q1 I'm sorry that Sally can't come.

抱歉，莎莉不能來。

正解 A. I don't mind. 我不介意。
B. Please say it again. 請再說一遍。
C. You're welcome. 不客氣。

Q2 He's late. He'll be here soon.

他遲到了，但很快就會來了。

A. See you later. 待會見。
B. So soon? 這麼快？
正解 C. It doesn't matter. 沒關係。

Q3 I'm sorry for the trouble.

很抱歉給您添麻煩了。

正解 A. Never mind. 別在意。
B. What would you like? 你想要什麼？
C. Don't talk to me. 別跟我說話。

Q4 Pardon me? What did you just say?

對不起? 你剛剛說什麼？

正解 A. Forget it. 算了。
B. I say what I mean. 我是說真的。
C. Have you forgotten what I said? 你是不是忘了我說的話？

Q5 What happened to you?

你發生了什麼事?

A. It happens. 常有的事。
B. I'm doing fine. 我很好。
正解 C. It's nothing important, really. 沒什麼事，真的。

Q6 Do you mind if I open the window?

你介意我打開窗戶嗎？

A. Don't say so much. 別說這麼多。
B. It's not important. 不是什麼重要的事。
正解 C. No, go ahead. 不介意，你開吧！

Q7 What do you want to drink?

你要喝什麼？

A. Let me get you some tea. 我幫你倒些茶。
正解 B. You can decide it. 你決定就好。
C. I'd love some. 好，來一些。

Q8

Do you know that Philip is leaving?

你知道菲利浦要走嗎？

正解 A. We'd better hurry. 我們得趕快。
B. I don't care. 管他的。
C. Did he? 他走了？

Q9

Do you have any idea who he is?

正解 你知不知道他是誰？

A. Who cares! 管他的！
B. I'll take care of it. 我來處理。
C. What do you think about it? 你覺得如何？

Q10

Sorry, I can't help with dinner.

正解 對不起，晚餐我幫不上忙。

A. Oh, that's no problem. 喔，沒問題。
B. I just want to help. 我只是想要幫忙。
C. I have no idea. 我不知道。

主題 **32**	猜 測

Q1

Is it all right?

這樣妥當嗎？

正解 A. It's all done. 都做好了。
B. I guess so. 應該是吧！
C. I'll write it down. 我會寫下來。

Q2

Does it matter how we get here?

我們怎麼到的要緊嗎？

A. We'll get there by a taxi. 我們會搭計程車去。
正解 B. As usual. 一如往昔。
C. I guess not. 應該沒關係。

※〔註〕(A) 回答的關鍵重點錯誤，應該回答究竟「有沒有關係」，而不是搭乘哪種「交通工具」。(B) 的錯誤在於說話時機應該是在發話者之前，而非之後。正確

Q3 答案 (C) 的回應偏向否定，但不完全肯定。

Will the teacher come?

正解 — 老師會來嗎？

A. It's possible. 可能會。
B. That's easy! 那很簡單！
C. We'd better tell the teacher. 我們最好告訴老師。

Q4 ## Do you think that's possible?

你覺得有可能嗎？

A. Pass me the ball, please. 請幫我傳一下球。
正解 — B. It's better. 這比較好。
C. I don't know. 我不知道。

※〔註〕(A) 為利用類音字組 possible / pass... ball 的錯誤。(B) 應該把 better 改成 possible 或 impossible 才對。(C) 表示自己不能妄下斷語，此為較合理的回應。

Q5 ## You will help me out, right?

正解 — 你會幫我的，對嗎？

A. That all depends on what it is. 那要看是什麼事。
B. You're welcome. 不客氣。
C. I'm fine. 我很好。

※〔註〕help out 幫助～擺脫困難。

Q6 ## You are going to travel, aren't you?

正解 — 你要去旅行，對嗎？

A. Not this summer. 這個夏天不去。
B. Not last winter. 去年多天沒有。
C. Do I? 我有嗎？

※〔註〕利用否定附加問句的問法，表示說話者認為自己的認知是對的，可是由正確答案 (A) 得知，其實並不然。(B)、(C) 都是時間點的錯誤。

Q7 ## Will he come back?

他會回來嗎？

正解 — A. He's at home. 他在家。
B. Maybe not. 也許不會。
C. He may not. 他不可以。

Q8 How long will Jimmy be out of school?

吉米會「脫離」學校多久？

A. There's only half an hour left. 只剩半小時了。
B. Sooner or later. 遲早的事。
正解 ► C. I guess "forever". 我猜是「永遠」。

※〔註〕問句關鍵詞 How long...?，回答應該是一段時間，而非一個時間點，故合理答案為 (C)。

Q9 I bet you were the best in the class.

我敢說你是班上最優秀的。

A. I just want to help people. 我只是想要幫助大家。
正解 ► B. Well, I did get an A. 嗯，我是得了個 "A"。
C. I will cheer for you! 加油！

※〔註〕bet [bɛt] 與某人打賭。

Q10 Have you got your work done for today?

今天要交的作業你做好了嗎？

A. We should work hard everyday. 我們應該每天努力不懈。
B. I don't go to work on weekends. 我週末不上班。
正解 ► C. No, but maybe the teacher won't ask for it.
沒有，可是或許老師不會收作業。

※〔註〕問句為現在完成式，問的是到目前為止，做作業這件事是否已經完成。
(A)、(B) 回答的都是每天固定的做法；(C) 為正確答案，簡明的回答 No 表示還沒完成，接著的是答話者的猜想，這實際上不過是在找藉口安慰自己罷了。

主題 **33** 尋求認同

Q1 Is it good?

這好嗎？

正解 ► A. Yes, I like it. 好，我喜歡。
B. Yes, he's nice. 是，他人很好。
C. No problem. 沒問題。

Q2 Is it alright?

可以嗎？

正解 ► A. No problem. 沒問題。
B. That's right. 沒錯。
C. That's all. 就這樣了。

Q3 Are you sure?

你確定？

A. That's you, not me. 是你，不是我。
B. Yes, we share everything. 是，我們分享所有。
正解 ► C. Yes, it's all right. 確定，可以。

※〔註〕類似音有 "sure [ʃʊr] / share [ʃɛr]"。

Q4 Is it that bad?

那麼糟嗎？

A. Yes, it's a bed. 是，那是一張床。
B. Yes, it's a bat. 是，那是一隻蝙蝠。
正解 ► C. I'm afraid so. 恐怕是。

※〔註〕類似音有 "bad [bæd] / bed [bɛd]"；同字異義的字 bat [bæt] 有「蝙蝠」和「棒球棍」兩種完全不同的意思。

Q5 I don't believe you.

我不相信你。

A. I can't believe it, either. 我也不相信〔這件事〕。
正解 ► B. But it's true. 但這是真的。
C. But we are leaving. 但是我們要離開了。

Q6 Take a look at this picture. How is it?

看看這張照片，如何？

正解 ► A. You did a great job. 你拍得很棒。
B. May I take a picture of you? 我可以拍一張你的照片嗎？
C. I'd like some more, please. 我還想要一些，謝謝。

主題 **33** 強調短句 v 尋求認同

Q7 Is my work O.K.?

我的作品可以嗎？

A. Oh, we're sorry. 喔，我們很抱歉。
B. No, no way. 不，絕對不行。
正解 — C. Not too bad. 還不賴。
　　※〔註〕work [wɜk] 成果；著作；作品。

Q8 Should I go?

我應該去嗎？

正解 — A. Yes, go ahead. 應該，去吧！
B. Do you play golf? 你打高爾夫球嗎？
C. It's better than nothing. 寥勝於無。

Q9 Shall we tell him?

我們要告訴他嗎？

正解 — A. Sure. He's our friend. 當然要，他是我們的朋友。
B. I'm sorry. 對不起。
C. It's terrible. 眞糟糕。

Q10 I can't do this.

我辦不到啊。〔我不能這麼做。〕

A. Do you think I'm stupid? 你以爲我很蠢嗎？
B. What is wrong with you!? 你到底是有什麼毛病啊!?
正解 — C. Of course you can. 你當然可以。

主題 **34**　　　　表達認同

Q1 It's a good book.

這是一本好書。

A. Yes, it's novel. 是，這是一本小說。
B. I like to read a book on weekend. 週末時我喜歡看看書。
正解 — C. You're right. 沒錯。

Q2 The house is big.

正解► 這個房子很大。

A. It sure is. 的確是。
B. How is it? 如何？
C. What is it? 這是什麼？

Q3 Let's go to a party.

我們去參加派對吧！

A. It was great. 派對很棒。→ [過去式]
正解► B. Yeah, I went. 是，我去了。→ [過去式]
C. What a great idea. 這意見太好了！

Q4 Let's go for a ride.

我們去兜風吧！

正解► A. Right, we'll ride a bike. 對，我們將騎腳踏車。
B. That sounds nice. 聽起來很不錯。
C. Have a nice trip. 旅途愉快。

※〔延伸例句〕We went for a ride in the car. 我們開車去兜風。

Q5 It's hard work to plant trees in the desert.

要在沙漠裡種植物是很困難的事。

A. Yeah, it's my plan. 是啊，這是我的計畫。
正解► B. It seems great! 似乎很棒！
C. I agree. 我認同。

Q6 Do you like it, too?

你也喜歡嗎？

A. Yes, I'm. 是，我是。
正解► B. There's nothing I can say. 我沒什麼好說的。
C. Yes, I'm just like you. 喜歡，就和你一樣。

Q7 Do you really like it?

你真的喜歡？

正解 ► A. Yes, Very much. 對，非常喜歡。

B. Yes, it's very noisy. 對，真的很吵。

C. Yes, we're alike. 對，我們很像。

※〔註〕like 除了有動詞「喜歡」的意思之外，形容詞的意思是「相像的」，alike 也是「相像的」的意思，但是兩者用法不盡相同。請見以下例句：

Ex: Are you *like* your brother? 你像你哥哥嗎？
Ex: Are you and your brother *alike*? 你和你哥哥像嗎？

Q8 How does it sound?

聽起來怎樣？

正解 ► A. Sounds good. 聽起來很好。

B. I'm sorry to hear that. 我為你感到難過。

C. I can't agree more. 我非常同意。

Q9 It looks like a warm place.

看來像是個溫暖的地方。

A. Yes, Luke won the first place in the game. 是啊，路克在比賽中得到第一名。

B. Yes, she has a warm heart. 是啊，她是個熱心腸的人。

正解 ► C. Yes, I think so too. 是啊，我也這麼認為。

※〔註1〕warm 除了表「溫暖」之外，還有「熱心」的意思。place 除了表「地方」之外，名次的說法也可以用：the first place 第一名、the second place 第二名……來表示。

※〔註2〕類音字組有 "look [lʊk] / Luke [luk]"，"warm [wɔrm] / won [wʌn]"。

Q10 I like this movie.

我喜歡這部電影。

正解 ► A. So do I. 我也是。

B. So am I. 我也是。

C. Nor do I. 我也不。

主題 **35** 不完全肯定

Q1 The soup is delicious.

這湯很可口。

正解 ► A. Really? 真的嗎？
B. Isn't it delicious? 這不美味嗎？
C. Is she? 她是嗎？

Q2 That's a good idea.

那是個好主意。

正解 ► A. Is it? 是嗎？
B. No, I have no idea. 不，我不知道。
C. That' too bad. 那太糟糕了。

Q3 He's coming today.

他今天會來。

A. Will he? 他會來嗎？
正解 ► B. Are you sure? 你確定嗎？
C. Has he? 他來了嗎？

Q4 She has a good voice and sings beautifully.

她有副好嗓子，歌唱得很好。

A. I don't know she's divorced. 我不知道她離婚了。
B. Is she getting better? 她好多了嗎？
正解 ► C. Is that true? 真的嗎？

※ 〔註〕類似音組是 "voice [vɔɪs] / divorced [dəˋvɔrst]"。

Q5 He's a famous actor.

他是有名的演員。

A. Really? He's a waiter? 真的嗎？他是個服務生嗎？
正解 ► B. Is that so? 是這樣嗎？
C. Isn't he famous? 他並不出名嗎？

※ 〔註〕類似音組是 "actor [ˋæktɚ] / waiter [ˋwetɚ]"。

Q6 That's a nice dress. It looks good on you.

那件洋裝很美，妳穿起來很好看。

A. Thanks. Don't bother. 謝謝，不麻煩了。

正解 B. I'm not myself today. 我今天不太對勁。

C. Do you think so? 你這麼認為嗎？

Q7 Will we make it on time?

我們有辦法準時到嗎？

正解 A. Yes, we'll be there. 是，我們會到。

B. I hope so. 希望會。

C. Are you sure? 你確定嗎？

Q8 You love your brother, don't you?

正解 你愛你哥哥，不是嗎？

A. Not always. 並非總是如此。

B. I enjoyed it. 我樂在其中。

C. Let me guess. 我猜猜看。

Q9 Of the countries you've been to, which do you like best?

在去過的國家中，你最喜歡哪一個國家呢？

A. I like Seattle best. 我最喜歡西雅圖〔城市名〕。

正解 B. Oh, I've been to lots of countries. 喔，我去過了很多國家。

C. It's hard to say. Each country is different. 這就很難說了，每個國家都各有特色。

Q10 Chinese is pretty difficult, isn't it?

正解 中文很難，對吧？

A. It seemed that way at first. 剛開始的時候可能是。

B. Are they? 他們是嗎？

C. I'm not Chinese. 我不是中國人。

※〔註〕Chinese 有「中文」和「中國人」的意思。

主題 36 不認同

Q1 I think math is harder than English.

我覺得數學比英文難。

A. No, math is harder than English. 不，數學比英文難。
B. You did it wrong. 你做錯了。
正解 C. I don't think so. 我不這麼認為。

※〔註〕正確答案為 (C) 表示不認同對方的說法。如果把 (B) 的 did 改成 said，也就可以表示不認同對方。

Q2 Don't you like it?

你不喜歡嗎？

A. Don't you? 你不〔喜歡〕嗎？
正解 B. No, I don't. 對，我不喜歡。
C. I believe so. 我相信。

Q3 They have better players, so I believe they will win.

他們有較優秀的選手，所以我相信他們會贏。

正解 A. Not really. 不見得。
B. Do they play badly? 他們球打得不好嗎？
C. They don't pray at all. 他們根本就不禱告。

※〔註〕類似音 "play [ple] / pray [pre]"。

Q4 It's too far to walk there.

太遠了，我們走不到那裡的。

A. Me, too. 我也是。
B. Not only two. 不只兩個。
正解 C. No, it's not. 不，不會。

※〔註〕(A) 把談論主題從「事」變成了「人」。(B) 則是類似音 too / two 錯誤。(C) 為正確的回答，以 be 動詞簡答的方式斬釘截鐵地否定對方的說法。

Q5 I don't think we can trust him.

我不認為我們可以信任他。

正解 — A. Of course we can. 我們當然可以。

B. Trust me, you can make it. 相信我，你做得到。

C. Believe it or not. 信不信由你。

※〔註〕原來發話者的意思是否定的口吻，(A) 的回答卻是正面的，否定了發話者的負面意見。(B)、(C) 出現了 trust「信任」和 believe 「相信」，中文意思相似，但意義卻是不同的，因此要特別小心使用。

Q6 I'm going to ask him to quit smoking.

我要去要求他戒煙。

A. No, you may not. 不，你不可以。

正解 — B. It's no use. He won't listen to you. 沒用的，他不會聽你的。

C. He kept on smoking all the time. 他還是無時無刻抽著煙。

Q7 Let's watch TV.

我們看電視吧！

正解 — A. It's too late. 太晚了。

B. See you later. 再見〔待會見〕。

C. What did you see? 你看到什麼了？

Q8 She said she would lend me her car.

她說她會借我車的。

A. It's the right time. 時機到了。

B. She will never sell her car. 她絕不會賣車的。

正解 — C. It's impossible. 不可能。

Q9 You can fix the machine, can't you?

你可以把機器修好的，對吧？

正解 — A. Sorry to let you down. 對不起，讓你失望了。

B. No, I don't have a fax machine. 不，我沒有傳真機。

C. I believe in you. 我相信你。

※〔註〕類音字組有 fix the machine [fɪks ðə məˋʃɪn] / fax machine [fæks məˋʃɪn]。

Q10 Why don't we give it up?

我們為什麼不放棄呢？

正解 → A. Never think about it. 想都別想。
B. OK, I'll give it a try. 好，我會試試看。
C. I can't forgive you. 我不能原諒你。

主題 37　提供或尋求協助

Q1 Can you do it?

你可以做嗎？

正解 → A. Sure thing. 沒問題。
B. I did it. 我做到了。
C. Go ahead. 儘管去〔做〕。

※〔註〕(B) 是助動詞的錯誤；(C) 為角色混淆的錯誤，對方是請「你」做某事，
而不是自己要做某事。(A) 才是合理回應，意思等於 Sure. I can.。

Q2 Will you do it for me?

你會幫我做嗎？

正解 → A. With pleasure. 很樂意。
B. Yes, it's for you. 對，這是給你的。
C. It will do. 行得通。

※〔註〕發問者是在談「做一件事情」，而不是「一件東西」，故 (B) 錯；(C) 則是
主詞錯誤，主詞由 I 變成了 it。(A) 才是合理回應，表示願意幫對方做某事。

Q3 Can you help me do this ?

你可以幫我做這個嗎？

正解 → A. No, do it yourself. 不行，你得自己做。
B. This will help. 這能幫〔你〕。
C. There's no hope for me. 我沒希望了。

※〔註〕(B) 這主詞從人(you) 變成了事物 (this)；(C) 則出現了類音字的錯誤
help / hope 。(A) 為合理回應，堅決地拒絕了對方的請求。

Q4 Pardon me, Sir. Can you tell me what time it is?

對不起，先生。你可以告訴我現在的時間嗎？

A. Let me think it over. 讓我想想考慮一下。

正解 B. Sorry, I don't have a watch. 對不起，我沒有手錶。

C. I've got plenty of time. 我不趕時間。

※〔註〕think it over = think about it 仔細想想；考慮

Q5 Do you understand?

你了解嗎？

正解 A. Can you show me an example? 可不可以舉個例子？

B. I'll try it on. 我會試穿看看。

C. I can hardly hear you. 我聽不到你的聲音。

Q6 Help! Can somebody help?

救命啊！有誰可以幫忙？

正解 A. What's wrong? 出了什麼事？

B. Could you tell me how to do? 你可以告訴我怎麼做嗎？

C. Excuse me. 對不起。

Q7 Can I help you?

需要幫忙嗎？

A. Who are you? 你是誰？

B. You can't. 你不可以。

正解 C. No thanks, I'm just looking. 哦，不用了謝謝。我隨便看看。

Q8 I'll turn on the light.

我來開燈。

正解 A. No, don't bother. 不，別麻煩了。

B. Turn right here. 這裡右轉。

C. You have no right. 你沒有權利。

※〔註〕類音字組 "light [laɪt] / right [raɪt]"。

Q9 Shall I open the window for you?
要我把窗子打開嗎？

正解 ► A. Yes, please. That would be very kind of you.
是的，你真好心。
B. We need to get help. 我們要去找人幫忙。
C. This is difficult. 這很難。

Q10 Would you like me to answer the phone?
你要我來接電話嗎？

A . It's not the answer. 這不是答案。
B. I'll help you. 我會幫你。
正解 ► C. If you wouldn't mind. 如果你不介意的話。

※〔註〕(A) 出現了同字異義的錯誤，answer 的意思從動詞「接聽（電話）」變成了名詞「答案」。(B) 則為角色混淆之錯誤，對方已經提議要幫忙，自己又說要幫對方，實在不合理。(C) 為正確的回應，客氣地接受對方的幫忙。

主題 **38** 強調短句 ▽ 請求許可與允諾

主題 **38** 請求許可與允諾

Q1 Can we buy this teapot?
我們可以買這個茶壺嗎？

A. It's tea time. 下午茶時間到了。
正解 ► B. It depends on you. 由你決定。
C. Make yourself home. 請不要拘束。

Q2 Can I borrow this book?
我可以借這本書嗎？

正解 ► A. Sure. Take it. 當然，拿去。
B. I'm sure you borrowed it. 我確定你借走了。
C. Lend it to me, please. 請借給我。

Q3 May I eat some cake?

我可以吃些蛋糕嗎？

A. Get me some, please. 請幫我拿一些。
B. I'd love some. Thanks. 好，給我一些，謝謝。
正解 C. Please help yourself. 請自己來。

※〔註〕(A)、(B) 同樣是要求要蛋糕的人，故為角色混淆的錯誤。(C) 為正確答案，回應者的身分可能是某個餐會的主辦人。

Q4 May I come in?

我可以進來嗎？

A. Stay there. 待在那裡。
B. I'll be right back. 我馬上回來。
正解 C. Come on in. 進來吧！

Q5 Could I see the room?

我可以看一下房間嗎？

正解 A. Sure. Come follow me. 當然，請隨我來。
B. Oh, I can't believe you're saying this. 不敢相信你會這樣說。
C. We don't have enough money. 我們的錢不夠。

※〔註〕這段對話應該是房屋出售或房間出租的情境，回應者應是屋主，(B)、(C) 的回答太不合情理。(A) 為正確答案。

Q6 Shall I read it?

我要唸嗎？

A. You should study hard. 你該用功讀書。
正解 B. Yes, read it aloud. 是，大聲唸。
C. You're the class leader. 你是班長。

※〔註〕類音字詞 "read [rid] / leader [`lidə]"；特別要注意 "study" 是「研究、研讀」，"read" 是「閱讀」的意思，中文意義看起來很相似，但是英文意義卻是不同的。

Q7 May I come with you?

我可以跟你們去嗎？

正解 A. That's OK with me. 我是無所謂。
B. I'm OK. 我〔身體狀況〕很好。
C. This is going nowhere. 毫無進展。

Q8 May I have one of these?

可以給我一個嗎?

正解► A. Of course you may. 你當然可以。
B. You won these? 你贏得這些?
C. You're welcome. 不客氣。

※〔註〕(B) 的錯誤是同音異字 one / won;(C) 為回應別人道謝的語句,也是錯誤選項。(A) 為正確答案。

Q9 Do you mind if I take one away?

你介意我拿一個走嗎?

正解► A. No, go ahead. 不介意,你拿去吧!
B. Save it! 省省吧!
C. I didn't mean to do it. 我不是故意那樣做的。

※〔註〕(B) 的回應很無禮,非最佳選項;(C) 則是主題不符。(A) 為正確答案,意思是告訴對方就這麼做吧!

Q10 Can I try?

我可以試嗎?

A. Try me. 試試看〔我的忍耐度〕。
B. It fitted you very well. 很適合你。
正解► C. Why don't you? 為什麼不呢?

※〔註〕Can I try? 這句話是 Can I try to do something. 的意思,與 (A) Try me. 完全不同;(B) 的回應則可能是把 try 聽成了 try on (the dress)「試穿(洋裝)」的結果。(C) 為正確回應,意在鼓勵對方放手一試。

主題 **39** 建 議

Q1 What should we do for dinner tonight?

晚上要吃什麼?

A. We'll have dinner at 7:00. 我們會在七點用餐。
B. How about watching a movie? 看場電影如何?
正解► C. How about eating out? 出去吃如何?

Q2 I can't decide what to wear.

我無法決定該穿什麼。

A. Keep in mind. 牢記在心。
正解► B. What about this? 這個如何？
C. I can't make up my mind. 我下不了決心。

Q3 How do I get to your office?

我要怎麼到你公司？

正解► A. You may take a taxi. 你可以搭計程車。
B. You should go back. 你應該回去。
C. You can get it. 你會得到的。

Q4 Let's go for a drive somewhere this week-end.

這個週末我們開車去兜風吧！

A. Come out and play! 出來玩玩嘛！
B. I'll buy the tickets. 我會買票。
正解► C. That's a good idea. 這是個好主意。

※〔註〕提議者已經說出提議的內容，也就是 go for a drive，(A) 卻反倒只說要出去，所以不是最好的選項。既然是開車兜風，就不需要買票，故 (B) 錯誤。(C) 為正確答案，表示回應者十分贊成對方的提議。

Q5 I wish I knew about painting.

真希望我知道怎麼繪畫。

正解► A. Why don't you learn? 你何不學呢？
B. You knew it. 你知道的。
C. How did you know? 你怎麼知道的？

Q6 I'd like something for a sunburn.

我想找擦曬傷用的產品。

A . Bring an umbrella. 帶把傘。
B. I don't like this. 我不喜歡這樣子。
正解► C. You might try this. 你可以試試這個。

※〔註〕發話者的意思是是如果已經曬傷了要怎麼辦，如果建議者建議帶把傘，就太不合理了，故 (A) 錯。(B) 則錯在動詞 like 的用法不一致，原來 I'd like... 等於是 I would like...，是 I want... 「想要」的客氣說法，與這裡「喜歡」的意思不同。(C) 則給予具體建議，故為正確答案。

Q7 Should I take the bus?

我應該搭公車嗎?

A. Yes, I'll go. 是,我會去。

正解 B. No. It's only a three-minute walk. 不,走路只要三分鐘。

C. You should take the chance. 你該把握機會。

※〔註〕(A) 的主詞、助動詞與動詞皆錯;(C) 錯在主題不符,由搭乘交通工具,變成了把握機會。(B) 正確,表示不需要搭公車,走路就會到了。

主題 39 強調短句 v 建議

Q8 Why don't you check there?

你何不到那兒問問?

A. Thank you for asking. 謝謝您的詢問。

正解 B. I'll write you a check for the car. 我會開支票給你買車。

C. Okay. Thank you very much. 好,非常謝謝你。

※〔註〕(A) 不是一個需要獲得資訊的人的回應,所以錯誤;(B) check 的意思從動詞的「查問」,變成了名詞的「支票」。(C) 為正確答案。

Q9 I don't feel good. I've got the flu.

我不舒服,我感冒了。

正解 A. You should drink more water. 你要多喝水。

B. Where did you get the flute? 從那兒來的笛子?

C. Here's some fruit you want. 你要的水果在這兒。

※〔註〕類音字組 "flu [flu] / flute [flut] / fruit [frut]"。

Q10 You look tired. Try to get some rest.

你看起來好累,試著休息一下。

正解 A. I wish I could. 我希望可以。

B. Have you been to the doctor? 有沒有看過醫生了?

C. Get ready for bed. 準備睡覺囉!

※〔註〕(B)、(C) 同為提議者而非回應者的說法,故為一角色混淆的錯誤;(A) 為正確答案,意思是他可能根本無法休息,有失眠的情況,或者是工作太多,挪不出足夠的時間休息。

Q1 Did he say when he would be home?

他有沒有說什麼時候會回家？

正解 A. He didn't say. 他沒說。

B. He'll be back. 他會回來的。

C. I happened to overhear what he said. 我碰巧無意間聽到他說的事。

Q2 Is this important?

這很重要嗎？

A. Yes, it's difficult. 對，這很難。

B. Yes, that's easy! 對，那很簡單！

正解 C. Yes. Learn it by heart. 重要，要背起來。

※〔註〕發問者是問某事「重不重要」，(A)、(B) 完全脫離主題。(C) 為正確答案，表示某事的重要性極高。

Q3 Is everyone here today?

今天每個人都來了嗎？

A. You don't know me? 你不認識我？

正解 B. Jimmy Taylor is absent. 吉米·泰勒缺席。

C. I understand it now. 我現在了解了。

※〔註〕Is everyone here today? 通常是在課堂上點名，或開會一開始要確定所有該參與的人是否到齊了，故答案為 (B)。

Q4 Have you made the sandwiches yet?

你做好三明治了嗎？

正解 A. I'll start right away. 我馬上開始做。

B. No chance at all. 毫無機會。

C. How many? 有多少？

Q5 We have your size, but not in that color.

我們有你的尺寸，但是沒有你要的顏色。

A. Who do you think you are (talking to)? 你以為你是誰？

正解▶ B. Can you order one for me? 你可以幫我訂一件嗎？

C. No more excuses. 別找藉口。

Q6 What do you mean by that?

你那樣說是什麼意思？

正解▶ A. I mean it's expensive. 我是說這很貴。

B. I know what you mean. 我知道妳的意思。

C. I really mean it. 我是認真的。

Q7 I'm going tomorrow.

我明天離開。

A. How can you tell? 你怎麼知道？

正解▶ B. For sure? 確定？

C. This is the answer. 這就是答案。

※〔註〕既然發話者說的是「自己」要離開，當然自己知道，故 (A) 為不合理回應；(C) 則完全離題；(B) 為正確答案，表示很訝異會聽到這個消息。

Q8 That's all that happened.

事情就是這樣。

正解▶ A. Is that all? 就這樣？

B. What did you say? 你說了什麼？

C. What have happened to you? 發生了什麼事？

Q9 She left ten minutes ago.

她十分鐘前離開了。

A. Will she come? 她會來嗎？

B. Don't give me your excuses. 別找藉口。

正解▶ C. Did she say why? 她有沒有說什麼？

※〔註〕發話者已經說「她」離開了，(A) 又問「她」是不是會來，所以不合理；(B) 談論的事情已經全然離題；(C) 為正確答案。

主題 **40** 強調短句 v 確認

Q10 I saw that magic show.

我看了那場魔術表演。

A. How was your show? 你表演得如何？

B. Can't you see me? 你看不到我嗎？

正解 C. Yeah? Tell me more about it. 眞的嗎？再多告訴我一點。

※〔註〕(A)、(B) 都是談論對象轉移的錯誤。正確答案爲 (C)，顯然回應者對這場 magic show 十分感興趣，而且尙未去觀看過。

Q11 Well, do you have something cheaper?

嗯，你們有沒有便宜一點的？

A. What's the difference? 有什麼不同？

B. This one is more expensive. 這個比較貴。

正解 C. Yes, how about this one? 有，這件怎麼樣？

問 > 什麼地方

Conversation 1.

W: Where are you going, Steven?
M: I'm going to Taipei Train Station.
W: Are you going by taxi?
M: No, I'm going to take a bus.

Q1: Where is Steven going?

A. Taipei Train Station.
B. The taxi stand.
C. The bus station. ◀━正解

中文翻譯

| 簡短對話 1 | 女人：你要去哪裡，史蒂芬？
男人：我正要去台北火車站。
女人：你要搭計程車去嗎？
男人：不，我要搭公車。 | >>> | 問：史蒂芬要去哪裡？
A. 台北火車站。
B. 計程車招呼站。
C. 公車站。 |

※〔註〕對話第二句就回答要去的地方（Taipei Train Station）了，緊接的話題繞著其他交通工具（taxi、bus）打轉，故意要混淆視聽罷了！

Conversation 2.

W: Hi, Sam. I phoned you yesterday, but you were out.
M: I was with Cindy. We had a good time at the park.

Q2: Where was Sam yesterday?

A. At Cindy's home.
B. At his home.
C. At the park. ◀━正解

中文翻譯

| 簡短對話 2 | 女人：嗨，山姆。我昨天打電話給你，可是你出去了。
男人：我和辛蒂在一起。我們在公園很愉快。 | >>> | 問：昨天山姆在哪裡？
A. 在辛蒂家。
B. 在自己家。
C. 在公園。 |

※〔註〕最後一句話才真的說出所在地"at the park"，故選 (C)。

Conversation 3.

W: Kyle. Are you going to Paris or Beijing?
M: I've decided to go to Paris. What about you, Mary?
W: I can't make up my mind right now.

Q3: Where has Mary decided to go?

A. Paris.
B. Beijing.
C. She hasn't decided where to go yet. ◀ 正解

中文翻譯

簡短對話 3	女人：凱爾，你要去巴黎還是北京？ 男人：我決定去巴黎。那妳呢，瑪莉？ 女人：我還下不了決心。	⟫⟫⟫	問：瑪莉決定去哪裡？ A. 巴黎。 B. 北京。 C. 她還沒決定要去哪裡。

※〔註〕對話中談到的地點都是「男子」Kyle的選擇。問題卻是問「女子」Mary要去哪裡，本題型要注意的是人稱問題。

Conversation 4.

W: Peter, did you ever live in America?
M: No, I studied in London for two years. Now I'm working in Taipei.

Q4: Where is Peter now?

A. In Taiwan. ◀ 正解
B. In London.
C. In America.

中文翻譯

簡短對話 4	女人：彼得，你住過美國嗎? 男人：沒有，我在倫敦讀了兩年書，現在則是在台北工作。	⟫⟫⟫	問：彼得現在在哪裡? A. 在台灣。 B. 在倫敦。 C. 在美國。

※〔註〕Taipei是Taiwan的首都；London是England的首都；Washington D.C.是America的首都。
※〔註〕這題要注意的是「時態」問題，過去住過London，在那裡念書 (studied)，但問題是問現在住哪裡。

主題 2　　　問 > 什麼人

Conversation 1.

M: Where is Ted? Jenny, do you know?

W: He's in the library, Mike.

Q1: Who is Mike looking for?

A. Jenny.
B. The library.
C. Ted. ◄━━ 正解

中文翻譯

簡短對話 1	男人：泰德在哪？珍妮，妳知道嗎？ 女人：他在圖書館，麥克。	>>>	問：麥克在找誰？ A. 珍妮。 B. 圖書館。 C. 泰德。

※〔註〕這一題問的是 Who「人」的問題，對話中出現了三個人名，內容是 Mike 在問 Jenny 知不知道某個人（Ted）在哪裡，故選(C)。

Conversation 2.

W: I come to work by MRT, so I'm always on time.

M: The buses are always late, so I usually ride a motor-bike.

Q2: Who usually goes to work by bus?

A. The man.
B. The woman.
C. Neither of them. ◄━━ 正解

中文翻譯

簡短對話 2	女人：我搭捷運來上班，所以我總是準時到。 男人：公車總是晚到，所以我通常是騎機車。	>>>	問：誰通常搭公車上班？ A. 男人。 B. 女人。 C. 兩人都沒有。

※〔註〕雖然男子提到了 bus 這個字，但其實他是在抱怨公車不準時。對話中的兩人，都不是搭公車上班，所以答案為 (C)。

Conversation 3.

W: Let's eat out tonight.
M: I don't feel like going out.
W: I'll treat you.
M: No. I'll pay for myself.

Q3: **Who will pay for the dinner?**

A. The woman.
B. The man.
C. Both of them. ◀━ 正解

中文翻譯

| 簡短對話 3 | 女人：今晚我們去吃館子吧！
男人：我不想出去。
女人：我請你。
男人：不，我自己付。 | ▶▶▶ | 問：誰會付晚餐的錢？
A. 女人。
B. 男人。
C. 兩人都會。 |

※〔註〕雖然女子說她會請客"I'll treat you."，但是男子回絕了"No, I'll pay for myself."，這表示兩人會各付各的，答案選 (C)。

Conversation 4.

W: What did your parents think of the show?
M: My father disliked it, but my mother liked it.

Q4: **Did the man's parents like the show?**

A. Both of them like it.
B. Neither of them liked it.
C. His mother liked it, but his father didn't. ◀━ 正解

中文翻譯

| 簡短對話 4 | 女人：你父母覺得那場秀怎麼樣？
男人：我父親不喜歡，可是我母親喜歡。 | ▶▶▶ | 問：男子的父母喜歡那場秀嗎？
A. 兩個人都喜歡。
B. 兩個都不喜歡。
C. 他母親喜歡但父親不喜歡。 |

※〔註〕對話中提到兩個人去看 show，其中一人（the man's father）不喜歡，另一人（the man's mother）卻喜歡，故選 (C)。

主題 **3**　問 > 什麼種類

Conversation 1.

M: Hi, Diana. What are you reading?
W: Oh hi, Bill. I'm catching up on my math. There is a test tomorrow.

Q1: What is Diana studying?

A. Math.　　正解
B. A novel.
C. A test paper.

中文翻譯

簡短對話 **1**	男人：嗨，戴安娜。妳在讀什麼？ 女人：喔，嗨，比爾。我在惡補數學，明天要測驗。	≫≫	問：戴安娜在研讀什麼？ A. 數學。 B. 小說。 C. 考卷。

※〔註〕catch up on～（努力趕上～）
※〔註〕Diana 並沒有直接回答她在 reading 或 studying 什麼，她用了一個動詞片語 catch up on my math，表示她在惡補數學。

Conversation 2.

Boy: Mom, I want some soda.
W: Sorry. We've got no soda. We only have some milk and a bottle of fruit juice.

Q2: What is the family out of?

A. Soda.　　正解
B. Milk.
C. Fruit juice.

中文翻譯

簡短對話 **2**	男孩：媽，我要喝汽水。 女人：對不起，我沒有汽水。只有一些牛奶和一瓶果汁。	≫≫	問：這一家人缺了什麼東西？ A. 汽水。 B. 牛奶。 C. 果汁。

※〔註〕問句中的片語 "be out of sth." 與對話中母親的回答 "have got no sth." 意思是一樣的，這家人已經沒有 soda 了，喝光了。

Conversation 3.

M: Betty, why are you so nervous?
W: I have an English spelling contest in 10 minutes.

Q3: What is Betty going to take part in?

A. She is good at English spelling.
B. The spelling contest. ── 正解
C. Betty is nervous.

中文翻譯

| 簡短對話 3 | 男人：貝蒂，妳為什麼這麼緊張？ 女人：十分鐘後我有一場英文拼字比賽。 | >>> | 問：貝蒂即將參加什麼？ A. 她的英文拼字很厲害。 B. 拼字比賽。 C. 貝蒂很緊張。 |

※〔註〕問題問的是貝蒂要"take part in"參加的是什麼，故答案為 (B)。

Conversation 4.

M: Hey, I'm going shopping for CD's. Would you like to come along?
W: No, I'm going to the video shop.

Q4: What does the man want to buy?

A. To a video shop.
B. To a CD shop.
C. To buy some CD's. ── 正解

中文翻譯

| 簡短對話 4 | 男人：嘿，我要去買 CD，妳想一起來嗎？ 女人：不，我要去錄影帶店。 | >>> | 問：這個男的要去買什麼？ A. 去錄影帶店。 B. 去唱片行。 C. 去買 CD。 |

※〔註〕這一題如果能聽到問題的關鍵字 What，就一定會選到正確的答案 (C)。其他兩個選項的問題關鍵字都是 Where。

<table>
<tr><td>主題 4</td><td>問 > 做什麼</td></tr>
</table>

Conversation 1.

M: Are you going to the movie tonight?
W: No, I'm going to watch a volleyball game at home.

Q1: What is the woman going to do tonight?

A. Go to the movie theater.
B. Watch TV. ◀ 正解
C. Play the volleyball.

中文翻譯

| 簡短對話 1 | 男人：妳今晚要去看電影嗎？
女人：不，我要在家看排球比賽。 | >>> | 問：這名女子今晚要做什麼？
A. 去電影院。
B. 看電視。
C. 打排球。 |

※〔註〕What ... the woman... do...?，問的是「女子」要做的事，女子回答"watch a volleyball game at home"是打算在家「看電視」的意思。

Conversation 2.

W: Jim, did you go to Ann's birthday party yesterday?
M: Yes, I did.
W: What about the food?
M: It was delicious.

Q2: Where did Jim go yesterday?

A. He had dinner with Ann.
B. He went to Ann's party. ◀ 正解
C. He threw a birthday party.

中文翻譯

| 簡短對話 2 | 女人：吉姆，你昨天去了安的生日派對嗎？
男人：是，我去了。
女人：食物如何？
男人：很美味。 | >>> | 問：昨天吉姆去了哪裡？
A. 他和安共進晚餐。
B. 他去了安的派對。
C. 他辦了一場生日派對。 |

※〔註〕對話一開始就說出答案了"go to Ann's birthday party"，故選 (B)。注意：Jim是去參加別人的party，不是自己舉辦"throw"了一個party，不可選 (C)。

Conversation 3.

M: I'm going to the supermarket, Mom.
W: Please get some fruit. We don't have it much.

Q3: What does the mother want the son to do?

A. To go shopping with her.
B. To get more money.
C. To buy some fruit. ◀━ 正解

中文翻譯		
簡短對話 **3**	男人:媽,我要去超級市場。 女人:麻煩買一些水果,我們沒什麼水果了。	問:這位母親要她的兒子做什麼? A. 和她去購物。 B. 拿多一點錢。 C. 買一些水果。

※〔註〕女子(媽媽)要男子(兒子)去超級市場時順便 "get some fruit",故選 (C)。

Conversation 4.

M: Help yourself to more food, Melody.
W: Oh no, thanks. Can I have some tea, please?

Q4: What did the man ask Melody to do?

A. To help him to get some food.
B. To have some more food. ◀━ 正解
C. To drink some tea.

中文翻譯		
簡短對話 **4**	男人:自己再拿點吃的吧!美樂蒂。 女人:喔不,謝謝。我可以喝點茶嗎?	問:這名男子要美樂蒂做什麼? A. 幫他拿些食物。 B. 再多吃點。 C. 喝些茶。

※〔註〕從這段對話知道男子是主人,女子是客人,當主人的會客氣地請客人多吃一些 "have more food",不要客氣,自己動手 "Help yourself...",故選 (B)。

主題 5　問 > 點鐘・時間

Conversation 1.

M: It's already 5:45. Why isn't your sister here yet?
W: I told her to be here at 5:30. What happened?

Q1: What time did the woman tell her sister to come?

A. At 5:45.
B. At 5:35.
C. At 5:30. ← 正解

中文翻譯

簡短對話 1	男人：五點四十五分了，妳妹妹怎麼還沒來？ 女人：我告訴過她五點三十分到的，發生了什麼事？	>>>	問：女子告訴她妹妹幾點來？ A. 五點四十五分。 B. 五點三十五分。 C. 五點三十分。

※〔註〕對話中出現了兩個時間，但女子的回答正是答案 I told her (= my sister) to be here (=come here) at 5:30，答案為 (C)。

Conversation 2.

M: Oh, it's ten o'clock.
W: Don't worry. The clock is fast. You still have 15 minutes.

Q2: What time is it now?

A. It's ten o'clock.
B. It's a quarter past ten.
C. It's a quarter to ten. ← 正解

中文翻譯

簡短對話 2	男人：喔，十點了。 女人：別擔心，這個時鐘快了，你還有 15 分鐘。	>>>	問：現在幾點？ A. 十點。 B. 十點十五分。 C. 九點四十五分。

※〔註〕時鐘指十點，實際上卻快了十五分鐘，表示現在是九點四十五分 nine forty-five，另一種說法就是答案 (C) 的說法 "a quarter to ten"。

Conversation 3.

W: What time does the store open?
M: It opens at 10:00 A.M.
W: How late does it stay open?
M: It stays open until 9:00 P.M.

Q3: **What time is the store closed?**

    A. At 10:00 P.M.
    B. At 9:00 A.M.
    C. At 9:00 P.M.   正解

中文翻譯

| 簡短對話 3 | 女人：這家店什麼時間開始營業？
男人：早上十點開始營業。
女人：會開到多晚？
男人：一直到晚上九點。 | >>> | 問：這家店幾點打烊？
A. 晚上十點。
B. 早上九點。
C. 晚上九點。 |

※〔註〕男子最後一句話說 "It (= the store) stays open until 9:00 P.M."，意思等於 "The store closes at 9:00 P.M."，所以答案為 (C)。

Conversation 4.

M: It's Monday today. I hope the science museum is open.
W: Don't worry. It's open 9:00 a.m. to 6:00 p.m. weekdays, and 9:00 a.m. to 12:00 a.m. Saturdays, closed Sundays.

Q4: **When is the science museum open on Sunday?**

    A. 9:00 a.m. to 6:00 p.m.
    B. 9:00 a.m. to 12:00 a.m.
    C. It is closed.   正解

中文翻譯

| 簡短對話 4 | 男人：今天是星期一。我希望科學博物館有開放參觀。
女人：別擔心，它的開放時間：平日是早上九點到下午六點，星期六是早上九點到十二點，星期天休館。 | >>> | 問：科學博物館在星期天的開放時間是什麼時候？
A. 早上九點到下午六點。
B. 早上九點到十二點。
C. 休館。 |

※〔註〕science 科學；museum 博物館；science museum 科(學)博(物)館
※〔註〕這題的時間點很多，但其實女子最後一句話 "It's ... closed Sundays"，就是答案。

| 主題 6 | 問 > 日期 |

Conversation 1.

W: How time flies! Tomorrow is Monday.

M: I have to spend the whole day doing my homework today.

Q1: What day is today?

A. It's Monday.
B. It's Sunday. ◀━ 正解
C. It's Saturday.

中文翻譯

| 簡短對話 1 | 女人：時間過得真快，明天就是星期一了。
男人：我今天得花一整天做功課。 | >>> | 問：今天星期幾？
A. 星期一。
B. 星期天。
C. 星期六。 |

※〔註〕女子說 "Tomorrow is Monday."，表示 "Today is Sunday."，故答案為 (B)。

Conversation 2.

W: Jack. Would you like to go swimming?

M: Not today, Tina. My family is going picnicking.

W: Well .... How about Friday then?

M: That sounds fine.

Q2: When will Jack go swimming?

A. Today.
B. Not Friday.
C. On Friday. ◀━ 正解

中文翻譯

| 簡短對話 2 | 女人：傑克，你想去游泳嗎？
男人：今天不行，蒂娜。我們家人要去野餐。
女人：那……星期五呢？
男人：應該可以。 | >>> | 問：傑克什麼時候會去游泳？
A. 今天。
B. 不是星期五。
C. 星期五。 |

※〔註〕picnic 野餐；go picnicking = go on a picnic 去野餐
※〔註〕Jack 回應 "fine"，表示 go swimming 的時間就是 Friday，答案為 (C)。

Conversation 3.

M: When can I come to see the doctor?
W: The doctor will be busy this week. Wait... Wednesday is OK.

Q3: When can the man come to see the doctor this week?

A. On Wednesday. 正解
B. Any day.
C. Next week.

中文翻譯

| 簡短對話 **3** | 男人：我什麼時候可以來看醫生？ 女人：醫生這星期很忙。等一下⋯⋯星期三可以。 | >>> | 問：本週男子何時可以看醫生？ A. 星期三。 B. 任何一天都可以。 C. 下星期。 |

※〔註〕女子可能是診所的 receptionist，負責接聽電話和招呼病患的接待員，她最後說"... Wednesday is OK."，故男子可在這一天來看診，答案爲 (A)。

Conversation 4.

M: When is your son's birthday?
W: On March 4. Mine, too.
M: No kidding! So is mine.

Q4: What date is the man's birthday?

A. In March.
B. In April.
C. On March 4. 正解

中文翻譯

| 簡短對話 **4** | 男人：妳兒子的生日是什麼時候？ 女人：在三月四日。我也是。 男人：眞的？我也是！ | >>> | 問：男子的生日在幾月幾日？ A. 在三月。 B. 在四月。 C. 在三月四日。 |

※〔註〕When...... 的問法可以只回答月份；但是 What date...... 的問法，除了月份之外，還要回答出確切的日期。
※〔註〕女子說 "Mine, too."，男子說 "So is mine."，都表示他們的生日都在 March 4，而且 What date 的回答一定要是確切的日期，所以答案是 (C)。

主題 7　問 > 季節・月份・氣候

Conversation 1.

W: What's your favorite season?
M: I like summer best. I like water sports. How about you?
W: I like spring more. Too much sun bothers me.

Q1: What season does the man like best?

A. Spring and summer.
B. Spring.
C. Summer. ← 正解

中文翻譯

簡短對話 1	女人：你最喜歡什麼季節？ 男人：我最喜歡夏天，我喜歡水上運動。妳呢？ 女人：我比較喜歡春天，我不喜歡曬太多太陽。	>>>	問：男子最喜歡什麼季節？ A. 春天和夏天。 B. 春天。 C. 夏天。

※〔註〕bother 使困擾。Ex: Stop bothering me! 別煩我了！
※〔註〕男子與女子各自說了自己喜歡的 season，因此聽問題的時候就要注意究竟是問誰，這題是問 the man，所以男子的回答就是答案 "I like spring."。

Conversation 2.

W: It's freezing today, isn't it?
M: The radio says the sun will come out later.
W: The temperature will stay above 10 in the day-time, but at night it will fall below 7.

Q2: What's the weather like?

A. It's freezing and rainy.
B. It's sunny and hot.
C. It's freezing but sunny. ← 正解

中文翻譯

| 簡短對話 2 | 女人：今天冷颼颼的，對吧？
男人：聽收音機說等一下太陽會出來。
女人：白天氣溫在十度以上，夜間又降到七度以下了。 | >>> | 問：天氣如何？
A. 又冷又下雨。
B. 艷陽高照。
C. 雖然冷但是有陽光。 |

※〔註〕女子的第一句話 "It's freezing."，加上男子的回應 "... the sun will come out..."，所以答案為 (C)。

Conversation 3.

W: Was it cold here last winter?

M: Yes, it was. And December is much colder than January and February.

Q3: **Which month was the coldest month last winter?**

    A. December. ◀—正解

    B. January.

    C. February.

中文翻譯

| 簡短對話 3 | 女人：去年冬天這裡冷嗎？
男人：冷啊，而且十二月比一月和二月冷多了。 | >>> | 問：去年冬天哪個月份最冷？
A. 十二月。
B. 一月。
C. 二月。 |

※〔註〕男子說 "December is much colder..."，所以答案為 (A)。

Conversation 4.

W: It's very cold now.

M: Yes, it is. November and December were cold enough. I don't think the cold weather will be over before February.

Q4: **In which month are they talking?**

    A. January. ◀—正解

    B. February.

    C. November.

中文翻譯

簡短對話 4

女人：現在很冷。
男人：是啊，11月和12月已經夠冷了，我想冷天氣在二月前是不會結束的。

>>>

問：他們是在哪個月份對話的？
A. 一月。
B. 二月。
C. 十一月。

※〔註〕這題要注意時態的說法，男子說 "November and December were cold...." 又說 "...over before February."，介於十二月和二月中間的月份，那當然就是 January，故選 (A)。

談論天氣的開場白

加分必背

1. What bad / good weather! 多糟（好）的天氣！

2. Lovely day, isn't it? 好天氣，不是嗎？

3. It looks like rain, don't you think so? 看來像是要下雨了，你不認為嗎？

4. It's hot for this time of year, don't you think so? 對於每年的這個時候來說太熱了，你不認為嗎？

主題 8 問 > 數字與計算問題

Conversation 1.

W: What's your telephone number? Is it 3281-6547?
M: No, it's 3218-6574.

Q1: What is the man's phone number?

A. 3218-5467.
B. 3218-6574. 正解
C. 3281-6547.

簡短
對話
1

女人：你的電話號碼是幾號？
是 3281-6547 嗎？
男人：不，是 3218-6574。

>>>

問：男子的電話是幾號？
A. 3218-5467。
B. 3218-6574。
C. 3281-6547。

※〔註〕注意問題問的是 "the man's"，所以男子回答的電話號碼才是答案，故選 (B)。

Conversation 2.

W: Tim, are you eighteen?
M: No, my sister is eighteen. I'm only fifteen.
W: You're so young.

Q2: How old is Tim's sister?

A. She is fifteen years old.
B. She is 3 years younger than Tim.
C. She is 3 years older than Tim. ◀ 正解

中文翻譯

簡短
對話
2

女人：提姆，你 18 歲嗎？
男人：不，我姐姐 18 歲，
我只有 15 歲。
女人：你真年輕！

>>>

問：提姆的姐姐幾歲？
A. 她 15 歲。
B. 她比提姆小三歲。
C. 她比提姆大三歲。

※〔註〕問題問的是 "Tim's sister"，Tim 的回答 "my sister is eighteen."， 接著他又說 "I'm only fifteen."，表示他的姐姐「大」他三歲，答案為 (C)。

Conversation 3.

W: How much are these coffee cups, please?
M: $200 each, or $300 for the two.

Q3: How much does one coffee cup cost if you buy two?

A. $200.
B. $300.
C. $150. ◀ 正解

中文翻譯

| 簡短對話 3 | 女人：請問這些咖啡杯多少錢？
男人：每個 200 元，兩個 300 元。 | >>> | 問：如果你買兩個咖啡杯，每個要花多少錢？
A. 兩百元。
B. 三百元。
C. 一百五十元。 |

※〔註〕這個問題有點難，不能直接在對話裡直接找到數字，必須做一點算術。前提是你要一次買兩個杯子比較便宜，" $300 for the two"，平均一個只要 "$150"，故答案為 (C)。

Conversation 4.

W: What's the time by your watch, Peter?

M: It's half past seven, but my watch is seven minutes slow.

Q4: What is the right time?

A. Seven thirty.
B. Seven twenty-three.
C. Seven thirty-seven. ── 正解

中文翻譯

| 簡短對話 4 | 女人：彼得，你的手錶幾點了？
男人：七點卅分，但是我的手錶慢了七分鐘。 | >>> | 問：正確時間為何？
A. 七點三十分。
B. 七點二十三分。
C. 七點三十七分。 |

※〔註〕這題同樣要一點算術，Peter 手錶上的時間是 "half past seven" = 7:30，但是彼得的錶慢了七分鐘，所以時間要再加 7 分鐘才對，故正確時間為 7:37，答案選 (C)。

主題 9 　　比　較

Conversation 1.

W: I'm Mary. I'm thirty.

M: I'm Ben. I'm ten years older than you.

W: Really? You look younger than me.

Q1: Who is younger?

A. Ben is younger.
B. Mary is younger. ━正解
C. They're of the same age.

中文翻譯

| 簡短對話 1 | 女人：我是瑪莉，我 30 歲。
男人：我是班尼，我比妳大 10 歲。
女人：真的嗎? 你看起來比我年輕！ | ⟫ | 問：誰比較年輕？
A. 班尼比較年輕。
B. 瑪莉比較年輕。
C. 他們兩個同年齡。 |

※〔註〕age 年齡；What's your age? = How old are you? 你幾歲?
※〔註〕Ben 說 "I'm ten years older...", 那麼當然是選 (B) Mary is younger.

Conversation 2.

M: Who is the tallest girl in your class, Alice?
W: Let me see. Mary is tall, but Jane is taller than Mary, and Rebecca is taller than Jane.

Q2: Who is the tallest girl?

A. Jane.
B. Mary.
C. Rebecca. ━正解

中文翻譯

| 簡短對話 2 | 男人：艾莉絲，誰是妳班上最高的女生？
女人：我想想看。瑪莉很高，可是珍比瑪莉高，莉貝卡又比珍妮高。 | ⟫ | 問：哪個女生最高？
A. 珍妮。
B. 瑪莉。
C. 莉貝卡。 |

※〔註〕Alice 的回應很有邏輯，出現的人名是一個比一個高 (tall--> taller--> tallest)，所以最後出現的人名 "Rebecca" 就是最高的人，選 (C)。

Conversation 3.

M: Excuse me. May I have a sheet of paper, please?
W: Certainly. Here you are.
M: Thank you. Oh, this is too small.

Q3: What does the man want?

A. He wants a sheep.
B. He wants a bigger sheet of paper. ◀━ 正解
C. He wants a smaller sheet of paper.

中文翻譯

| 簡短對話 3 | 男人：對不起，可以給我一張紙嗎？
女人：當然，拿去。
男人：謝謝。喔，這張太小了！ | >>> | 問：男子要的是什麼？
A. 他要一隻羊。
B. 他要一張較大的紙。
C. 他要一張較小的紙。 |

※〔註〕類音字 sheet [ʃit] 一張 / sheep [ʃip] 羊；綿羊
※〔註〕類似音 sheet（一張）/ sheep（羊），男子要的是 a "sheet" of paper，與 sheep 一點關係也沒有。至於要什麼樣的紙張？他最後說 "This is too small." 那就表示要 "bigger" 的，故答案選 (B)。

Conversation 4.

M: This dress is not as expensive as the blouse. Isn't it?
W: No. Neither is the handbag.

Q4: What is the most expensive?

A. The dress.
B. The blouse. ◀━ 正解
C. The handbag.

中文翻譯

| 簡短對話 4 | 男人：這件洋裝沒這件女襯衫貴，對吧？
女人：沒錯，連這個手提包都沒女襯衫貴。 | >>> | 問：最貴的是什麼？
A. 洋裝。
B. 女襯衫。
C. 手提包。 |

※〔註〕not as expensive as = cheaper than
※〔註〕要聽懂這段對話有三個重點：
1) "X" is not as expensive as "Y" = "Y" is more expensive
2) ... is not... Isn't it? 回答 "No" 表示對方說的「沒錯」。
3) Neither is "Z" = "Z" is not as expensive as "Y" = "Y" is more expensive
結論就是：最貴的 (the most expensive) 東西是 "Y"，答案為 (B)。

主題 **10** Yes-No 問題

Conversation 1.

W: Did you get the letter, Jack?
M: What letter?
W: Well, no news is good news.

Q1: Did Jack get the letter?

A. Yes, he did.
B. No, he didn't. ← 正解
C. We don't know.

中文翻譯

簡短對話 **1**

女人：傑克，你有收到信嗎？
男人：什麼信？
女人：嗯，沒消息就是好消息。

>>>

問：傑克有收到信嗎？
A. 有，他收到了。
B. 不，他沒收到。
C. 我們不知道。

※〔註〕news 表「消息、新聞」。
※〔註〕Jack 的回應 "What letter?"，表示他根本不知道有什麼信件，也就是說他並沒有收到信，故答案為 (B)。

Conversation 2.

M: Where do you work, Susan?
W: I worked in a museum near a library before, but I began to work in a school three months ago.

Q2: Did Susan ever work in a library?

A. No, she didn't. ← 正解
B. Yes, she did.
C. Yes, she worked in a library for three months.

中文翻譯

| 簡短對話 2 | 男人：妳在哪裡工作，蘇珊？
女人：我以前在靠近圖書館的博物館工作，可是三個月前我開始在學校工作了。 | >>> | 問：蘇珊曾在圖書館工作過嗎？
A. 不，她沒有。
B. 有，她有。
C. 有，她曾經在圖書館工作過三個月。 |

※〔註〕Susan 在回答男子的問話中提到了三個地點 museum、library、school，但是仔細聽她說的是 "a museum near a library"，圖書館只是讓男子了解她以前工作的那個博物館確實的位置而已，並非她工作的地方，所以答案為 (A)。

Conversation 3.

M: Lucy, you should rest for a while. Even ten minutes would be fine.

W: No way. There's so much work to do.

Q3: Is Lucy going to take a rest?

A. No, she doesn't like working.
B. Yes, she has to work.
C. No, she has to work.　正解

中文翻譯

| 簡短對話 3 | 男人：露西，妳應該休息一下，即使十分鐘也好。
女人：不行，有這麼多工作要做。 | >>> | 問：露西要休息嗎？
A. 不，她不喜歡工作。
B. 是，她必須工作。
C. 不，她必須工作。 |

※〔註〕rest（休息）當動詞時，等於名詞用法的 take a rest。
※〔註〕Lucy 回應的很明白 "No way."，表示要休息根本是不可能的事，答案為 (C)。

Conversation 4.

W: What's the matter?

Boy: I can't find my mother. I don't know the way home.

Q4: Can the boy go back home by himself?

A. He can't find his mother.
B. Yes, he can.
C. No, he can't.　正解

| 簡短對話 4 | 女人：怎麼了？
男孩：我找不到媽媽，我不知道回家的路。 | | 問：男孩可以自己回到家嗎？
A. 他找不到媽媽。
B. 是，他可以。
C. 不，他沒辦法。 |

※〔註〕這個對話應該是小男孩迷路時，女子熱心詢問他發生了什麼事。男孩說找不到媽媽，「自己」不知道怎麼回家，即 "He can't go home by himself."，答案為 (C)。

主題 11　混淆音

Conversation 1.

W: Have you seen Ms. Smith recently, Stephen?

M: No, Sandy. I heard that she has gone back to New York.

Q1: Who has gone back to America?

A. Stephen.

B. Ms. Smith. ◀━正解

C. Sandy.

| 簡短對話 1 | 女人：史蒂芬，你最近有看到史密斯女士嗎？
男人：沒有耶，珊蒂。我聽說她已經回去紐約了。 | | 問：誰回去美國了？
A. 史蒂芬。
B. 史密斯女士。
C. 珊蒂。 |

※〔註〕Smith / Stephen / Sandy 三個字首發音都是 [s]，易造成混淆，對話者談論是 Ms. Smith 回紐約（美國城市）的消息，答案為 (B)。

Conversation 2.

M: Don't you think Blake runs the fastest?

W: He's faster than Frank, but slower than Eric.

Q2: Who runs the slowest?

A. Blake.

B. Frank. ◀━正解

C. Eric.

中文翻譯

簡短對話 2	男人：你不認為布萊克跑得最快嗎？ 女人：他比法蘭克快，但是比艾瑞克慢。	>>>	問：誰跑得最慢？ A. 布萊克。 B. 法蘭克。 C. 艾瑞克。

※〔註〕Mike, Frank, Eric 三個名字的字尾都是 /k/，易造成混淆。這一題除了要聽懂三個人名之外，還必須馬上反應出相反詞 fast/slow 的關係，最後還得知道比較詞的用法，跑步速度快慢依序為 Frank is fast; Blake is faster; Eric is the fastest，答案為 (B)。

Conversation 3.

M: What can I do for you, ma'am?

W: I'm looking for a coat for my daughter.

Q3: What does the woman want to buy?

A. A dog.

B. A coat. ◄— 正解

C. A cat.

中文翻譯

簡短對話 3	男人：我能為你服務嗎，女士？ 女人：我想為我女兒買件外套。	>>>	問：這名女子想買什麼？ A. 一隻狗。 B. 一件外套。 C. 一隻貓。

※〔註〕dog / daughter 聲音相似，只相差在字尾；coat / cat 則只相差在中間母音，所以容易混淆，但女子要買的其實是 a coat，答案為 (B)。

Conversation 4.

M: Could you wrap it up for me?

W: Sure. Is there anything else I can get for you?

M: That should be it. Thank you.

Q4: What did the man buy?

A. A recorder.
B. A pair of shoes.
C. We don't know. ◀ 正解

中文翻譯

| 簡短對話 4 | 男人：妳可以幫我包起來嗎？
女人：當然。您還需要我幫你拿點其他的東西嗎？
男人：這樣應該夠了，謝謝。 | ⟫⟫⟫ | 問：這名男子買了什麼？
A. 一台錄音（影）機。
B. 一雙鞋子。
C. 我們不知道。 |

※〔註〕類似音組 wrap / recorder、should / shoes，但對話中根本沒提到男子買了什麼東西要店員幫他包裝，因此答案要選 (C)。

主題 **12** 推 測

Conversation 1.

W: I hope you like this place.
M: I love it. Do they have sushi?
W: Sure!
M: Great. I'd like to try it.

Q1: Where are they?

A. In a restaurant. ◀ 正解
B. In a toy shop.
C. In a shoe store.

中文翻譯

| 簡短對話 1 | 女人：我希望你喜歡這個地方。
男人：我喜歡，他們有壽司嗎？
女人：當然！
男人：太好了，我想吃看看！ | ⟫⟫⟫ | 問：他們在哪裡？
A. 在餐廳。
B. 在玩具店。
C. 在鞋店。 |

※〔註〕這個題目並沒有直接說出這個地方是哪裡，但由 sushi（壽司是一種日本米食）可知，對話在討論「吃」的問題，三個選項裡只有 (A)「餐廳」與情境相符，故選 (A)。

Conversation 2.

W: The wind is blowing through the door. Do you feel cold, Vincent?

M: Oh, I see. I'm terribly sorry.

Q2: What will Vincent do?

A. He will open the door.
B. He will answer the door.
C. He will close the door. ◄ 正解

中文翻譯

| 簡短對話 2 | 女人：風從門口吹進來，你覺得冷嗎，文生？
男人：喔，我知道了。真的很對不起！ | | 問：文生會做什麼？
A. 他會打開門。
B. 他會去應門。
C. 他會關上門。 |

※〔註〕男子因為風吹進屋裡造成女子不適而向她道歉，因此可以推測，唯有 close the door（關上門）風才不會吹進來，故選 (C)。

Conversation 3.

M: How was everything at school today?

Girl: I got 100 on my math test.

M: I'm so proud of you!

Q3: What does the girl do?

A. She's a student. ◄ 正解
B. She's a teacher.
C. She studies English.

中文翻譯

簡短對話 3	女人：妳今天在學校過得如何？ 女孩：我數學考了一百分。 女人：我真為妳感到驕傲！	>>>	問：女孩是做什麼的（工作）？ A. 她是一位學生。 B. 她是一位老師。 C. 她研讀英文。

※〔註〕從對話中兩個關鍵詞 school、math test 推測，唯有「學生」是可能的身分，其他兩種身分都無法從對話中判斷出來，故選擇最佳答案為 (A)。

Conversation 4.

M: Ms. Patrick, when do you usually go to work?

W: I work at home because I'm a writer. And I go to bed about seven o'clock in the morning.

Q4: When does Ms. Patrick usually work?

A. She works at midnight. ——正解

B. She works at home.

C. She works as a writer.

中文翻譯

簡短對話 4	男人：派翠克女士，妳通常是什麼時候去上班？ 女人：我在家工作，因為我是個作家，而且我早上七點上床睡覺。	>>>	問：派翠克女士通常在什麼時候工作？ A. 她在半夜時工作。 B. 她在家工作。 C. 她當一位作家。

※〔註〕女子最後一句話說 " I go to bed about seven o'clock in the morning."，推測她早上應該都是在睡覺，晚上工作，是一位夜貓族，答案選 (A)。

主題 **13**	健　康

Conversation 1.

M: I have a stomachache.

W: Oh, that's too bad. Have you seen a doctor?

M: I'm on my way to the clinic.

W: Take care. Bye.

Q1: What's wrong with the man?

A. He's bad.
B. He's a doctor.
C. He got a stomachache. ← 正解

中文翻譯

| 簡短對話 1 | 男人：我胃痛。
女人：啊，真慘。看醫生了嗎？
男人：我正要去診所。
女人：保重，再見。 | >>> | 問：這名男子怎麼了？
A. 他很壞。
B. 他是個醫生。
C. 他胃痛。 |

※〔註〕"What's wrong with +（某人）?" 所指的是某人正在為某事所困擾，大部份的情況是身體的病痛問題，中文意思接近「（某人）怎麼了？」、「（某人）有什麼不對勁？」，因此 (C) 為合理答案。

Conversation 2.

M: Sara has been absent for a few days. What's wrong with her?

W: She's got the flu and is home in bed now.

Q2: Why is Sara absent?

A. She is sick. ← 正解
B. She is wrong.
C. She is not home.

中文翻譯

| 簡短對話 2 | 男人：莎拉有幾天沒來了。她怎麼啦？
女人：她得了流行性感冒，現在正在家裡養病。 | >>> | 問：莎拉為什麼缺席？
A. 她病了。
B. 她錯了。
C. 她不在家。 |

※〔註〕女子說 She's got flue. 感冒了就是生病了，故選 (A)。

Conversation 3.

M: I have to go to the hospital after school.
W: Are you sick?
M: No, I'm not. My mother is in the hospital.
W: I hope she will get well soon.

Q3: **Who's in the hospital?**

    A. The man.
    B. The woman.
    C. The man's mother. —[正解]

中文翻譯

簡短
對話
3

男人：下課後我必須到醫院去。
女人：你生病了嗎？
男人：不，我沒有。我母親住院
了。
女人：我希望她能早日康復。

>>>

問：誰在住院？
A. 這名男子。
B. 這名女子。
C. 這名男子的母親。

Conversation 4.

M: Good afternoon, Ms. Stone. Do you feel better?
W: Yes, thank you. But I've still got pains in my back.

Q4: **What is the relationship of the man and the woman?**

    A. Father and daughter.
    B. Doctor and patient. —[正解]
    C. Teacher and student.

中文翻譯

簡短
對話
4

男人：午安，史東女士。覺得好些嗎？
女人：是，謝謝。可是我的背還是會痛。

問：這一對男女是什麼關係？
A. 父親與女兒。
B. 醫生和病患。
C. 老師和學生。

※〔註〕在講 relationship（關係）的時候，所有的名詞前面都不加任何冠詞（a, an, the）。
※〔註〕由男子對女子的稱謂 "Ms. Stone" 看出兩人的關係應該不親密，故 (A) 不對；再由女子的回應中提到 "pains in my back" 看出 (B) 應該是較合理的答案。

醫生為病患檢查身體的說法

1. Open your mouth and say "Ah".
   張開你的嘴巴「啊～」。
2. I want to take your temperature.
   我想量一下你的體溫。
3. Let me listen to your heart.
   讓我聽一下你的心跳。

主題 **14**　　　**會面與道別**

Conversation 1.

M: Clair, I just saw Lisa.

W: Really, where?

M: On the other side of the room.

W: Let's go say hello.

Q1: Whom did the man see?

A. Clair.
B. Lisa. 正解
C. Holly.

中文翻譯

簡短對話 **1**	男人：克萊兒，我剛剛看到麗莎。 女人：眞的嗎？在哪？ 男人：在房間的另一頭。 女人：我們去打個招呼。	問：這名男子看到誰？ A. 克萊兒。 B. 麗莎。 C. 荷莉。

※〔註〕男子說 "I just saw Lisa."，答案爲 (B)。利用在同一句話裡說出兩個人的名字，造成聽力上的混淆。通常一個人要對某人說話的開場都是叫對方的名字，但這個名字並不是對話雙方在談論話題的主要對象，必須小心。

Conversation 2.

（門鈴聲）

M: Hey Julie, you look great.

W: Thanks. You're handsome, too.

M: So are you ready to go to the party?

W: Sure, Joe. Where's your car?

Q2: Where are they talking?

A. At Julie's home.　　**正解**

B. At the party.

C. In Joe's car.

中文翻譯

簡短對話 **2**	男人：嘿，茱莉，妳看起來眞美。 女人：謝謝，你也很帥。 男人：那妳準備好去派對了嗎？ 女人：當然，喬。你的車在哪兒？	問：他們在哪裡講話？ A. 在茱莉家。 B. 在舞會上。 C. 在喬的車裡。

※〔註〕男子說 "... ready to go to the party?"，也就是說他們還沒抵達舞會現場，女子說 "Joe. Where's your car?" 表示他們還沒進到 Joe 的車內。正確答案爲 (A)。

Conversation 3.

M: I really must be going now.

W: Can't you stay a little longer?

M: I really can't.

W: OK. Drive carefully. Bye.

Q3: What is the man doing?

A. He's saying goodbye. ← 正解
B. He's driving.
C. He is going to stay longer.

中文翻譯

| 簡短對話 3 | 男人：現在我真的該告辭了。
女人：不能再待久一點嗎？
男人：真的不能再待了。
女人：好吧，小心開車，再見。 | 問：這名男子在做什麼？
A. 他在道別。
B. 他在開車。
C. 他會待久一點。 |

※〔註〕選項 (B)、(C) 都重複了對話中的一些內容，但答案都剛好相反，也就是說 He's NOT driving. 而且 He's NOT going to stay longer.。由男子說 I really must be going now. 判斷出正確答案為 (A)。

Conversation 4.

W: Sorry, I've got to go now.
M: So soon?
W: Yes, I have to be home by 3 o'clock. I have a piano class.
M: OK. See you later.

Q4: Why is the woman leaving?

A. She will be leaving by 3 o'clock.
B. She has a piano class. ← 正解
C. She has a piano.

中文翻譯

| 簡短對話 4 | 女人：對不起，我現在必須走了。
男人：這麼快？
女人：是啊，我必須在三點以前回到家。我要上鋼琴課。
男人：好吧，再見！ | 問：為什麼這名女子要離開？
A. 她會在三點前離開。
B. 她有鋼琴課。
C. 她有鋼琴。 |

※〔註〕女子說 "I have a piano class."，因為有鋼琴課，所以要離開，答案選 (B)。這題選項同樣是利用對話中的部份內容刻意設計，如果沒有仔細聽，即可能因此誤選。

主題 15　　　用 餐

Conversation 1.

W: Bill, what would you like to drink?
M: I'd like some water, please.
W: Anything else?
M: Well. Some cake, please.

Q1: What would Bill like to eat and drink?

A. Some bread and water.
B. Some cakes and coffee.
C. Some cakes and water. ──正解

中文翻譯

| 簡短對話 1 | 女人：比爾，你想喝什麼？
男人：我想喝點水，謝謝。
女人：還要其他的嗎？
男人：嗯……，來點蛋糕，謝謝。 | >>> | 問：比爾要吃什麼？要喝什麼？
A. 麵包和水。
B. 蛋糕和咖啡。
C. 蛋糕和水。 |

※〔註〕男子一開始就說 "I'd like some water."，然後他又說 "Some cake, please."，故正確答案為 (C)。

Conversation 2.

W: I am so full. The duck was excellent.
M: I hope you saved room for dessert.
W: Oh no, dessert?

Q2: How does the woman feel?

A. She feels hungry.
B. She feels like eating some dessert.
C. She feels full. ──正解

簡短
對話
2

女人：我好飽喔，那道鴨肉眞棒。
男人：我希望你還吃得下甜點。
女人：哦，不，甜點？

>>>

問：這名女子覺得如何？
A. 她覺得餓。
B. 她覺得想吃些甜點。
C. 她覺得很飽。

※〔註〕room（空間）；save room（留下空間）意指留下胃（stomach）的空間來吃其他東西。

Conversation 3.

W: There's a new restaurant open nearby.
M: What kind of food do they have?
W: Italian. Would you like to try?
M: Certainly. Let's go.

Q3: **What will they probably have?**

A. Pizza and spaghetti. ◄── 正解
B. Fried chicken and soda.
C. Rice and fish.

簡短
對話
3

女人：附近開了一家新餐廳。
男人：他們賣哪種食物？
女人：義大利菜。要試試看嗎？
男人：當然要，走！

>>>

問：他們可能會吃什麼？
A. 比薩和義大利麵。
B. 炸雞和汽水。
C. 米飯和魚。

※〔註〕因爲他們要前往的是一家「義大利」餐廳，(A) 是義式餐廳最可能提供的餐點。(B) 可能是 fast food restaurant（速食店）裡的菜色，(C) 則可能是亞洲餐廳裡的菜色，例如 Chinese / Japanese / Korean / Thai restaurant（中國／日本／韓國／泰國餐廳）。

Conversation 4.

M: Good morning. What would you like?
W: A cola for me and a coffee for my friend.
M: Would you like anything to eat with that? A pancake or a sandwich?
W: No, thank you.

Q4: What does the customer want?

A. Cola and coffee. ──〈正解〉
B. Coffee and cake.
C. Pancake and sandwiches.

中文翻譯

| 簡短對話 4 | 男人：早安，您想點什麼？
女人：我要一杯可樂，我朋友要一杯咖啡。
男人：除了這些，您還要來點吃的嗎? 薄烤餅或三明治？
女人：不用，謝謝。 | >>> | 問：這名顧客要什麼？
A. 可樂和咖啡。
B. 咖啡和蛋糕。
C. 薄烤餅和三明治。 |

※〔註〕女顧客一開始點了飲料，她說 "A cola... and a coffee...."，接下來店員雖然提供了食物的選擇，但她拒絕了。正確答案爲 (A)。

Column

中式早點	
饅頭	steamed buns
蛋餅	egg cakes
飯糰	rice and vegetable roll
豆漿	soybean milk
燒餅	clay oven rolls
油條	fried bread stick

加分必背

主題 16　　購　物

Conversation 1.

W: May I help you?
M: Yes. Do you have this jacket in size 40?
W: I'm not sure. Let me look in the stockroom.
M: Thanks.

Q1: What is the man looking for?

A. A shirt.
B. A jacket. ◀ 正解
C. A coat.

中文翻譯

| 簡短對話 1 | 女人：我能爲你服務嗎？
男人：是。你們這件夾克有四十號的嗎？
女人：我不確定，我查一下倉庫。
男人：謝謝。 | ≫≫ | 問：男子在找什麼？
A. 襯衫。
B. 夾克。
C. 外套。 |

※〔註〕男子問店員 "Do you have this jacket...?"，由此清楚地知道他想買一件夾克，答案爲 (B)。

Conversation 2.

M: Hi, are you being helped?
W: No, I'm not. I'm interested in some scarves.

Q2: What is the man?

A. He's police officer.
B. He's a shop salesman. ◀ 正解
C. He's a fashion designer.

中文翻譯

| 簡短對話 2 | 男人：嗨，有人爲您服務嗎？
女人：不，沒有。我想找些圍巾。 | ≫≫ | 問：男子的職業是什麼？
A. 他是警察。
B. 他是店員。
C. 他是服裝設計師。 |

※〔註〕本題的說法 "Are you being helped?"="May I help you?（有需要幫忙嗎？）"。再由女子回答 "I'm interested in some scarves." 得知答案爲 (B)。

Conversation 3.

M: Can I try these pants on?
W: Yes, you can. The fitting room is over there.
M: They don't fit. Please show me bigger ones.

Q3: Do the pants fit the man?

A. He doesn't look good on them.
B. They are too big.
C. They are too small. ←正解

中文翻譯		
簡短對話 3	男人：我可以試穿這件褲子嗎？ 女人：可以，試衣間在那裡。 男人：這件不合身，妳能再給我看看大一點的?	問：褲子對男子而言合身嗎？ A. 他穿起來不好看。 B. 太大了。 C. 太小了。

※〔註〕男子試穿 (try on) 後發現褲子不合自己的尺寸，說 "... show me bigger ones."，要求再試穿大一點尺寸的，也就是說試穿過的這一件太小了，答案爲 (C)。

Conversation 4.

W: Would you like some help?

M: Do you have the book "Harry Potter and the Goblet of Fire"?

W: Yes, it's right here. It's on sale.

Q4: Where is this dialogue taking place?

A. In a book shop. ←正解
B. In a library.
C. In a VCD shop.

中文翻譯		
簡短對話 4	女人：需要服務嗎？ 男人：你們有「哈利波特第四集～火盃的考驗」嗎？ 女人：有，就在這裡，正在特價！	問：這段對話是在哪裡發生的？ A. 在書店裡。 B. 在圖書館。 C. 在錄影帶店。

※〔註〕男顧客問 "Do you have the book...?"，由此判斷對話發生的地點不是 (A) 就是 (B)；接著女店員又說 "... It's on sale."，圖書館不會拍賣書，所以正確答案爲 (A) 書店。

店員讚美顧客用語

1. It suits you well. 這很適合你。
2. You look good in it. 你穿起來很好看。
3. It looks good on you. 穿在你身上很好看。
4. The skirt matches your pink blouse.
   這件裙子很搭妳的粉紅色女襯衫。
5. The necktie goes with your blue shirt.
   這條領帶和你的藍色襯衫很搭。

主題 17　約定・預約

Conversation 1.

M: I'm going to miss you.

W: Me too. Let's keep in touch.

M: Yeah. Don't forget to write me.

Q1: Who's the woman?

A. She is Miss Yu.
B. She is the man's Miss Right.
C. We don't know. ◀ 正解

中文翻譯

| 簡短對話 1 | 男人：我會想妳的。
女人：我也是。保持聯絡喔！
男人：對，別忘了寫信給我！ | >>> | 問：這名女子是誰？
A. 她是尤小姐。
B. 她是男子的夢中情人。
C. 我們不知道。 |

※〔註〕Write me. 就是「寫信給我」的意思，是美語人士常用來提醒對方要保持聯絡的說法。

Conversation 2.

M: Excuse me. My name is Adam Ford. I have an appointment with the dentist at 3:30.

W: Yes, Mr. Ford. The dentist will be ready to see you in a minute. Have a seat.

M: Thank you.

Q2: **Who will the man see?**

    A. Mr. Ford.
    B. No. 4.
    C. The dentist. ◀ 正解

中文翻譯

| 簡短對話 **2** | 男人：對不起。我叫亞當・福特。與牙醫師約在三點半見面。 女人：好的，福特先生。醫生待會就準備好與您會面。請坐。 男人：謝謝您。 | >>> | 問：男子將見到誰？ A. 福特先生。 B. 四號。 C. 牙醫。 |

※〔註〕appointment [ə`pɔɪntmənt] 約定
      dentist [`dɛntɪst] 牙科醫生
      have a seat 坐下 = take a seat

Conversation 3.

W: You'll be here for two nights. Is that correct, Mr. Katz?

W: Yes, that's correct.

Q3: **When will Mr. Katz leave the place?**

    A. The day after tomorrow. ◀ 正解
    B. Tomorrow.
    C. Today.

中文翻譯

| 簡短對話 3 | 女人：你會在這裡兩晚。正確嗎，蓋茲先生。
男人：是，沒錯。 | >>> | 問：蓋茲先生什麼時候會離開這個地方？
A. 後天。
B. 明天。
C. 今天。 |

※〔註〕女子說 "You'll be here for two nights..."，意思就是男子 (Mr. Katz) 再過了兩晚後會離開，也就是「後天」，答案為 (A)。

Conversation 4.

W: I'd like to book a flight to Taipei, please.

M: Surely, ma'am. What date?

W: June 6.

Q4: How will the woman go to Taipei?

A. On June 6.
B. By plane.　正解
C. Ride a train.

中文翻譯

| 簡短對話 4 | 女人：我要訂往台北的班機，謝謝。
男人：沒問題，小姐。哪一天？
女人：六月六日。 | >>> | 問：男子將如何到台北？
A. 六月六日。
B. 搭飛機。
C. 坐火車。 |

※〔註〕flight [flaɪt] 班次；班機，book a flight to + 地點，「預訂前往（某地點）的班機」，flight 還可以改成 train（火車）或 bus（巴士）。

※〔註〕對話一開始女子就說 "I'd like to book a flight...."，訂機票的原因當然是要搭乘前往台北，所以答案為 (B)。

主題 18　學校

Conversation 1.

M: The English lesson is so interesting. Don't you think so, Lily?

W: No, I think it's boring. I like math more.

Q1: Which is more interesting for Lily?

A. Neither English nor math is interesting.
B. Math. 正解
C. English.

中文翻譯

| 簡短對話 1 | 男人：英文課眞有趣。妳不這麼認爲嗎，莉莉？
女人：不，我覺得它很無聊，我比較喜歡數學。 | >>> | 問：對莉莉而言什麼學科比較有趣？
A. 英文和數學都無趣。
B. 數學。
C. 英文。 |

※〔註〕女子 (Lily) 說 "I like math more.，換句話說就是 "Math is more interesting."，答案爲 (B)。

Conversation 2.

M: Your Japanese is good. When did you begin to learn Japanese?

W: Two years ago. I met a very good teacher.

Q2: How long has the woman learned Japanese?

A. She begins to learn Japanese.
B. She has learned Japanese for two years. 正解
C. She met a very good Japanese teacher.

中文翻譯

| 簡短對話 2 | 男人：妳的日文很好，妳是從什麼時候開始學日文的？
女人：兩年前。我遇到了一位好老師。 | >>> | 問：女子已經學了多久的日文？
A. 她開始學日文。
B. 她已經學了兩年的日文。
C. 她遇到了一位好的日文老師。 |

※〔註〕以 How long...? 起始的問句問的是維持了多久的一段時間，由於女子說 "Two years ago." 開始學日文，答案爲 (B)。

Conversation 3.

M: Excuse me. Where can I find the English teachers' office?

W: It's on the second floor-between the math teachers' office and the Chinese teachers' office.

M: Thank you.

Q3: Where does the man want to go?

    A. To the English teachers' office.
    B. To the third floor.
    C. To the Chinese teachers' office.

中文翻譯

| 簡短對話 3 | 男人：對不起，請問英文老師的辦公室在哪裡？
女人：在二樓，數學老師辦公室和中文老師辦公室中間。
男人：謝謝你。 | 問：男子想去哪裡？
A. 去英文老師的辦公室。
B. 去三樓。
C. 去中文老師的辦公室。 |

※〔註〕男子一開始就問 "Where can I find the English teacher's office."，也就是說他想去英文老師辦公室卻不知道路，所以答案為 (A)。

Conversation 4.

W: What score did you get in French, John?
M: I got 98 at first, but the teacher found a mistake and changed it into 95.

Q4: What was the man's score?

    A. It was 95.
    B. It was less than 95.
    C. It was 98.

中文翻譯

| 簡短對話 4 | 女人：約翰，你的法文幾分？
男人：原本有 98 分，可是老師發現了一個錯誤，就把分數改成 95 分了。 | 問：男子的分數是幾分？
A. 95 分。
B. 低於 95 分。
C. 98 分。 |

※〔註〕對話中提到老師給錯分數，後來又改成95分，也就是男子真正該得的分數，所以答案為 (A)。

主題 19　　　　工　作

Conversation 1.

W: What does your wife do, Ian?

M: Lillian used to be a nurse, but she quit the job three months ago. Now she looks after our new baby.

Q1: What is Lillian's job now?

A. She is nurse.
B. She is looking for a job.
C. She is a housewife. ←正解

中文翻譯

| 簡短對話 1 | 女人：伊安，你太太的工作是什麼？
男人：莉莉安曾經是名護士，可是三個月前她辭職了。現在她在照顧我們剛出生的孩子。 | >>> | 問：莉莉安現在的工作為何？
A. 她是一名護士。
B. 她正在找工作。
C. 她是一位家庭主婦。 |

※〔註〕Now she looks after our new baby.，換句話說她目前只有在家帶小孩，所以答案為(C)。

Conversation 2.

W: Something must have bothered you.

M: I'm having a meeting with the manager. She is unhappy with me.

W: What's wrong?

M: I was absent for the Tuesday meeting.

Q2: What is bothering the man?

A. He has a meeting on Tuesday.
B. He is unhappy with the meeting.
C. The manager is angry. ←正解

中文翻譯

簡短對話 2

女人：一定有什麼是困擾著你。
男人：我要和經理開會，她對我很不高興。
女人：怎麼了？
男人：星期二的會議我缺席了。

>>>

問：什麼事正困擾著這名男子？
A. 他在星期二有場會議。
B. 他對會議不高興。
C. 經理在生氣。

※〔註〕男子說 ".... the manager. She is unhappy...."，換句話說經理生氣 (angry) 了，答案為 (C)。

Conversation 3.

W: How was your interview with the company?
M: It's tomorrow. I'm worried.
W: Don't worry. You should do fine.
M: I hope so.

Q3: **What are they talking about?**

A. About finding a job. ——正解
B. About hopes.
C. About running a company.

中文翻譯

簡短對話 3

女人：你跟公司的面談如何？
男人：是明天。我很擔心。
女人：別擔心，你會做得很好。
男人：我希望如此。

>>>

問：他們在談論什麼？
A. 找工作。
B. 希望。
C. 經營公司。

※〔註〕女子一開始就打開真正的話題 "How was your interview with the company"，也就是在找工作，答案為 (A)。

Conversation 4.

W: I'm going to quit my job, Jeff.
M: Why?
W: I'm going to Paris to study. I want to become an artist.

Q4: What does the woman do?

A. An artist.
B. Pianist.
C. We don't know. ← 正解

中文翻譯

| 簡短對話 **4** | 女人：傑夫，我想要辭職。
男人：為什麼？
女人：我要到巴黎念書，我
想當藝術家。 | >>> | 問：女子的工作為何？
A. 藝術家。
B. 鋼琴家。
C. 不知道。 |

※〔註〕注意聽問句的時態 "What does... do?" 是現在式，問的是女子「現在」的工作，對話中女子只提到要辭職，以及未來想成為藝術家，並沒有說出目前的工作為何，所以答案為 (C)。

主題 20　　　　社　交

Conversation 1.

W: Would you like some cookies or cake?
M: I like both, but I'd just like something to drink now.

Q1: What does the man want now?

A. Cookies and cake.
B. Some drinks. ← 正解
C. Something that can eat.

中文翻譯

| 簡短對話 **1** | 女人：你要來點餅乾或蛋糕嗎？
男人：我兩樣都喜歡，可是我現
在只想喝點東西。 | >>> | 問：這名男子現在要什麼？
A. 餅乾和蛋糕。
B. 飲料。
C. 可以吃的東西。 |

※〔註〕男子雖然回答女子他餅乾和蛋糕兩樣都要，但他說現在(now)只想要喝點東西 would like something to drink，故答案是 B。

Conversation 2.

M: Jane. Help yourself to more food, please.
W: No, thanks. I'm full.

Q2: What did the man ask Jane to do?

A. To help him to get some food.
B. To have some more food. ←正解
C. To leave some food.

中文翻譯

| 簡短對話 2 | 男人：珍，自己動手再多吃點。
女人：不，謝啦，我很飽了。 | >>> | 問：男子要珍做什麼？
A. 幫他拿食物。
B. 多吃點。
C. 留一點食物。 |

※〔註〕Help yourself to more food 是再多吃點東西的意思，所以答案是 B.。

Conversation 3.

M: Anna. Everybody is singing and dancing. Why are you here?
W: I'd rather stay out for a while. Why do people smoke at all? It's so smoky in there.

Q3: Why is Anna staying out?

A. She doesn't like dancing.
B. She doesn't like people in there.
C. She doesn't like people smoking in there. ←正解

中文翻譯

| 簡短對話 3 | 男人：安娜，大家都在唱歌跳舞，妳怎麼在這裡？
女人：我寧願出來待一會兒。人們究竟為什麼抽煙？裡面好燻喔！ | >>> | 問：為什麼安娜待在外面？
A. 她不喜歡跳舞。
B. 她不喜歡裡面的人。
C. 她不喜歡裡面的人抽煙。 |

※〔註〕對話中 I'd rather ～是「寧願～」的意思。Anna 用疑問句 Why do people smoke 來表示她留在外面 stay out 的原因。

Conversation 4.

W: I think it's about time we got going.

M: Already? Won't you have more coffee?

W: I'd love to, but I have to get up early tomorrow.

Q4: **What is the relationship between the man and the woman?**

A. Singer and audience.

B. Shop owner and customer.

C. Host and guest. ——正解

中文翻譯

| 簡短對話 4 | 女人：我想差不多是該告辭的時候了。
男人：要走了？不再喝點咖啡嗎？
女人：我是很想，但我明天得早起。 | >>> | 問：男子和女子的關係為何？
A. 歌手和觀眾。
B. 商店老闆和顧客。
C. 主人和客人。 |

※〔註〕audience [`ɔdɪəns] 觀眾
　　　owner [`onɚ] 物主；所有人
　　　host [host] 主人

解答 短文聽解

第一類 廣播

主題 1　交通工具上

Q1 Please look at the following three pictures.
Listen to the following announcement. Where does it take place?

This is Captain Josh. We are now flying at a height of about 2000m. As the weather condition turns bad, we are expecting turbulence during the flight. Please stay in your seat and have your seat belt fastened. Meals will be served in 15 minutes. Thank you for your cooperation.

解答 C

我是機長喬許。我們現在的飛行高度約為兩千米，由於天氣轉壞，飛行中將有氣（亂）流，請坐在您的位子上並扣上安全帶。餐點將在十五分鐘後供應，謝謝你的合作。

※〔註〕在飛機上聽到之廣播內容是常考的題目，大概分為「起飛前」、「飛行途中」及「即將降落」三種階段的題型，本題考的是在飛行途中的廣播，關鍵字是 flying，「坐遊覽車 / 高鐵」，我們說 take / ride on a coach or high-speed train，廣播中的 turbulence 是另一關鍵字，指「亂流」，故正確答案為 C。

Q2 Please look at the following three pictures.
Listen to the following announcement. Where does it probably take place?

Good morning passengers. The next train to Yilan is arriving in two minutes. Please stay behind the yellow line until the train makes a complete stop. Thank you and have a nice journey.

解答 C

 各位乘客早安，下一班到宜蘭的列車將在兩分鐘進站。請在黃線後等候直到列車完全停妥，感謝您的搭乘並祝您旅途愉快。

※〔註〕仔細看過三張圖後，考生要有 MRT（捷運）、City（市）及 train station（火車站）或 train platform（火車月台）的概念，本廣播內容的關鍵字為 train，且出現兩次，所以正確答案為 C。

Q3 Please look at the following three pictures.
Listen to the following conversation. Where might you hear this?

Good morning everyone! Welcome to Japan. I am your tour guide, Diana. And Mark, our handsome driver, who's now driving us to the hotel, is going to take us safely to those well-known scenic spots in Tokyo for the following five days. Let's give him a big hand.

解答 A

大家早！歡迎來到日本。我是你們的導遊戴安，還有正在載我們到飯店的帥氣司機馬克，接下來的五天他會安全地帶我們到東京著名的景點遊覽，讓我們以熱烈的掌聲歡迎他。

※〔註〕本題考對話的場所，破題點在 ...driver is now driving... to the hotel，「司機正開往飯店」，代表旅客跟導遊正在遊覽車上，所以正確答案為 A。

主題 2 電台

Q1

Please look at the following three pictures.
Listen to the following talk. Where can you hear this talk?
This is FM 92.6, Taipei Music. I am Christine sharing lovely music with you from 2 to 4 every weekday. Next is the last song for today. Do join me on air tomorrow at the same time.

解答 B

 這裡是 FM92.6 台北音樂台，我是克莉絲汀，每周一到周五下午兩點到四點跟你分享美妙的音樂。接下來是今天最後一首歌曲，明天同一時間繼續與你空中有約。

※〔註〕電台廣播類型的考題，考生只要聽到 FM 或 Radio，答案就能百分百確定，本題一開始就清楚說明 this is FM92.6，故本題正確答案為 B。

Please look at the following three pictures.
Listen to the following talk. What might be the background?
Good evening dear audience. I'm your night host Ben. Thank you for tuning in to FM 99.9, your best LOHAS broadcast. Today I would like to talk about how to choose a good bike. And you are welcome to call in to share your own buying and biking experiences.

解答 A

親愛的聽眾朋友晚安，我是你的晚間主持人小班。謝謝你們收聽FM99.9 —你最好的樂活電台。今天我們要討論的是如何選購好的腳踏車（小摺），歡迎打電話進來分享你購買小摺和騎車的經驗。

※〔註〕本題問「背景」back-ground 為何？關鍵字在 FM99.9，聽到 FM 考生一定知道是電台，另外 audience（聽眾）、tune in（收聽）、broadcast（廣播），都是破題字，也是「電台廣播」類題型常出現的字，本題正確答案為 A。

主題
2
廣播ｖ電台

Q3 Please look at the following three pictures.
Listen to the following talk. Who is the speaker?
Welcome back to Love Radio. I'm Jenny, your weekend DJ. The song you just listened to is from Jay. Jay released his new album last week and I am glad to have him in the studio in the second hour. Stay tuned in for more Jay.

解答 B

中文翻譯 歡迎回到愛戀電台，我是你的周末 DJ 珍妮。剛聽到的歌曲來自傑爾。傑爾在上星期推出全新大碟，而今天很高興他將在節目第二小時中出現，想知道更多的傑爾，別轉台。

※〔註〕本考題屬變化型，考 Who（誰）而不是常出現的 Where、What place，破題點在 I'm Jenny, your...DJ「我是你的 DJ」，當然 radio（這裡指電台）、stay tuned 都有助於確認答案，本題正確答案為 B。

主題 3　百貨公司・賣場

Q1　Please look at the following three pictures.
Listen to the following announcement. Where will you most probably hear this announcement?
Welcome to Love Mall. We would like your attention, please. A customer is looking for her 6-year-old daughter, who is wearing a purple dress and white shoes. If you happened to see her around, please accompany her to our information counter on the 1st floor. Your help is much appreciated. Thank you and wish you a wonderful shopping day.

解答　A

中文翻譯　歡迎來到愛戀購物中心，我們需要您的留意。有一位客人在找她六歲的女兒，小朋友身穿紫色洋裝跟白鞋子，如果您看到她在附近，請陪同她到一樓的服務台。感謝您的幫忙，愛戀購物中心祝您購物愉快。

※〔註〕先仔細看完三張圖，考生應該知道 shopping center / mall（購物中心）、police station（警察局）以及 restroom（洗手間）等單字，所以當聽到第一句 Welcome to Love Mall，答案就已經揭曉，最後的 ...wish you a wonderful shopping day，shopping 一字讓答案更為明確，故本題正確答案為 A。

Q2 Please look at the following three pictures.
Listen to the following announcement. At what place might you hear this announcement?
Good day customers, thank you for shopping at SMART Super. To celebrate the 20th birthday of SMART, customers are offered a lucky draw coupon for every $300 purchase. The biggest prize is $200,000 in cash. Try your luck at your nearest SMART supermarket.

解答 B

 顧客好，感謝你惠顧 SMART 超市。為慶祝 SMART 二十歲生日，顧客每單筆購買滿三百元即可獲得摸彩券一張，最大獎是現金 20 萬元，趕快到你附近的 SMART 超市試試運氣。

※〔註〕「超級市場」是supermarket；「傳統市場」是market，本題的關鍵字當然是 super 及 market，出題者故意把 supermarket 的 super 拆出來擺在前面出現，是希望讓題目更符合國外的文化與習慣，考生也可從中學習。本題正確答案為 B。

Q3 Please look at the following three pictures.
Listen to the following announcement. Where might you hear this?
Sale! Sale! Sale! We are offering a summer offer on every item from July 1st to July 8th. Women's clothes are up to 50% off. Gentlemen are able to buy one tie and get one free. Kids under ten years old are free to enjoy their time in our toy land while you shop.

解答 C

 降！降！降！從七月一日到七月八月每樣商品夏日大特惠。女仕服飾五折起，男仕領帶買一送一，你家十歲以下的寶貝，在你選購時可免費在我們的玩具樂園中盡情玩樂。

※〔註〕咖啡店 coffee shop / café；夜市 night market；百貨公司 department store，考生聽到 sale，馬上可知跟「打折，優惠」有關，圖中三個地方都有可能聽到這樣的訊息，但接下來的 women's clothes、ties 都不可能出現在咖啡店，而夜市也不會有 toy land（玩具樂園），所以正確答案為 C。

第二類 留言

主題 4 親友間

Q1
Please look at the following three pictures.
Listen to the following message. What are the parents going to do?
Hey sweetheart, your mom and I are taking the afternoon train to your place. Don't bother to pick us up. We will meet you at the Grand Hotel at 6, ok? Can't wait to see your birthday present, right? See you later. Love you.

解答 C

 嗨！甜心，妳媽媽跟我正在搭下午的火車到妳那裡。不用麻煩來接我們，我們六點在格蘭飯店見，好嗎？等不及看妳的生日禮物，對吧？待會見，愛妳。

※〔註〕本題考「父母將做什麼」，關鍵句在 We will meet you at the Grand Hotel...，代表爸媽將要跟女兒碰面，接著爸爸提到生日禮物的事，應該是要為女兒慶祝生日，所以正確答案為 C。

Please look at the following three pictures.

George left a message to Sam. Where might Sam probably go after hearing the message?

Sam, I'm George. I've been calling for the past few hours. Brad was hit this morning and is now in the operation room. Please call back as soon as you hear my message. This is not something funny.

解答 B

 山姆，我是喬治。我打了好幾個小時電話給你，小布今天早上出車禍，現在人在手術室，聽到我的留言請馬上回我電話，這不是鬧著玩的。

※〔註〕本題考「聽完留言後，Sam 會去哪」，關鍵字在 was hit（被撞／打）以及 operation room（手術室），Sam 的朋友 Brad 人在醫院，而根據 George 在留言中緊張憂心的語氣，所以可推知 Sam 在聽完留言後將起往醫院，故本題正確答案為 B。

Q3

Please look at the following three pictures.

Listen to the following message. Where is Carol?

Time to get out of your bed, Carol. It's bright and sunny out-side, just perfectly fit for a walk or ride. You're not going to waste your life in bed. I'm on the way to your place. See you in a minute.

| 解答 | A |

是時候起床了，凱蘿。外面陽光普照，很適合去散散步、騎腳踏車。你不能賴在床上浪費生命，我現在在去你家的路上，馬上見。

※〔註〕本題考「Carol 現在在哪？」，破題字是 bed，也出現了兩次— get out of bed（滾出床／起床）、waste your life in bed（在床上睡覺浪費生命），所以本題正確答案為 A。

主題 **5**　公事

Q1　Please look at the following three pictures.
Listen to the following message. How is Peter going to deliver the report?

Peter, this is Ryan. I need you to do me a favor. I'm out with my client. Could you kindly bring me the annual report which is left on my desk? I need that by one and please meet me at 12:30 at the café around the corner. A million thanks.

解答 A

　彼得，我是雷恩，我需要你幫我忙。我現在人在外面見客戶，可以麻煩你幫我把我忘在桌上的年度報告送過來嗎？我下午一點就要這份報告，麻煩你十二點半在轉角的咖啡店跟我碰面，萬分感謝。

※〔註〕本題考「Peter 要如何送交報告？」，首先考生聽到 I'm now with my client，就可知 Ryan 不在公司，所以 C 不對。而破題點是 meet me at...the café...，故本題正確答案為 A。

Q2 Please look at the following three pictures.
Kate's boss left her a message. What might she probably do after listening to the message?
Morning Kate, I got an emergency call from Mr. Jackson early this morning. As you might guess, I am now heading to the airport. Please cancel all the meetings and appointments originally scheduled. Please keep your cell phone on and stay alert to my emails.

解答 B

 早呀，凱特。今天一早我接到傑克森先生的緊急電話，妳應該猜得到我現在正趕往機場。麻煩妳取消所有原定的會議及會面，手機開著，還有注意我發給妳的電子信件。

※〔註〕本題考「女人在聽完老闆的留言後會做什麼?」，破題句為 cancel all meetings and appointments…老闆因為有急事臨時出差，請他的祕書或助理取消所有會議，所以女人接下來忙著打電話（或 email）通知取消事宜，故本題正確答案為 B。

Q3

Please look at the following three pictures.

Judy was sick and she left a message to her supervisor. Where might Judy be?

Good morning, Mrs. White. This is Judy. I'm afraid I need to ask for a sick leave today. I had a fever and diarrhea. My doctor kept me here in the clinic for further check-up. Sorry for the absence and I'll be back to the office as soon as I can.

解答 B

懷特女士早安，我是茱蒂，我今天恐怕要請病假。我發燒又拉肚子，醫生把我留在診所做進一步檢查。很抱歉今天請假，我會盡快回來上班。

※〔註〕本題考「Judy 生病留言給她的主管請假，她現在人在哪裡？」，首先聽到 ask for a sick leave（請病假），就代表 Judy 不可能在辦公室，所以 C 不對。剩下醫院跟診所，破題字就是 clinic，指「診所」，而 Judy 說 doctor kept me in the clinic，所以本題正確答案為 B。

主題 **6**　　　　　　　　　　　　**提醒**

Q1
Please look at the following three pictures.
Listen to the following message. What is suggested?
Dear customer, your account at City Telecom shows a balance of $2500. Please cover the balance within 72 hours or your communication service will be suspended. Thank you for using City Telecom.

解答 A

中文
翻譯
親愛的用戶，閣下在城市電信的帳戶尚有餘款 $2500 未付。請於七十二小時內繳納，否則您的通話服務將被停止。感謝您使用城市電信服務。

※〔註〕本題問「建議何事？」，關鍵字是 balance、cover the balance。balance 在此為「餘款」，它本身有「餘額」之意，但因為電信公司 Telecom 提到 cover the balance（補繳餘額），故代表這是一通提醒繳費的留言，而最後…or your communication service will be suspended 就是建議用戶補繳費用，故本題正確答案為 A。

Please look at the following three pictures.

Q2 Listen to the following message. On what kind of product might you hear this?

Good day, you have five new messages. Listen to messages, please press 1. Delete messages, please press 2. Main menu, please press 9. To leave, press 0 or hang up.

解答　B

您好，您有五通新留言，要聽留言請按 1，刪除留言請按 2，回到主目錄請按 9，離開請按 0 或掛斷。

※〔註〕本題考「你會在哪一種產品中聽到此留言？」，筆電暫時沒有幫忙留言的功能，所以 A 不對。本題破題字為 hang up，指「掛斷」，能「掛上」的只有手機跟電話，所以本題正確答案為 B。

主題

6

留言 ∨ 提醒

Q3 Please look at the following three pictures.
A credit card company left a message to a customer. What can be told from the message?
Dear customer, thank you for shopping with Metro Credit card. Your latest purchase amount is \$10,000 at Mountain Restaurant. Please confirm or check with our staff at 080-565-656.

解答 B

 親愛的用戶,感謝你使用大都會信用卡消費。你最新一筆消費是在山頂餐廳,金額爲 \$10,000,請確認或來電 080-565-656 查詢。

※〔註〕本題考「一信用卡公司留言給一名用戶,我們可以從留言中得知什麼訊息?」,A 指兩個人在餐廳用餐,雖然留言提到 Restaurant,但我們無法確定用戶跟幾個人在用餐,所以 A 不對。而 C 描述用戶在購物,也許真的有,但留言中完全沒有提到。本題關鍵句爲 thank you for shopping with Metro Credit,代表用戶剛剛用 Metro 信用卡刷卡消費,所以本題正確答案爲 B。

第三類　簡短談話

主題 7　問「什麼地方」

Q1 Please look at the following three pictures.
Listen to the following short talk. What might be the place?
Good evening guys. This should be the biggest live concert you have ever seen. Thank you to all the fans from Taiwan, Japan, Hong Kong and Singapore. Are you ready to rock? Let's do it!

解答 A

 大家晚安。這應該是你們看過最大的現場演唱會，謝謝從台灣、日本、香港還有新加坡來的粉絲樂迷，你們準備好一起搖滾了嗎？我們來吧！

※〔註〕演唱會是 concert；戲院是 theater、cinema；舞台劇是 play，當考生聽到 the biggest live concert 時就可確定答案，本題正確答案為 A。

Q2 Please look at the following three pictures.
Listen to the following short talk. What place is probably mentioned?

Hello everyone. You might be amazed by the spectacular appearance of this building. It's no different to a palace. Truth is this highly protected building had been a palace since 1900 and was only renovated into a historical museum in 2002.

解答 C

 大家好，這座建築物宏偉的外觀或許讓你驚豔，因為它跟皇宮沒兩樣（它就像是一座宮殿）。其實這座受到高度保護的建築物從 1900 年以來確實曾是一座宮殿，一直到 2002 年才改建翻新為歷史博物館。

※〔註〕本題有一定難度，考生必須仔細聽取細節，首先看完三張圖後，要有這些單字概念－城堡是 castle；皇宮是 palace；博物館是 museum。palace 一字雖然出現兩次，但是指「（美得跟）宮殿無疑 no different to a palace」、「自 1900 年（到 2002 年）它曾是一座皇宮...had been a palace since 1900...」，所以這座 building（建築物）不是宮殿更不是城堡，它現在已 renovated（翻新）成一座 museum（博物館），所以本題正確答案為 C。

Q3 Please look at the following three pictures.
Listen to the following short talk. Which place suits the description best?

Thank you, Mr. Lee, for your statements. Next, the opposition will be given three minutes to deliver their arguments. Captain of the opposition, please proceed to the front. You may start when you hear the ring.

解答 A

 謝謝李先生的陳述,接下來反方將有三分鐘的時間提出他們的反駁。反方隊長,請到前面來,聽到叮一聲後,可以開始辯論。

※〔註〕本題考「哪一場合最符合以下描述?」, the opposition 是考生要認識的字,在辯論比賽中是指「反方」,儘管考生不懂 the opposition 的意思,簡短對話中的 arguments(辯駁,反駁)、captain of the opposition(反方隊長)都是破題字,所以本題正確答案為 A。

主題 8　問「做什麼」

Q1
Please look at the following three pictures.
Listen to the following short talk. What will Sarah do on Friday?

Sarah has a busy week. On Monday and Wednesday morning, she has to teach a new English class. She can't wait to meet her new students. On Tuesday, she's going to have dinner with a friend. Yet Sarah put off a date with Chris on Friday night because the next day is a big day. She is having a huge party at home in the afternoon and there's so much to prepare before that.

解答 B

中文
翻譯
莎拉這星期非常忙碌，星期一跟星期三早上她要為新的英文課程授課，她已等不及跟新學生見面。星期二她跟朋友吃晚餐，不過莎拉延後了跟克里斯星期五的約會，因為隔天是大日子，她隔天下午要在家舉行大型宴會，在這之前有很多事情要準備。

※〔註〕本題考「Sarah 星期五要做何事？」，考生必須注意聽關於 Friday（星期五）前後之內容，對話中提到 put off a date with...on Friday，指「延後與……的約會」，所以 A 不對。接下來說 because the next day is a big day...having a huge party，這裡的 next day 是指隔天，星期六 Saturday 將在家宴客，所以 C 不符。而最後一句...ther's so much to prepare before that 是確認答案，因為星期六是宴客的大日子，所以在之前要好好準備，故本題正確答案為 B。

Q2 Please look at the following three pictures.
Listen to the following short talk. What might Mr. Henson plan to do?

Christmas is around the corner. This year, Mr. Henson wants to give his family a surprise. He's going to buy a toy car for his two kids and decorate the house with a Christmas tree and ribbons for his wife.

解答 C

 聖誕節將至，今年，漢森先生想要給他的家人一個驚喜。他打算替兩個小孩買一台玩具汽車當作聖誕禮物，還要幫太太買聖誕樹和緞帶佈置家裡。

※〔註〕本題考「Mr. Henson 的計畫做什麼？」，Mr. Henson 計畫在 Christmas 給家人一個 surprise，所以他「打算」，也就是 he's going to...，buy a toy car 跟 decorate the house with a Christmas tree...都是答案，故本題正確答案為 C。

Q3 Please look at the following three pictures.
Listen to the following short talk. What might Wendy probably do next?
Wendy came home to find the door unlocked. Her living room was a mess, the drawers were opened and her favorite bottles of wine were gone. Worst of all, the cash and jewelry kept under her pillow were all stolen.

解答 B

 溫蒂回家發現大門沒有鎖上,她的客廳一團亂,抽屜都被打開,她最愛的酒全部不見蹤影。最糟糕的是,她放在枕頭底下的現金跟珠寶都被偷走了。

※〔註〕本題考「Wendy 接下來將做什麼?」,本題考生只要聽懂 find the door unlocked(發現門沒有鎖)還有最後一個字 stolen(被偷),就能破題。溫蒂回到家發現客廳一片混亂 a mess,酒不見了 wine were gone,錢跟珠寶被偷了 cash and jewelry were stolen,因為門沒有鎖而遭小偷光顧,所以接著她一定是去報案,故本題正確答案為 B。

主題 **9** 　　　　　　　　　　　**推測**

Q1 Please look at the following three pictures.
Listen to the following short talk. What can be expected from Lucy?
Lucy is worried about Pitt. Since he was taken for a walk yesterday, he has looked pale and hasn't eaten much. Pitt used to bark loudly but now he is real quiet. Lucy is going to take Pitt to a place.

解答　C

 中文
翻譯　露西很擔心小皮，自從昨天帶他去散步回來，他看起來很蒼白，胃口也不好（吃不多），小皮平常吠叫得很有力，現在他真的很安靜，露西打算帶他到一個地方。

※〔註〕本題考「推測 Lucy 帶 Pitt 到何處？」，根據三張圖的提示，Pitt 到底是人還是狗，關鍵字為 bark（吠叫），所以本題正確答案為 C。

Q2

Please look at the following three pictures.
Listen to the following short talk. What might Marie buy?
Marie is moving to her new apartment next month. Her friend Ann promised to buy her a set of furniture which includes a couch and two armchairs. So Marie is looking for an item to go with the sofas, something she can put coffee or tea on.

解答 A

 瑪麗下個月要搬到新公寓，她的朋友安答應送她一組家具——一張長沙發以及兩張扶手椅，所以瑪麗在找一件搭配沙發椅的單品，一件可以讓她擺放咖啡或茶的家具。

※〔註〕本題考「瑪麗要買什麼？」，Marie 的朋友 Ann「答應買一張長沙發跟兩張扶手椅給她」promised to buy her a couch and two armchairs，所以 B 不對。破題句為 ...looking for ...something she can put coffee or tea on，「一種她可以擺放 put on 咖啡或茶的東西」，所以不會是 coffee maker（咖啡機），而是要買一張 tea table / coffee table（茶几），故本題正確答案為 A。

Q3 Please look at the following three pictures.
Listen to the following short talk. What can be told about Mark's girlfriend?

Mark had a date with his girlfriend. He booked a nice restaurant and had some lovely roses ready. On the way to the restaurant, he passed by a candy shop. His girlfriend has a sweet tooth, so he went in.

解答 A

 中文翻譯 馬克跟女朋友約會,他訂了一家很棒的餐廳,也準備了一些漂亮的玫瑰花,在去餐廳的路上,馬克經過一家糖果店,他女朋友很愛吃甜食,所以他走了進去。

※〔註〕本題考「從簡短對話中可得知馬克的女朋友是怎樣的人?」,馬克為了這次約會準備了花,可見她女朋友應該是喜歡花的,所以 C 不對。馬克 pass by (經過) 一家 candy shop (糖果店),他沒有考慮就 went in (走進去),可見他是要買東西給女朋友,本題破題字是 sweet tooth,就某人 has a sweet tooth 是指「他 / 她很愛吃甜食」,故本題正確答案為 A。

第四類 其他

主題 10 綜合問題

Q1 Please look at the following three pictures.
Listen to the following short talk. Which is Lena?
Lena is my best friend. We have known each other for ten years. She has small eyes and has short hair. We both like sports and love to put on jeans and T-shirts. We seldom go shopping.

解答 C

妮娜是我最好的朋友，我們已認識了十年。她眼睛小小的，頭髮很短，我們兩個都喜歡運動，愛穿牛仔褲跟 T-shirt，我們很少去逛街買東西。

※〔註〕Lena has short hair（Lena 是短頭髮），所以 A 不符。兩個女生喜歡運動 like sports 而不太愛逛街 seldom go shopping，所以答案已很明顯，本題正確答案為 C。

Please look at the following three pictures.

Q2 Listen to the following short talk. Which picture matches the talk?

Little Angel Kindergarten is one of the most beautiful schools in the city. There is a huge fountain at the center of the square, and a playground is on the left. Classrooms and office buildings are on the right hand side, surrounded by a lovely garden.

解答　C

中文翻譯　小天使幼稚園是本市最漂亮的學校之一，學校廣場中央有一座大型噴水池，左邊是操場，右手邊是被美麗花園圍繞的教室及辦公大樓。

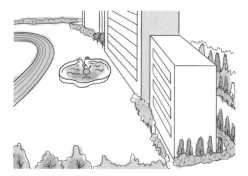

※〔註〕看完三張圖後，考生如果知道 playground（操場）、building（大樓）、fountain（噴水池）這幾個重要的單字，那麼一定能答對，不過其實只要知道其中一個單字，還是可以得分。操場只有一個 a playground，所以 A 不符。而且對話中提到 a playground on the left「操場在左手邊」，所以 B 不對，故本題正確答案為 C。

Q3
Please look at the following three pictures.
Listen to the following short talk. Which picture is the best match?
Jane bought a gift for her sister's baby. It was baby pajamas with adorable strawberry prints on it. And it goes with a pair of socks.

解答 A

珍買了一份禮物給她姐姐的嬰兒，那是嬰兒的睡衣，上面有可愛的草莓圖案，還有搭配一雙襪子。

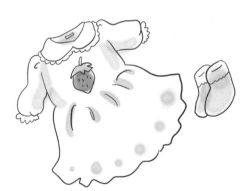

※〔註〕pajamas 是睡衣，baby pajamas 當然就是嬰兒穿的睡衣，所以 C 不符。本題破題點有兩個，一是 strawberry prints（草莓圖案），另一個是 goes with a pair of socks（搭配一雙襪子），本題正確答案為 A。

國家圖書館出版品預行編目資料

全民英檢初級聽力測驗題庫解析 / 國際語言中心
委員會編著. --初版.--【臺北縣中和市】：
國際學村, 2009.10
　面；　　　公分

ISBN 978-986-6829-45-1　（平裝）

1. 英語　2. 問題集

805.1892　　　　　　　　　　　98012854

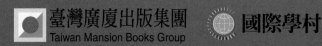

全民英檢初級聽力測驗題庫解析

英檢初級聽力測驗1000《精修版》

作者 WRITER	國際語言中心委員會
出版者 PUBLISHING COMPANY	台灣廣廈出版集團 TAIWAN MANSION BOOKS GROUP 國際學村出版
發行人 / 社長 PUBLISHER / DIRECTOR	江媛珍 JASMINE CHIANG
地址 ADDRESS	235新北市中和區中山路二段359巷7號2樓 2F, NO. 7, LANE 359, SEC. 2, CHUNG-SHAN RD., CHUNG-HO DIST., NEW TAIPEI CITY, TAIWAN, R.O.C.
電話 TELEPHONE NO	886-2-2225-5777
傳真 FAX NO	886-2-2225-8052
電子信箱 E-MAIL	TaiwanMansion@booknews.com.tw
網址 WEB	http://www.booknews.com.tw
總編輯 EDITOR-IN-CHIEF	伍峻宏 CHUN WU
執行編輯 EDITOR	周宜珊 JOELLE CHOU
美術編輯 ART EDITOR	許芳莉 POLLY HSU
製版 / 印刷 / 裝訂	東豪 / 廣鑫 / 紘億 / 明和
法律顧問	第一國際法律事務所 余淑杏律師
代理印務及圖書總經銷	知遠文化事業有限公司
地址	222新北市深坑區北深路三段155巷25號5樓
訂書電話	886-2-2664-8800
訂書傳真	886-2-2664-8801
出版日期	2014年8月初版7刷
郵撥帳號	18788328
郵撥戶名	台灣廣廈有聲圖書有限公司

（購書300元以內需外加30元郵資，滿300元（含）以上免郵資）